Praise for *The Sis...*

"A well-written portrait, not just of grief but also of the pain of realizing you didn't really know someone you thought you were close to... A heavy but powerful read that tackles big topics."

—*Booklist*

"The story reads like *Go Ask Alice*... As Allie learns the many sordid secrets of her sister's concealed life, she begins to understand the powerful influence her sister had on her and struggles to find her own voice."

—*Kirkus Reviews*

"A powerful story of redemption, forgiveness, love, and the ability to persevere."

—*VOYA*

Praise for *The Homecoming*

"A stirring close-up of a family haunted by emotional trauma."

—*Kirkus Reviews*

"The overall message of relying on family and friends for support is clear, and John's pain and confusion are palpable."

—*School Library Journal*

"This engaging story will appeal to all readers and will help troubled teens realize that there can be help out there for what's going on in their lives."

—*School Library Connection*

"Ramey has penned a rare raw, emotion-packed romance from a male perspective, with themes of empowerment and self-actualization."

—*Booklist*

THE

SECRETS

WE BURY

Also by Stacie Ramey

The Sister Pact
The Homecoming

THE

SECRETS

WE BURY

STACIE RAMEY

sourcebooks
fire

Published by Sourcebooks Fire, an imprint of Sourcebooks, Inc.
P.O. Box 4410, Naperville, Illinois 60567-4410
(630) 961-3900
Fax: (630) 961-2168
sourcebooks.com

Library of Congress Cataloging-in-Publication data is on file with the publisher.

Printed and bound in the United States of America.
BVG 10 9 8 7 6 5 4 3 2 1

CHAPTER 1

Compulsively stirring my coffee in Nowhereville, New Jersey, I recognize I'm going to have to do a lot of explaining when Emily gets here. Well, assuming she's figured out my code and picked the right coffee shop.

I look at my burner cell and check the time. 12:02. Not super late. Especially not for my cousin, who is less governed by rules than I am but still hates being tardy. *Tardy* is her word, not mine. Although I totally approve, because it feels specific to the situation of meeting with someone. I hate nondescript words.

Cell in hand, I'm hit with a new, burning desire. Text Mom. Tell her I'm okay. Tell her that I'm sorry I do these things that only make sense to me. Like that time we went to my great-aunt's farm. The older cousins wanted to scare us younger ones, so they told us there was a big pit where the previous farm's horses were buried. We were warned to stay away. So of course, that's the first place we went. The place was nasty. It smelled. There were thorns everywhere, but that didn't stop me from digging and going deeper into the pit. They had to call the fire department to have me removed from what was really a sinkhole used as a large animal grave. My brother, Brad, and Emily's sister, Abby, got in huge trouble. Emily had burns on both hands from trying to pull me out by the rope I had tied around my waist. I was so freaked out about the bones I found, about the smell of death and all the animals buried, that they had to sedate me. Good times.

Man, I was a pain in the ass. Once I set my mind on doing something, I couldn't veer from whatever stupid thing I'd decided to do. Mom never understood that I couldn't control my obsessive behavior. But it wasn't her fault. I am a lot to handle.

I start to type. Mom, I'm sorry. I was always sorry after I'd upset Mom. But for some things, like not following clear-cut rules, rules like *Don't dig where you shouldn't* or *Don't run away from home*, saying sorry doesn't help, so I delete the text.

Emily and I are more like brother and sister than cousins. From the time we were little, we were always together, only interested in what the other one was doing, never paying attention to anyone else. Ignoring the older siblings and cousins, especially.

"We would hang out with other people if anyone else was remotely interesting," I always said. Emily agreed. Of course.

But this time, I'm not sure she'll agree with what I've got planned, so I have to tell her the right way, which is never easy for me. Words come to me like pictures stored on a hard drive that cycle in front of me constantly. I can't always control which ones I choose as they spew out of my mouth. They call that *verbal impulsivity*. It comes along with a slew of other labels doctors have given me over the years. Whatever you call it, for me, choosing the right words is an exquisite sort of pain.

2

"Be brief," Dad used to tell me. "Let people catch up to your brain."

He said that to make me feel better. Like none of my dysfunction was my fault.

The waitress approaches, lifting the coffeepot and her eyebrows.

I shake my head, drink my coffee, and think about how I can explain my plan to Emily in a way she'll get behind Operation Wild Thing.

The taste of coffee paired with the drizzling rain sends my mind back to a time when our families were on the Cape and everyone was at the beach. Emily and I hung at the house, because I needed some away-from-the-rest-of-them time. A fly buzzed around my head, the sound making me insanely edgy. So edgy, apparently, I was sitting there with my hands over my ears. Maybe even rocking a little. Okay, rocking way too much.

Emily yanked me out of the house by my arm and into the fresh air. We stood on the dock behind Uncle Bill's house. The sky was overcast, and the breeze kept the gnats and mosquitos away.

I rubbed my shoulder joint. "That used to be attached, you know!"

She punched me in the arm. "The fly is going after the crumbs, not you, Dylan, you big dork."

"I knew that." I did. It's just that buzzing puts me in such a constant state of make-it-stop that I can't do the simplest thing, like figure out I can walk away. But Emily does. And she gets me.

If I was the kind of person who blushed, I would have blushed then.

It started to drizzle. "Come on," I said, going around the side of the house. "They'll be home soon." I tapped my leg. "Max, we're going for a walk."

The rottweiler Dad brought home for me when I was six jumped up from his spot on the grass to join me.

"Wait for me." Emily ran inside and grabbed a rain jacket— yellow London Fog, because she wanted to be like her mom back then. "I can't believe with all of the things you hate touching and the things you hate touching you, you don't mind the rain."

She was right. I didn't mind the rain. Never had. It was like nature's drumming. I was obsessed with drumming. Not actually playing the drums, but listening to them as loud as I possibly could. A therapist had explained I liked the sound because I could feel them before I could hear them. Whatever the reason, they calmed me, for sure. Just like the rain did that day.

Now, a good five years later, sitting in a coffee shop in a tiny town in New Jersey, I wonder if I'll feel Emily's presence before I hear her. I sent her an email the other day using the fake account I set up for us before I ran away from home and the alphabet code we used when we were kids.

> Zelda,
> I have something big to tell you. Huge. Meet me. Next letter. Tell me when and where. But do it soon.
> Yorik

Yorik,
Coffee. 12:00 3 on the list on TLD. You always
scare me.
Z

I stare at my coffee. My Dad used to drink his coffee black. "Like my heart," he always said. The rest of my immediate family uses a dash of cream and definitely no sugar. I like my coffee light and sweet. Is it any wonder we don't get along?

The waitress appears again. Alice, as her name tag says, refills my cup. I'm supposed to thank her, even though she doesn't seem to mind our nonverbal exchange. But then she goes and ruins the silence. "You want anything else?"

I shake my head, pour in more cream, and wait for it to swirl around my cup like the thoughts that swirl around my mind. After coffee, that is. Without coffee, I am stuck in a fog of nothingness, like my brain knows it's supposed to be processing information but just doesn't feel like it.

Emily always said coffee was going to be my undoing. My Kryptonite or some bullshit. But it's not like I'm at a loss for things that destroy me. The list is long. Starting with sounds. Like Brenda White's shoes scraping against the floor of my kindergarten classroom over and over again. *Scrape scrape scrape scrape.* Pause. *Scrape scrape scrrrapppe.* Is it any wonder I flipped my shit and hid under the desk? Or Josh Mellon's *click click click* of his pen during exams in physics. I could have told him flicking his pen wasn't going to get him the right answers. Or…

The door opens. I look up. Not Emily.

The refrigerator at the front of the shop hums, and that makes me want to cover my ears, but the best way to deal with unwanted sounds is to tune them out by playing louder ones. I scroll through my playlist: Rolling Stones, Led Zeppelin (best band ever). Dad and I agreed about that. I guess I get distracted by listening to the drum solo in "Moby Dick" for the zillionth time, because shoes appear in my field of vision next to my table and stop. Em's shoes. Running shoes. Since I'm planning the biggest running-away-from-home plan ever, I find that ironic.

Emily puts her raincoat on the back of her chair, giving me a second to acclimate to her presence. Her coat is a navy-blue North Face, because Emily is all about being serious now. *Serious as a heart attack, motherfucker.* "Hey," she says.

"Hey, yourself." I wave. Stiff-handed (my usual).

She punches me in the arm. It's a trick of hers. The punch floods my body with enough input that I can actually handle being hugged. She leans in. Emily smells like she has since she was five years old: cherry Life Savers, rain, Dial soap. It's weird to know what soap your cousin uses, but I'm not being creepy. I can literally detect the scent of more than a dozen different brands of soap. It's awesome to be me.

I wrap my hands around her shoulders and hold for five seconds. That's the usual amount of time that people who are related to each other hug. I don't hate it for the first one or two seconds, but by the fourth second, I'm like, *Seriously, can we be done?* But I let her hold it longer, because I know most human beings don't mind physical contact for five full seconds. Some even allow seven. Sick bastards.

Emily grabs the biscotti off my plate, the extra one I'd ordered because I knew she'd take mine when she got here. She bites a hunk of it, oblivious to the crumbs she's sent flying, and says, "You were counting, weren't you?"

My eyes go to my coffee. "No comment." I take a drink, slurp on purpose. She laughs. God, it's great to hear that laugh.

"So, what's the big emergency?" she asks as she motions for the waitress.

"I never said emergency."

"You said, 'Soon.' That's definitely heightened language for you." She puts air quotes around the word *heightened*. The waitress approaches. Waits.

"You have mochaccino?" Emily asks.

The waitress rolls her eyes, taps her pen on her pad. "We don't have crappuccinos here. Just real coffee. For people who like coffee."

"Alice!" the woman in the front of the shop yells, clearly having overheard her.

Alice scowls. "Our frappé machine is down at the moment. May I get you something else?"

"Bring her a double espresso, whipped cream, lots of whipped cream." My hand palms the sugar packet dispenser. "Don't worry. We have enough of this to make it palatable."

Emily nods. "Oh, and a menu." Then to me. "You look

skinny." She pulls out a wad of cash. Yes, a wad. The bills are all crumpled, and change flies everywhere. "Babysitting money. It's on me."

When the waitress's steps tell me she's out of earshot, I reach for Emily's hands, trying to grab the mess of bills sticking out everywhere, trying to contain her chaos. I need her to focus on what I'm saying, so my hands clamp over hers. "I'm going to hike the Appalachian Trail," I say.

She drops the money on the table. "What?"

"I've decided. You can't talk me out of it."

The waitress returns, stands, pad perched. I read that as a little hostile, but I've no idea why. And like with most human interactions, I really don't care.

Emily stares at me as if she's suddenly gone mute, selectively mute, which is one of the other labels those doctors tried to stick on me. I close Emily's menu, aim my voice at Alice the waitress. "She's going to need a few minutes."

Alice huffs and moves on. I point at her moody retreat. "Did she seem a little…?"

Emily stares at me like—I don't know. Facial expressions? They're fuzzy for me. Muscular patterns? Those I can read. Like how Emily's gripping her closed menu like it's the only stable thing in an insane world. Obviously, she's angry. Her fingers are turning white because she's exerting so much pressure with her grip on that innocent menu. I'm the only one who can piss off Emily that much. So she must be mad because of the Appalachian Trail. Got it. So of course I say, "What? It's totally safe."

She throws her head in her hands, then looks up. "Sure it is. Why not? Why don't I just put my life on hold and join you?"

I stir my coffee, only it doesn't need stirring because I've mixed my cream in completely and it's a nice homogenous blond. "That's ridiculous. You like your life." I take a sip, which must really piss her off, because she reaches for my cup, a tactic Emily only resorts to when she's about to go nuclear. I move my cup out of her reach. "Hold up, psycho." Then I lean forward. Leaning forward makes you seem earnest. "I have to. It's my only choice."

"You could come home," she says, but she knows I can't.

The last school they sent me to had a special unit for "emotionally challenged" kids. I only agreed to go there because it was Emily's school. The teachers and counselors had a big meeting, and they said if I didn't do well, I'd have to go to a school that had a more "therapeutic environment." And I guess forcing the faculty to have to evacuate the entire school from the auditorium after losing it during an assembly qualifies as "not doing well." Yeah. But honestly, me sitting in class with a bunch of kids who are more messed up than I am? Not. Going. To. Happen. Not if it's up to me. Which it will be in six months when I finally turn eighteen. Which is why I ran away from home to begin with.

I hold her hands again, this time because I need her to believe me. My hands over hers doesn't make me feel as closed in as if she put hers on mine, but even this brief contact is only possible because it's her, Emily. I soften my voice, which also indicates concern. "They're getting closer." I look into her eyes. "They almost caught me at a coffee shop in New York."

She nods. She knows Mom's detectives are pretty motivated. "I told you coffee was your Achilles' heel." A skinny tear drips down her cheek, and part of me considers what it means to cry thin tears versus big fat ones. Has anyone done a study on the size of tears in relation to the emotional load they bear? I look away, mostly to contain the smirk I'm sure is on my face since I'm depersonalizing the situation, as usual. She pulls her hands back. Uh-oh. She noticed.

"Damn it, Dylan. Stop playing me." She sounds sad, and that makes me feel bad.

"I'm sorry," I whisper.

She stares at me. She can count the number of times on one hand that I've said that two-word combination to anyone. Actually, I remember each and every time. Two before this. The last one when it was too late.

I lean back. "I'm not playing you. If I stay here, Mom's guys will find me. In six months, I can make my own decisions. Do you know how long it takes to hike the Appalachian Trail? Six months. That means something."

It's hard for her to argue with Dylan logic. "Okay, that does seem coincidental, but you've never hiked before."

I break out the book I bought about hiking the trail and slide it across the table. "First line, 'So you've never hiked before? No problem.'"

She raises her eyebrows but can't keep from smiling. "That's a stupid first line."

"I thought it was kind of catchy myself."

"The wilderness isn't some kid-invented adventure," she says. "What if something happens to you?"

"It won't," I say. *Because bad things can't happen to you after the worst thing already has.* "I just need time. And I always considered doing this anyway."

"Liar."

True. That was a lie. This is the kind of thing Dad and my brother, Brad, and maybe my cousin, Christian, would do, planning for months, needling me because no way I would ever want to join them. "But I feel like it makes sense."

"You could get lost."

I almost choke on my biscotti. "It's a *trail.*" I trace an imaginary straight line on the table. "I mean, point A to point B."

"People get lost. They've gotten lost on the trail before. There've been people—"

"I know. I realize that, but, Em, the thing is, I'm trying to get lost, aren't I?"

"Only for six months! Not for—"

"I'll come back. I have to. We've got Max's revenge. You know I wouldn't miss that."

Max hated Halloween with a passion. Barked his little head off. So, we'd have an anti-Halloween every November 1. We'd hang out on the floor with him all day, no matter what day of the week it was. Take off school. Cancel all plans and do what the dog liked best. Which was to lounge with us while we watched movies. Usually the Harry Potter ones, which never got old.

"Every November," she says solemnly. "So, when are you going?"

"The normal time. When most people do."

She looks at me like I'm confusing her. Or annoying her. Or—

Then she whacks me on the arm with her spoon. "When?"

"Next week. April 15."

This time, fat tears fall down her face, and she swipes them away fast. Those are the kind of tears that sting. But she knows she can't argue with me now. That detail was my wild card.

"You're such a dick."

"I know, but I'm a dick with a profound sense of irony."

CHAPTER 2

Dad was an accountant at one of the big firms. "Big Four," his coworkers always said, like they were the original six hockey teams in the NHL. It didn't crack up Dad when I said, "Original four, baby. You made it to the major league." I used to use air quotes around the original four part too, thinking Dad would respond to that level of funny, but the joke missed every time. Every time.

A smile creeps on my face, and I cover my mouth the way Emily does when she's trying to act like some smart-ass thing I said wasn't funny even though it clearly was. Except everyone on this bus couldn't care less about my screwed-up sense of humor.

The rain pounds the road, and it makes me wonder how the bus driver can see where he's going. I know I wouldn't be able to if I was driving, which I never will. Sensory processing disorder. I acquired that label after my assembly freak-out.

"You can't listen to everything people say about you," Brad told me the following week when he was dropping me off at school. "It's gonna suck having to rely on other people your whole life. You should learn to drive."

A knife in the gut. Thanks for understanding, Brad. But I

also know that I was a pain-in-the-ass little brother to him. My behavior over the years always mystified him; he couldn't understand why it was so hard for me to just *live*, like everyone else did. If I had the answer to that little cosmic riddle, Brad…

Thunder rocks the air, followed by an impressive lightning strike, forcing me to focus on the here and now. It seems a little early in the season for lightning, but there's nothing I can do to calm myself except pull my long-sleeved flannel down to cover the inside of my wrist. I play with my black rubber bracelet, the one Emily had bought for each of us at the store in New Jersey where I'd stocked up for the hike. Had that been only yesterday?

"So it's like we're always together," she'd explained as she'd slipped it over my wrist. "I'll be with you the whole time, okay?"

I close my eyes and count the number of jars of instant coffee I transferred into Ziploc bags before stashing them in my backpack. Three. They're in my pack along with a sleeping bag, the rain pants Emily insisted I get, and four pairs of socks. My trail book said I needed two, but wet feet freak me out.

"These have good wicking action," Emily told me as she piled shirts of her choice in the cart, and I pretended not to be upset they weren't cotton. I've never worn anything but cotton. Ever. I was half considering scrapping my entire mission for my comfortable tees when a kid and mom passed us. The boy had to be about ten years old. His mother was complaining into her cell phone while he pushed their cart with a miserable look on his face.

"If he's getting suspended in fourth grade, what's next? Prison?"

That got me focused on my goal. I grabbed boxes of instant oatmeal, different flavors, all in bags (total, thirty), beef jerky (ten). Desperate to get the feel-good energy back into this day, I said to Emily. "Wicking action? That's word-of-the-day stuff right there."

"I know, right? That makes—"

"Twenty-eight points for you and fifty-six points for me. I'm still killing you on WOD ranking."

"But I'm catching up."

I raised my eyebrows at her, didn't say anything. Raised eyebrows are judgy enough without words.

"Slowly," she equivocated.

I didn't even have time to celebrate my win before Emily said, "Wicking action is going to be your friend. *Trust me.*" She laughed as she threw a tube of diaper rash cream into the cart. She showed me her phone. "I just Googled it."

I couldn't say I'd ever imagined buying diaper cream, but all the money I'd made fixing people's computers was really paying off. I'd squirreled it away in my room, so when I left home, I had more than $1,800 on one of those refillable credit cards. I gave Emily access to the account, knowing she could add money if I needed it. But I wasn't planning on needing it. I need to limit her involvement as much as possible.

We pushed my cart through the sporting goods store when Emily said, "Boxes. We need boxes so I can send you stuff."

"Yeah. No."

"Yeah. Yes."

"That was such a witty comeback."

She put her foot in front of the wheel of my cart. Stopped it cold. Stopped me cold. "Nonnegotiable."

"Negotiable."

"Non."

I tried to pull the cart backward, but she did some sort of ninja move that landed her other foot in front of the wheels.

"Okay, okay, you win. You can send me one box."

"I'll send you as many boxes as I like."

"You'll get me caught."

"I can be careful. You've been training me for this my entire life. Remember Operation Cookie Jar?"

I smile thinking of how we single-handedly stole, then eventually ate, an entire batch of homemade cookies at the Cape one year. We had to frame Max, which caused huge upset and a bunch of calls to the emergency vet because of the chocolate. I admit that was a big flaw in the plan, but that was when we were young and sharpening our team skills.

"Or Operation Air Freshener?"

We covered up the smell of brewing coffee in my room for years before anyone detected it, because we sprayed vodka into an essential oil air freshener. We used to sing the Febreze Noticeables commercial all the time, and no one guessed. But to be honest, most kids try to hide vodka, not coffee. Not how we roll. Although soliciting Sam, my swim-team buddy whose father always had those little bottles from the airline where he was a flight attendant to supply us, definitely increased my cred.

"Good times," I say.

"Besides, you almost got caught by yourself."

"I'm not entirely sure that wasn't your fault. The investigation into the New York coffee shop near capture is ongoing."

"Ass," Emily said and walked toward the underwear section, where I was sure more wicking garments would be picked out. "How could I possibly have tipped your hand when I didn't even know where you were?"

"Save your testimony for the formal inquiry."

She huffs.

"Relax. You'll get your turn to testify."

But then my stomach sort of soured. The thought of going six months without seeing Emily made me feel all weird inside.

———o———

A big bump on the road makes me bounce out of my bus seat, that second of propulsion enough to light the fires of panic in me. The steady thrumming of the bus's engine as it takes the rise of the hill pounds its way into my mind. It whines. And whines. We are climbing, climbing, and I have to not concentrate on how packed we all are on this bus. I have to try to shake off the nearness of the guy sitting next to me. He's probably around Dad's age. In good shape like Dad, but bulkier, which makes his form shift into my zone a couple of times.

I start to worry that Emily was right. I made a big mistake. I can't even make it through the nineteen-plus-hour bus ride to the start of the trail. I rip open a packet of Dramamine I picked up at the 7-Eleven next to the bus station. I gulp down the tablet with a Mountain Dew and get ready for the relief. When the chemicals relax the adrenaline in my body, it will reduce my vertigo, and let me settle in for a long nap. Headphones in, I pipe in my chill-out list: Gregorian chants, sounds of nature, sacred drums. I lean my face against the cool window. On planes I sit in the aisle seat. On the bus, it's the window. No idea why. That's just how it has to be. The sun drops below the horizon, and the lights of the cars we pass become elongated. I close my eyes.

Before I know it, I am woken by a jolt.

"Gainesville, Georgia."

I pull out my phone. It's registered to Xevon Drexil. 8:25. Let the adventure begin.

I wait on the sidewalk with the other passengers. The night air is chilly; the fumes from the buses make my stomach turn. Finally, I see my bags. The guy piling the luggage onto the side-walk is also Dad-aged, but not as tall. It's like I'm surrounded by an army of dads in all different shapes and sizes. The guy's partner is a kid, maybe a few years older than I am, and he's not working half as hard.

"Come on, Todd. Get in here," the old guy gripes, and that amuses me.

But then I hear my father's voice at the Cape that last time: "Stand up straight, Dylan. Shoulders back. Head high."

We were taking pictures, Mom's annual family picture.

"You're slouching, Dylan. Look strong."

People shuffle by me. One bumps into me. "Sorry, man."

I realize I'm sort of out of it. I grab my bags, and the bus guy puts out his hand. "Ticket?"

"Oh, yeah." I hand him my baggage claim ticket and a couple of dollars.

He nods, stuffs the cash in his pocket. "You thru-hiking?"

I wipe my hair out of my eyes. "Yeah."

"Good luck to you."

Then our conversation is done. He's moved on, and I'm in this weird fugue state, caught between what happened before and what's happening now—sensory dysfunction. *The Out-of-Sync Child*, that was the book Mom referred to again and again as my situation got thornier and thornier. Sensory dysfunction means I don't move through life the way other people do. So thru-hiking feels like the complete opposite of what I'm suited for. Which makes me want to do it even more.

My steps take me away, toward the shuttle that takes hikers to the hostel. A superblond, smiley guy looks up at me. "Hey, man, you hitting the trail tomorrow?"

I nod. I'm one of them. Only I'm not.

"Stow your gear." He points to the back of the shuttle.

I do and climb on board the small bus, trying not to obsess about how tiny it is. The blond guy sits next to another guy whose phone is out. This one has dark hair and a scowl on his face, even though his vibe says he's happy. So it must be a perma-scowl. Interesting. "Great weather conditions tomorrow," the scowl guy reports.

The third one tells some sort of joke that I miss, and they all laugh. It reminds me of when I was on swim team, and I feel like I'm with Sam and Taylor, my teammates, again. And then it's like a black hole surrounds me and fills me all at once. I miss those guys. Hiking the trails with them would be fun and cool and annoying all at the same time.

For the hundredth time, I wish I hadn't screwed up that whole situation. Swimming was the perfect sport for me. The feel of the water pressing in on me from all sides, the silence. Sam and Taylor stuck with me for most of high school. I don't blame them for bailing when my behavior rose to levels that were considered unsafe for myself and others. Unsafe for myself and others. Unsafe. For myself.

And others.

We pile out of the minibus, and I grab my gear, which comes out first since it was loaded last. I move to the side and let everyone else get their stuff and go ahead of me. It's the best way to lower expectations and make these kinds of social interactions easier. Let the water flow downhill. When the last of them has paid their bill, I step forward.

The clerk gives me a smile. "Sign in." He flips the book so it faces me. "Name and address. And person to notify."

I scribble Xevon. Just Xevon. Like Madonna.

"Legibly, if you can." The clerk chuckles good-naturedly and points to the mess I've made in the book. "You know, just in case we…"

"Right." I act like I'm trying to write clearly. Person to notify,

I put Zelda Sendak (a.k.a. Emily). For a second, I consider writing Emily's burner cell number or even her real one, but even the part of my brain that realizes a backup plan for actual emergencies would be wise knows I can't implicate Emily in any of my plans. Especially if they go bad.

I've taken so long making up a fake number that looks legit that the guys are banging down the stairs and out the front door as I'm finishing up.

"Hey, man! Come out with us!" Blond guy smacks me on the shoulder. "We'll wait while you throw your shit upstairs."

"Oh." I run my hand through my hair to give myself a second to deal. "I just…"

"You've got to eat. We left you the single."

"Huh?"

"Figured you'd like that, the single room."

"That'll be fifty-five dollars." The clerk puts the logbook away and waits for me to put the right combination of bills in his hand.

"Oh. Right. Thanks. I'm just gonna hit the sack. Very tired."

"It might be our last good hot meal for a while," he offers again.

My foot hits the first step. I can hear them standing, waiting for me. It's a weird thing to be able to do, but the Dramamine has infected me with its chemical stupor, so my senses focus on everything. *Everything.*

"You sure?" the blond guy calls. "Last chance."

A sound starts in my head. A drumbeat. A *bang*, a *thump*, a *bump*. A heartbeat. With an extra blip on the end. The rhythm

21

ricochets back and forth in my head until it bursts inside me, and the regret leaks out.

"Come on, he's not up for it. I'm starved."

Again, I think of the swim team. Taylor. Sam. *"You really killed the last fifty, Lone Wolf."*

Me, laughing because that's what guys do. The guys rearing back and howling. Me, joining.

Loneliness spreads through me.

The door bangs shut behind me.

"I'll go." The words slip out before I even know I've said them, but definitely too late, because obviously the guys are gone.

"They went to Hank's across the street," the clerk says. "You can catch up easy."

I take the steps two at a time, find my single, throw my backpack on the bed, and head back downstairs. I'll spend this last night with people. Plenty of time to be alone on the trail.

CHAPTER 3

Hank's is a small restaurant, tables out front, most of them taken, torches lit. I guess to keep the bugs away. I don't see my new hiker friends outside, so I push open the door, stepping into a world of noise and the smell of burgers. Good burgers. It's been forever since I've eaten more than a trail bar or a stale sandwich from a convenience store, so my stomach is screaming at me to give it real food.

A waitress pushes past me, tray over her head, but she's so short I have to lean sideways to avoid being decapitated, which makes a table of guys erupt laughing. "Over here," blond hiker guy calls. The rest of the table is cutting up.

I make my way over.

"By the way, I'm Drew. This is Lenny and Emerson." As he calls their names, the other dudes raise their hands in my direction. Drew points to the only empty chair at the table, next to Emerson and Lenny. There's no way I'm going to be able to squish in there without knocking some or all of their drinks off the table. Not with the level of Dramamine still in my system. Drew motions to the other guys. "Move down."

So they do. And it's immediately obvious who the alpha

dog is. I sit next to Drew, which is completely uncomfortable, because my back is facing the middle of the room. I hate that.

A tall redheaded waitress arrives without being summoned, a rag in her apron. She wipes the table and hands out menus. "We've got Miller, Miller Light, Yuengling, and Blue Moon on tap." She aims her attention at Lenny who calls out. "Big Sky IPA."

The waitress nods as each of the guys order. Then her eyes rest on me, even though I'm staring at the table, trying to decide if that dirty rag made it cleaner or just spread bacteria. "Coke," I say.

"Just Coke?" Drew asks. "You saving it for the trail?"

For two seconds, I contemplate ordering something to go in the Coke. It would help me fit in with the guys, for sure. And I guess with being on the go, my current beard situation makes me look a little older. But twenty-one? Do I chance it? Then I remember the Dramamine. That plus alcohol would probably not be a great mix. "Just Coke," I say.

"Good deal," the waitress answers.

She leaves and I worry that we are going to spend the next few minutes sharing our personal hiking goals or something, but then Drew says, "You're not shaving?"

My hand goes to my beard.

"It's kind of a tradition," the Emerson guy says. "We go into the woods clean shaven. We leave full bearded."

"It's stupid," Emerson says.

I agree with Emerson, but I'm pretty sure it's not a good time to say something like that. So instead I say, "So you guys have done this before, huh?"

"It's our third time," Emerson answers for the group.

The waitress brings the drinks and takes our food orders.

"Guess you must've liked the trail then." I take a drink of my Coke. Stupid meaningless drivel. God I hate myself and casual conversation right now.

They're all nodding and laughing, and by the time the food comes, they've each had a couple beers and are telling trail stories. I've managed to inch my chair over so that I'm sitting with my side to the door, not my back. It's a small gain, but I'll take it. Nobody notices that I'm not talking. Nobody cares. Everyone's happy. I take out my phone and text Emily: You wouldn't believe it. I'm out with three guys I just met, eating a burger. Not free range (don't tell Mom!) and my back is to the restaurant. Shiver.

Take a pic. I don't believe it.

That would be weird.

But bragging about it isn't?

No. Bragging about it is def weird. But less weird than documenting it.

B careful.

W the guys? They seem harmless.

On the trail.

It's a straight line.

Point A to B.

Exactly.

"So what do you think?" Emerson asks me.

"What?"

"For your trail name."

"My trail name?"

Drew smacks me on the arm. "How come we're the ones drinking and you're the one who's spacing out? No one uses their real name on the trail."

"The minute you step across that archway, you are whoever you want to be. Why do you think we walk five million steps to begin with?"

More laughing. The sound's starting to get to me, which means the Dramamine is wearing off.

"You want to pick your own name, though, or it could get dicey."

Even more laughing.

The waitress clears the dishes. "Another round?"

Lenny says, "One more for the road."

To me she says, "What about you?"

"Nah. Gonna call it a night."

She smiles and hands me my check. I pay in cash, tip included. I lean forward. "Thanks, guys."

I'm not sure if I'm supposed to say something else, but I've got nothing. So, I do my stiff-handed wave.

Drew tips his beer toward me. "Only five million steps, brah."

They all laugh some more.

I'm walking across the street when it hits me. Only five million steps. That's probably 4,999,999 steps more than I would normally plan as a leisure activity. These hikers are nuts. Then I wonder if I'm the stupidest person on earth. So, I text Emily again.

They say it's five million steps.

Nuh uh.

Uh huh.

Your feet r going to hurt.

Great prediction.

Maybe don't do all of them at once?

Funny girl.

I try.

It's a great hiding place. No one would believe to look for you there.

I almost don't.

You sure you don't want to go to school instead? You could sleep in a bed if you went to a school. Plus we won't be able to do our last summer b4 I go to college tour.

I know. Duck Tour.

Freedom Trail.

The Cape.

I know. Will have to resched. Gnite Z.

Gnite Y.

My head hits the pillow and I stare at the ceiling. Five million steps. Em's right. I'm an idiot. Is exerting my independence really worth all of this? Wouldn't going to a new school be easier than what I'm about to do? I roll over and punch the horribly flat pillow, fold it in half, and put the bunched part under my head. I remind myself that this cot is going to feel like living in style compared to sleeping in a tent. And then I remember, at least all of this is going to be on my terms. Mine. Not Mom's or that uberhelpful group of teachers and counselors who act like they are the only ones who know what I need.

CHAPTER 4

The walls in the hostel are pretty thin, and I can hear the guys getting ready to leave in the morning. Backpacks zip. Boots thud. I figure it's gotta be late since they were out drinking, but when I check my phone, it's only 7:30 a.m. Wow. These guys are serious about hitting the trail. Maybe I should be too.

My body is hyped from sleeping in a strange place. Plus, once I wake up, I can't go back to sleep anyway, so instead I check the weather. No rain today. Temps starting at sixty degrees, going to be cloudy but clear.

I stare at the date on my phone. April 15. This day usually signaled the end of the nightmare season for my family. Dad would work insane hours leading up to this day, and Mom always said tax season was going to kill him if she didn't first. I always thought that was unfair. She knew he was going to be an accountant before she married him. Just like he knew she was going to be a lawyer. The thing about being a lawyer, though, is there's no "season" to make lawyering harder or easier.

Now, April 15 is simply another day, and for me, it's as good a day as any to do the stupidest thing I've ever done in my life. I wait until there are no more voices or sounds outside my door to signal that my dinner mates are gone, and I go to take a shower, something I've come to consider a luxury since I've been on the run. I'm actually getting good with the grunge. Triple answer score. Yeah. You know, if this was one of Emily and my epic games of Scattergories.

In the bathroom mirror, I look at my scraggly beard. The others are going to shave before their hike. They said everyone does it. Do I really feel the need to conform? I head back to my room, wishing I'd bought shaving gear. I need to do this to fit in so I don't get caught as a runaway. But deep down, I know shaving my beard along with the other thru-hikers will let me be part of something bigger than I am. I like to act like I'm above all that, but the truth is, I miss my team, and maybe this is my second chance.

I run downstairs and find a different clerk at the desk. This one is wearing a blue beanie and has a super long beard, which makes me laugh at the irony of my next question. "Hey, do you guys have shave kits here?"

He leans over, opens a cabinet, and pulls out one of those cheap-ass travel kits with a throwaway razor and a tiny can of shaving cream. "Five dollars."

Back in my room, clean-shaven and freshly showered, packing is easy. However, dressing myself is a little harder. It takes me three attempts and one actual full-on self-talk to get myself into that polyester shirt that's supposed to be my lower layer. Luckily, they are tagless shirts, otherwise I'd be in *real* trouble. Once the shirt is on, my skin tingles like it's trying to pull away from the strange fabric. My armpits begin to sweat, which makes me feel cold and my skin hurt. I'm not sure I can do this, except I picture the conversation I'd have with the police officers. Sort of a bad *Scooby-Doo* moment… "I would have hiked the trail too, if it weren't for the wicking-action clothes…"

I walk around my room. Squat down. Stand up again. Walk some more. The fabric isn't terrible, it's just not cotton. It's tight enough to close off most of the air to my skin, but not tight enough to relieve my need for pressure. Then I realize, the backpack will help. So I put on the rest of my layers and then my backpack. At least this version of a weighted vest is normal, not like the one the occupational therapist made me wear in school years ago. The one I sometimes still miss and would wear if it didn't make me stand out so much. Man, I was a little freak.

Still am.

Obviously.

I'm down the steps in three seconds. I hand my key to the new clerk at the hostel desk, and I push my way out the front door.

I get a text.

Emily. A to B.

I answer. Z to Y.

Stay safe. Check in.

I will.

Then comes the one text she knows better than to send, but I guess she feels like it has to be said, in case it's the end of the world.

It wasn't your fault.

In this instance, I let her emoting slide. Then she sends another.
No one blames you.

I text back. I know. But really, I'm lying, because I blame me
and she knows that, even if she doesn't know why.

Liar.

I send her a stupid emoji that looks like a fox handing her flowers.
She sends back a dog chasing its tail.

So I send back. Conserving phone battery. Spk on the
other side.

It wasn't your fault. No one blames you. Those words are the
push I need to get me going. Each step I take will take me
farther from those sentences, create breathing space between
me and the sounds I can't forget. At least, that's my new hope,
the one that sprung up unexpectedly this morning as I was
getting dressed. Walking might help me feel better. Just like
swimming always did.

My phone in my backpack, I walk toward the entrance to the
trail. My nerves are building. My shoulders are tense, and my
hands are fisted. Enough to put dents in my palms from my
fingernails but not enough to draw blood.

A stone arch with a sign announces the approach to the trail
and diverts my attention. I'm pretty into rocks and bricks and
mortar, which I realize is a weird and overly selective interest,
but there it is. I'm so busy looking at the way they built the
stone arch that I almost miss the huge-ass tent set up to the left
of it with a group of people hanging out. Someone's playing a
guitar. I'm about to move past them, simply ignore the sons

of bitches who are destroying the one part of the trail I was actually looking forward to—complete isolation—but then I smell coffee, and I'm reminded that I haven't had any yet. Or breakfast for that matter.

The smell of a griddle, eggs, and bacon waft over to me. I approach the tent, feeling like one of Pavlov's dogs, but not caring. My stomach growls, deep. A plump Mom-aged woman ladles scrambled eggs onto a plate, which she holds out to me.

"How much?" I ask, not worrying so much about the cost, but the awkward series of movements it will take to get to my wallet, which is stuffed at the bottom of my backpack like the guides suggest.

She shakes her head. "It's free, dear."

The guy in front of me has a full beard and wild hair, which should mean he's been hiking for some time (though he is at the start of the trail), turns to offer these words of wisdom: "Trail magic."

"Trail magic?" I ask.

"From trail angels." He finishes as he adds a doughnut to the toast and tomatoes and sausage he's already piled on his plate. "People who generously donate time, money, supplies, and food to people who are hiking the trail. We—" He points to himself and then to me. "We inspire them to do random acts of kindness. Go us."

He catches me staring at his facial hair, which is kind of weird. So, I feel I have to ask. "You're just starting the hike?"

"Nah. I'm a flip-flopper."

I've got no idea what that means, but I nod like that makes total sense. I pile food on a plate, thinking of all of this new vocabulary. Flip-flopper. Thru-hiker. Trail names. Trail angels. Trail magic. It's all so cool and makes me feel proud of this world I had no idea even existed. It makes me wonder why more people don't drop out of their lives and hike the trail. Why kids don't routinely run away from bad homes and bad schools and live off the generosity of these strangers. Santa Claus requires obedience in exchange for gifts. Then there's that sick Elf on the Shelf nonsense. These people are feeding us simply because we are going to walk the trail. Booyah!

I don't spend too much time pondering the generosity of others, because I notice a big urn of coffee that calls me forward. I fill a cup. The smell of the coffee as it pours into the cup and the warmth in my hand as I palm it is all I need to make my brain start to wake up. After I've blanched my drink with cream, I pick a table with no one sitting at it, grateful that my friends from last night aren't here. Hopefully they've already moved on. The last thing I want to do is hike in a big group. Or any group for that matter.

The wind blows and it's chilly, and that makes the food better and the coffee more satisfying. Plus the food is good. Damn good. And free, which is also good. But more importantly, the hot coffee slides down my throat. My body hums, and for the briefest second, my mind is still and peaceful. Then I see her, a tall, thin girl with white blond hair that is cut super short. She looks about my age, making me wonder why she'd be doing this hike by herself. If Emily was here, she'd be pissed at me for the double standard and obvious discounting of the strength of women, but I can't help it. It seems wrong that she's alone, double standard or not.

This girl, whoever she is, has on a camo-colored baseball hat and is wearing a long-sleeve T-shirt and leggings. If it wasn't for her backpack, I'd be sure she wasn't a hiker. Doesn't she know the no-cotton rule?

Her movements are what really draw me in. She stands like she doesn't need to engage anyone. Like she believes in herself. I don't know exactly what makes me think this. Maybe it's the way she walks, head high, but eyes not scanning the environment. Simply in her head, eyeing whatever is in her immediate area.

She accepts food, with almost no eye contact exchanged, which makes me think she's smarter than most people. A hiker tries to talk to her and she doesn't answer. She takes a seat at the far end of the tent, facing outward. Maybe she's like me and wants to be able to keep everyone in front of her where she can see them. That makes me wonder even more about her.

She fiddles with a leather cord necklace. Pulls the sleeves of her shirt down over her wrists. These small movements tell me she's anxious, which is a direct dichotomy with the self-assuredness that she wears like her nonhiking clothes.

I've gulped down my breakfast, but she takes tiny bites. She stops to get a tiny notebook out of her backpack, and writes in it for less than a minute. Her expression is all straight lines. Mouth grim, but determined. Maybe. She shuts the book and stuffs it back into her backpack. Then she eats a little faster.

I realize I'm staring like a complete stalker, but this thought comes to me a second too late, because she catches me looking and shoots me a death glare that is impossible to misinterpret. My eyes go to my coffee, which I drain, then scoop up my garbage. I walk to the trash bins, careful not to look in her direction a final time, even though I'm dying to do just that.

I wave to the trail angels, then stare up at the stone arch that marks the entrance to the trail. My gaze scales the landscape, and for the first time, I really consider chucking the mission. Can I really do this? It's just one step. Then another. Until you get to some insane number of steps. Wow. This is nuts.

And then I remember how the guys told me the trail is where you can be whoever you want to be. And that means I don't have to be a runaway. I don't have to be the sad kid or the angry kid. I don't have to be the weird kid who always gets worked up about everything. I don't have to be the kid hiding under his desk. Or erupting during the assembly. I don't have to be the one disappointing my mother. Or my brother. Or Em, even though she'd never say it.

Setting goals always helps me, so I try to focus on a goal for today. The guidebooks say that you should aim for only eight to ten miles the first few days you hike the trail. That makes me want to get all competitive and go longer, but I'm not a hiker, and it's been years since I swam competitively. I remember the first time I had to do the forty laps we swam in an easy practice. I was winded and mad at Dad for making me go.

"You looked good out there."

My shoulders were heaving, and I was trying to slow my breathing a full five minutes after practice. "I'm hyperventilating. That's not good. That's the direct opposite of good. It's like my body," *cough, cough,* "is telling me to stop doing this. And my heart... It's beating like it's going to," *cough cough,* "explode." *Pause. Then, because he was just sitting there, smiling and nodding.* "I thought I was going to die."

"Now Dylan, logically you know I wouldn't make you do anything that would kill you. Also, there has never been a death at a swim team practice logged in any of the USA swimming pools. Look it up." *He handed me his phone.*

I typed in the question: Has anyone died at swim practice? Nothing. But even if no one died in the pool, it didn't mean they didn't want to die afterward. "I'm not going back."

"Okay."

"I'm serious. You can't make me."

"That's true. I can't. But I can promise you a few things."

Dad had a way of getting to me. "What?"

"Well, first of all, it will get easier and easier the more you swim, and soon, you'll be able to swim double what you did today without even trying."

That seemed unlikely, despite what I already knew about muscle growth and coordination from my years of occupational therapy. Which I hated. I was still holding Dad's phone, staring at the face, finger poised as if I was going to do another search of some kind.

"And I am willing to make a few deals with you if you are willing to give swim team a month's trial."

I flipped the phone over in my palm. Looked up at him, trying to not look interested, but I was sure my body's active listening posture, as described by my many therapists, was giving me away. "I'm listening."

"As long as you do swim team, you don't have to do occupational therapy."

Direct hit. But I wasn't going to give up so easily. "You said deals. Plural."

He laughed. "I know what I said. If you do swim team for a season, I will take you to Comic-Con."

I crossed my arms. "Mom won't like it."

"It's not up to her. It's a deal between two guys."

It's been a long time since that talk after swim practice. Almost eight years to be exact. Two since I competed on the team. But I know my body will remember how to do impossibly hard things. I still have my swimmer's V, broad shoulders, and strong legs, and muscle memory will kick in for sure. I tell myself what I used to tell myself at swim practice: *Just take the next lap.*

Just take the next hill. The next mile. The next hour. The next two hours. Let myself get good and lost in the woods. Each step takes me away from the coffee shop where I almost got nabbed. From Mom's detectives. From everything bad I've ever done.

CHAPTER 5

At first, all I notice is how heavy my pack feels as it presses down on my shoulders. Then how my foot slides a little in my boots, because the guy told me to buy them half a size too big "at least." The rugged terrain is difficult to maneuver, and I've got to look down all the time to make sure I don't trip or step on a snake. I'm not exactly sure what I pictured this to be like, but I didn't expect this. At times I walk along a forested trail, mostly flat with tree roots and downed limbs littering the ground. At other times, the trail leads uphill over rocks. I'm always looking for the white blazes, marks put along the trail that tell you where to go. Every time I pass one, a tiny bit of anxiety melts away. People have done this before me. Others will do it after me. Plus, it feels good to mark my progress by the white rectangles painted on the trees. These little details are the ones Dad would have pointed out for me if he was here. That makes me feel good.

I stop by a creek for a lunch of a PowerBar, one of the chocolate-covered peanut butter ones, and drink some water. It feels good to stop walking, and I listen to the sounds of nature, not through my headphones, but in real life. The sounds are calming—they remind me that there are aspects about this whole hiking-the-trail life that I already like. Sitting still makes my legs stiffen up, so I push myself to standing, put the pack back on, and walk some more.

I'm sweating, but it's cold and the wind blows and I shiver. It's not the actual hiking I mind. Hiking is like swimming. What I do mind is that my pants get caught on rocks and branches, disrupting my rhythm. I hate how my neck is damp and that it makes me feel like I'm sick.

I worry about bugs. A lot. So, my ears are listening in hard to make sure no insects are around me, ready to strike, that it is exhausting. The trail guides all said there are no bugs in Georgia at this time of year, especially when the wind blows, but I'm still on constant alert. Just in case.

I distract myself by putting in my headphones and playing the drums, the fast ones, on my phone. I match my walking to the rhythm of the sticks pounding and pounding. I make up this mantra in my mind. *Fourteen hours of battery. Fourteen hours of battery.* It's a stupid thing to chant, but I've got to remind myself that I can listen to music for part of the trail and for some of the nights, as long as I'm careful. It's seventy-eight miles to the first resupply town where I can recharge my phone.

I'm walking at a brisk-ish pace, and after a while, without my neurotic need to make sure no insects are threatening, it feels like being in the zone while swimming. Constant repetitive, unthinking movements. I picture Dad. How proud he would be of me. His eyes would almost close in approval with that pleased-with-me face.

Hard work and exercise make my body hum. A peaceful feeling fills me, and I don't ever want to stop. Only that's not normal or good. Or doable. My feet are really starting to hurt. I hear someone coming up behind me. So, I go off trail a few feet. Then a few more. I drop my pack, sit on a large rock, drink some water. Unzip my pack and get out my cell. It's 2:08. I've been hiking for so many hours already. Wow. My cell has two bars, remarkably. I want to tell Em. So I try to text her.

youll never believe how easy this has been!

But when I go to send it, I get a delivery failure message, which makes sense since I'm in the middle of fricking nowhere.

Now that I'm sitting, my legs feel a little shaky. I haven't eaten except the one PowerBar and that awesome send-off breakfast, so I open the top part of my pack and grab some dried apples. I drink more water. I'm almost out, so I'll have to find a water source and use my filtration system and tablets, which I'm pretty nervous about. Most people use one system or the other, but I'm a better-safe-than-sorry kind of person, especially when it comes to clean drinking water and gross stomach viruses. Blowout diarrhea in the deep woods? Not my dream.

Below me, I watch two hikers pass. An old Dad-aged guy and a kid who's probably his son. Glad I pulled off the trail. I check my mileage on my phone. 11.9 miles. I check my map. I'm almost at Cooper Gap.

I look around and wonder about setting up camp. I check my guide and my map; there's a flat camping area and one of those shelters about a half a mile from here.

I hike to where I want to set up camp and drop my pack. I take a drink of water and look out over the hillside. There's a brook nearby, and I think about refilling my water bottle. The sound of the rushing water is such a relief. If Emily was here, she'd understand that. The sound lifts the tension from my generally over-torqued body. I wish I'd gone camping with Dad, Christian (Emily's brother), and Uncle Steve, or even my brother, Brad, when I had the chance.

I don't want to think about that, so instead I get to work using my water filter. It slips at first and takes a few tries before I get the rhythm down, but then I pump the water and it actually goes in the bottle. It's strange to get excited about water, but I do. Then I drop in the tablets that are also supposed to make it safe to drink. I sit on a rock and wait for the water that looks so effing perfect, clean, and wonderful, but that is probably full of crap that'll kill me, to purify.

I take off my boots and my socks. My feet are definitely a little swollen with areas that are super red on the sides of my big toes. Great. I plunge my feet in the water and let that relief flood me. I think about washing my socks. And my body because I'm disgustingly dirty, definitely more dirty than I've ever been in my life.

Then I see her, the girl from earlier. She's about two hundred yards downstream from me, picking her way off trail. I wonder if this is a bathroom stop for her. It would make sense. You're supposed to leave at least that distance between water and catholes. She opens her backpack and takes an orange-handled trowel. I should look away, but I don't. Instead I crouch behind a rock like a total lurker.

I'm not well versed on trail etiquette, but I do know a few things. Watching someone take a poo or pee is definitely not cool. No need for social skills class to dissect that. So, I know that what I'm doing is wrong and I still do it. I keep watching her. Part of me wishes I could grab my binoculars to get a better look. Damn, I'm a sicko.

When she's done digging, I feel my heartbeat pick up a little. Is she going to get undressed right here? She doesn't. Instead, she reaches into the front pocket of her pack and takes out that little notebook that she wrote in earlier. Her face gets that same grim look I saw at the trail angel breakfast. She rips out a sheet from the notebook, then stares at it for ten seconds. Ten seconds is a long time to stare at anything, let alone a piece of paper with your writing. It's not like she has to figure out what the note says, I mean, she wrote it and all.

She rips the paper in half. And in half again. She puts the pieces into the ground and covers it with dirt. She stomps on it, packing the dirt tight. When she's done, she looks up at the sky, back to the creek, then—hands on her hips—she speaks, nodding as she does, like she's using self-talk or something. Some of the kids in my unit at my last school used to do that. It drove me crazy. But watching her do it now, I wish I could read her lips.

When she's done, she looks around, and I crouch lower. She goes to the stream and unpacks her water filtration system.

Should I approach her? Would she be angry that I was invading her space? She struggles a little with the pump. It slips and the water spills, then she kneels by the creek, crying. Except I know that she's not crying about the water, and that's a really weird thing to know about someone. Especially for me.

The right thing to do would be to leave her alone, but all I can do is stare. I understand the pain she's feeling. I feel it. And that means she and I have something pretty deep in common, aside from us hiking the trail. And maybe she's got similar reasons to be here. Not the not-wanting-to-go-to-school reason. The other, deeper one.

I watch as she eventually gets the water flowing. The wind gusts again and I shiver. I decide not to tempt fate any longer, backing myself away from the creek and toward a camping area, though the image of her burying that piece of paper and crying by the creek stays with me long after I've set up my tent and my stove. I'm still thinking about it when I take out my can of OFF! Deep Woods (evergreen scent), the only kind of bug spray I believe works, and I spray a huge area where I lay out my sleeping bag. I choke a little on the fog of the insect repellent, but I don't care. There is no way I'm sleeping in the woods without a little protection.

Housekeeping complete, my stomach growls—a long, deep rumble. It's definitely time for dinner. I light my stove, the one thing that isn't remotely difficult for me, having worked with Bunsen burners in chemistry class, and cook myself two delicious bags of mac and cheese. I'm not usually a huge mac and cheese fan, but man am I hungry. And mac and cheese is easy to carry and easy to make.

Mom used to always get so annoyed with me when I forgot to eat. Sometimes it would be all day. Sometimes longer. She'd complain to Dad, who would eventually just drop off a plate with food on my desk. Dad knew when I was working on something, anything, I did not want to be disturbed. I could be playing the computer in chess, reading Harry Potter, any of them, for the sixth or seventh time, playing sudoku. It didn't matter. When I was in my world, there was no way to enter it, unless maybe by dropping off a piece of Joey's Pizza, extra sauce, extra cheese. Sometimes I'd even look up and say, "Thanks, Dad." Other times, like when I was studying the astronomical charts of recent star deaths or weather charts, I'd just shovel the food in and not even acknowledge the receipt. But Dad was cool with that. Sometimes he'd mutter, "That's my little scientist." And I would feel understood on a profound level.

When I'm done eating, I wash out my bowl with my newly filled water bag and then dry the inside. I "pack out my trash," like the books say to, and put everything away, rewarding myself in my head for following the trail rules.

Once I pack everything up, I prepare to do the one thing I've been dreading since deciding to live this thru-hiking life; I head into the woods with a shovel. The trail books are really clear about this next part. There are rules you have to follow. Rules usually help me. But in this case, I'm worried they won't be enough.

I tell myself this isn't hard. It's just like going in a toilet. It's no big deal. Don't focus on the potential bugs. Don't worry about anything but this. First, I have to pick an ideal spot. Not too close to trees or leaves. Those have bugs, for sure. Crawling bugs. That's a deal breaker. I have to not think about bugs. But once you tell yourself not to think about something, it's all you *can* think about.

Once I find a decent spot, I dig the hole. It needs to be six to eight inches deep. I picture a medium Coke ICEE from Burger King and dig down far enough for one of those. That done, I take a deep breath. I dug a cathole. Check.

I look around to make sure there is no noticeable insect life. I listen carefully. No bug sounds. I drop my pants. But the very thing I've come here to do is now the last thing I can accomplish with tense muscles. I stand here, listening for invaders. Telling myself to stop being an idiot. Reminding myself it'll be less weight to carry if I do this. *Ha!*

Eventually, I give up. I fill in the hole so no unsuspecting animal or hiker falls in, and I tramp back to my tent where I wipe my sleeping bag with an insecticide wipe that Emily said I should be careful about using or some hiker will find me in my tent, legs in the air like a dead bedbug. I said, better a dead bedbug than a live one.

I crawl inside the soft sleeping bag. The guy at the store said I should have bought the down one, but the thought of all of those feathers sort of freaked me out. I felt I could live with the few extra ounces this bag cost me in pack weight.

Sleeping bags in general freak me out. It's a weird phobia to have, but there's no convincing me to give it up. They seem so confined. Exactly the kind of place where animals or rodents or other vermin would lie in wait for the unsuspecting hiker. I'm going to have to give myself a word-of-the-day point for vermin. I'll tell Emily when I'm able to text her.

I zip the bag open, check for bugs, zip it back up, and climb in. My toes stretch out, feeling for marauding mice or rogue spiders that my inspection may have missed. Finding none, I decide to lie on top of the sleeping bag. Seems safer somehow. Triple points! Booyah! But then I start to worry that by laying on top of the sleeping bag, it makes me even more vulnerable to the nasty bugs that have waited for this moment to attack. So I force myself under the covers. Even with the cushion-y sleeping bag, rocks poke my back through the layers of nylon and flannel. I remember when I was little, Mom used to smooth out my bedsheets so there were no wrinkles…and definitely no crumb attacks (what I called dirt or sand that scraped my knees). She'd wash my bedding regularly, and she'd even go over it with one of those lint rollers.

I try not to think about how much Mom must be worried. My biggest impairment is the one no one wanted to talk about. There are times that I know that I'm hurting someone I love, and I still do whatever it is that is hurting them, because I believe what I want or need at that moment outweighs every-thing else. I know that really sucks for other people. I wish I could change it, but I feel like it's written in my DNA some-how. Some people are just born assholes.

I put on my headphones and listen to the chill-out playlist, same as always: Chants, sounds of nature (double points for being ironic), and finally, drumming. I guess I'm more tired than I realize, because by the time the second track kicks in, my muscles loosen and I feel them melt into the sleeping bag. My eyes close, and I fall away from the music around me.

CHAPTER 6

I wake up to the sound of rain drizzling on my tent. It's peaceful, like the rushing creek yesterday, but this time instead of making me feel good, I feel incredibly sad. The weird thing is, feeling sad is also a relief, because, according to the counselor Mom made me see, it shows my conscience is working. I am sad. And I feel sad. These are good things, I guess. Although, normal people don't need to celebrate feeling this way. They just do it, at the right time, not a year later. But what can I say? My processing is slow. And better late than never, right? I lie in my sleeping bag—wishing I'd gotten that down sleeping bag. Freezing temperatures are more compelling than the fear of feathers. I kick myself for being so painfully me, and I try to ignore the urgent need to take a mighty piss.

The one time I let Dad talk me into camping with him, we went to one of those parks that actually have bathrooms and cabins and was far enough from civilization that nobody cared if you peed in the woods, but close enough that you could get a good piece of pizza if you were desperate. We camped in the tent in the woods to make it feel more real. It was like training wheels for camping, and I knew at thirteen, I was way too old to have to take baby steps. Bathrooms were one of my stipulations for camping of any kind. Having Emily camp with us was another condition for my agreement. Dad was always finding ways to help me say yes to activities I wanted to say no to.

"It's not so bad going in the woods," he said. "Not for guys anyway."

That made Emily giggle.

But I flat refused to find out if it was bad or not. Dad went into the woods while Em and I took turns using the bathroom.

The sounds at night were horrible. Bugs droning. Frogs croaking. I remember thinking how wild it sounded. How could anyone sleep outside like this? Why would anyone choose to? I slept that night in fits and starts, convinced as soon as I closed my eyes some horrid army of insects would walk all over me, my skin crawling with the thought. But Dad put his hand on my back while I tried to fall asleep, and I loved the way that felt. Strong and protective. Like he was holding me in place.

When I can't make myself lie here anymore, I unzip my tent and step out into the drizzle. It's colder than I thought it would be, but I make myself move. Pee. Then coffee. Coffee after pee. My new mantra. I grab my trowel, the one I took from the garage before I left home, dig a hole six inches down, and pee. Dad's right—peeing in the woods isn't terrible. But no other inspiration hits, so I cover the hole and pack the dirt. I remember the blond hiker girl burying that note. My gaze shoots in the direction of where she was when she buried it.

Before I know what I'm doing, I'm on my knees examining

the ground for evidence of the burial site. I'm pretty sure my position is right, but I don't see any fresh patches of disrupted ground. So I go back to where I was spying on her, because I've got to be honest with myself, I was spying. And now I'm spying even more, because I'm going to dig up whatever note it was she buried. That should stop me. It would stop a normal person. But. Yeah. I'm too focused to completely walk away.

From my new position, I can tell that I need to move about forty-five degrees to the left. I can almost hear Mrs. Horner, one of the therapists from over the years who took the time to explain socially expected behaviors to me. She also told me she believed I knew when I was going to do something inappropriate. If she were here with me now, she'd tell me there's still time to stop myself. There's still time to not give into the obsession. But, sorry, Mrs. Horner, restraint is not the order of the day, because within seconds of finding the burial ground, I'm pawing through the dirt, which is super weird, because I could use the trowel, but I'm worried about ripping the note. So, I go bare-handed into the dirt. Getting dirt under my nails and on my hands usually freaks me out, especially after that entire horse burial ground incident. But this time, all I can think about is finding that note. Once I get a few inches down, I slow my digging and carefully brush the dirt back like I'm an archaeologist or something. Finally, my fingers close around the thin pieces of paper, and I almost let out a shriek of excitement. *Eureka, baby!*

Except the ink has run and the words are illegible. I can pick out only a few letters. E K W O I hold the paper up to the light, but that doesn't help. Next time I won't wait so long before I dig up her notes. The *next-time* thought should be enough to scare me straight, but I'm pretty sure it won't. Not once my mind is committed to a course. I roll the paper up and put it in my pocket, careful not to rip it anymore. Maybe when it dries, I'll be able to figure out more letters or words.

I stare at my dirty hands. The soil caked on my fingers, drying and making them feel weird and horrible. And for what? Tiny strips of torn paper. Damp and smeared. I wipe my hands on my pants. Wipe them some more. But it's not enough. I rush to the stream and plunge my hands in the water, scrubbing them clean. The funny thing is that in addition to my being a complete stalker, I'm also more committed to finding out about this strange girl than anyone else I've met. Mom would be so proud, I'm taking an interest in my peers. That makes me laugh. Then my phone makes a noise. By some miracle, I'm getting service.

So proud of you. Keep going. It's Emily. Then, Also don't get eaten by a bear bc then I'll be in so much trouble.

I cover my mouth with my hand like Emily does when she's trying to hold in a laugh. I go to answer her, but it's such a perfect line, I want to leave it alone for now.

I put my phone in my pocket and head back to my camp. Coffee is waiting in that plastic bag, practically begging to be brewed. Along with my self-respect and dignity, I hope.

I start up my stove. Heat the water for coffee. Instant is not my favorite, but it'll do. I pour in sugar and fake creamer and stir, stir, stir. The water has to be superhot in order for the powder to mix in. One speck of unmixed powder and I'd be gagging like a mofo. It's nowhere near as good as the real stuff, but it still wakes up my brain enough that, as I'm stirring my oatmeal, I'm wondering about what I just did with that girl's notes, and how awful I would feel if someone did that to me. That does not stop me from pulling out the papers and trying to make sense of the letters I can see. I can guess at one word, "know," but that's all I've got.

I look at my phone again. It's 8:00 a.m. Being out in the wilderness has got me all "early to bed, early to rise." Like when I was on swim team. Man, those swim practices started at the crack of dawn. But that was me and Dad time, so I didn't care. While I was in the pool, he'd get coffee and doughnuts or some of those awesome cheese Danishes from that bakery near the rec center, so I'd get to chow before school without Mom yelling at either of us for eating junk.

"When you swim one hundred laps before school, you can eat whatever you like, am I right?" my dad would say, his mouth full of doughnut.

I'd always answer, "You're right." I was so happy being with Dad, I wouldn't even point out that he was eating the same stuff and hadn't done any of the swimming.

It was always hard to go back to school and life after the dreamy feeling of being underwater. Alone. In complete silence. It was perfection. But as Dad pulled up in front of my school, he'd say the same thing to me every day. "Man, Dylan, you really killed it at practice today, but now you're a little zoned out, huh?" Then he'd laugh. Shake my arm a little bit. "Wake up for school, though, okay? We don't want to answer to Mom if your teachers tell her you're having problems staying awake. She'll yank you off the swim team, and we'd have to give up our male-bonding mornings."

And I'd say, "Scattergories. Double score for double letters."

And he'd chuckle and say. "You and your games." But he'd say it like it was cool, like I was cool.

Alone in the forest, I shake my head. Drink more coffee. Take down my tent. Stash my gear. Pack out my trash. The snapping of twigs should rouse me from my focused fog, but it doesn't. So, it's a big surprise when I notice an actual *bear* in the woods behind me.

All of a sudden Emily's don't-get-eaten text is less funny, which makes it even more funny, in my head, at least. I'm not stupid enough to think the bear will be amused, though. My mind searches through all of the bear facts I read before embarking on this nice, long stroll in the woods. I've got at least ten website pages, memorized in full, displaying themselves in my head, ready for me to focus on. Great. *He died while choosing a page to read.* Perfect epitaph for my tombstone.

The bear stands to full height. He doesn't look too tall. Maybe, like, four feet. The image of those height markings on the door of banks comes to me. That's the way my brain works, making these strange pairings.

The bear stands taller. *Ruh roh.* That eliminates some of the research about harmless meetings in the wild, when bear and human exchange a bit of eye contact, then each go on their ways. Great.

This isn't going to be one of *those* stories. Obviously.

One of the websites talked about there being safety in numbers. Not helpful, since I'm on my own here. One site talked about not running. Fear has my feet planted in place, so I'm not going anywhere.

Twigs snap behind me, and for one terrifying second, I'm convinced that I'm surrounded by a family of bears. Or a gang of them. Which is actually called a sleuth of bears. A fun fact that would normally entertain the hell out of me, but right now I'm thinking, like bullies at school, they'll pants me and then kick me, then *tear me open.* Okay, so that happened before I was on the swim team and became built from all that training. Not the "tear me open" part, but the rest. Still, the bear in front of me doesn't seem to be wowed by my swimmer's V, and I'm guessing the bear behind me doesn't care either. I turn my head the tiniest bit to confirm my suspicion, and my jaw drops.

The blond girl is behind me, waving two big sticks over her head. She starts yelling. "Hey, bear! Go away! You don't want a piece of this!"

That triggers me to remember the internet page that talked about looking bigger, waving things like humans do, and making noises to scare off bears. This girl is definitely on top of her bear de-escalation strategy. Who am I to argue? I grab my backpack and wave it over my head. "Yeah, bear! Go back to your bear world!" *Bear world? God, I sound ridiculous.*

The bear stares at both of us. Ten seconds pass. Twelve. Sweat is rolling down my face, my neck, my back. The bear drops down to all fours and lumbers off.

His back to us, I freeze. Terrified. Grateful. Embarrassed. One day into my trip, and I needed a girl to save me from a bear.

"You gotta use the bear bags or poles." She sounds annoyed. "You could've gotten yourself *and* that bear killed."

I dry swallow, which makes my chest tighten and cramp. For once words fail me. I nod.

"Okay, then," she says and walks away.

The feeling in my legs return. I jog over to her. "Hey, thanks. You know, for um…"

"Saving your ass?" she offers.

"Yeah."

"Don't make me do it again." She points back to where my stuff is. "Like now. You just saw a bear and you leave your stuff to thank me? You ever camped or hiked before?"

"Um…"

She holds up her hand like a stop sign. "Save it. Obviously you haven't, which means I'm hoping you're doing a couple of day hikes and will be done. Don't make me run into you again, or I may just give you a trail name you'll never live down."

My eyes go to my gear. I don't want to fight off a bear again, but I also don't want to look like an idiot in front of this girl. "What kind of nickname?" I ask.

"Like *stupid-newbie* or *dumb-as-shit*." With that she stalks off.

I've never met anyone who has left me verbally defenseless. This girl is a big ball of enigma. She buries slips of paper that she cries over. She can fend off bear attacks and brainstorm trail names, but she wears cotton on a big hike. Cotton? The no-cotton rule is the first one in every single trail book out there.

I trudge back to my campsite, grateful the bear hasn't come back and made off with my stuff. More than anything, I wish I could talk to Em about this girl. She wouldn't believe I'm actually interested in someone. Not just someone. A girl.

CHAPTER 7

I make decent time through a very hilly part of the trail. My shoulders are a little sore from yesterday, but my quads, my calves, and the rest of me are purring. Almost like they've craved this level of exercise.

Every step I take, I feel my muscles building like when I was swimming.

I think of the last time I swam with the team. Like most things with me, everything was cool until it wasn't. Then it *really* wasn't. We'd practiced pretty hard that summer, and Taylor and Sam and I had all upped our games. Junior year was going to be our year.

The trouble started the first day of school, when I came home and Max didn't greet me. He always hated when we went back to school. Over the summer he'd get used to me hanging around the house all day. So, usually every year when I came home after the first day of school, he would take his frustration out on my room. He'd trash my bed. Throw my stuff on the floor. Raid my hamper. Every year, he made his misery known. After school, I'd always scratch him behind the ears and try to make up for it with treats, but I knew he was hurt.

But when I got home that day, not only didn't he come find

me, he wasn't in my room. And everything was as I'd left it that morning, even though I'd forgotten to put the extra lock on it that Dad devised to keep him out.

"Mom?" I called, since she'd come home early from work that day. "Mom, have you seen Max?"

"No, honey," she answered from the kitchen.

"Max!" I cried going from room to room. "Max!"

Mom joined in the hunt.

"Oh, honey…"

Those two words made me feel like I'd swallowed boulders. My legs lost their coordination. He'd collapsed in the laundry room. I stroked his muzzle. "It's okay, Max. It's okay."

The vet came to the house, because Max couldn't move and we couldn't lift him to the car. They took blood and Max didn't even notice. The vet found the tumors near his heart and under his ribs. They were so large they didn't even need an X-ray. By then, Emily was there. Mom talked to the vet about possible treatments, but I knew that would be horrible for him so I shook my head. The vet agreed. We kissed Max goodbye.

Dad told me that I didn't have to go to swim practice the next day, but that made no sense to me. Staying home wouldn't bring back Max. Wouldn't change that we hadn't noticed Max was sick, that he was getting lumps on his body. He had been slowing down. We had chalked it up to his getting older. If only I'd paid attention, at least I could've stayed home with him on his last day. But I hadn't. And swim practice wasn't going to change that.

But Dad was right about staying home, and I should have listened.

The swimmers shared the locker room with the wrestlers, and there was this guy Charlie who would never leave me alone. He was always like, "Hey, Dylan, swimmers are wimps. I could out-wrestle you any time."

I'd usually answer, "So what, dipshit. I can out-swim you."

"Wrestling is a man's sport. Why don't you have daisies on your cap for your synchronized swimming?"

I could've made fun of what wrestlers wore. That would have been easy enough, but that day I didn't feel like talking. I felt like shutting him the eff up, so I said, "Let's do it, Charlie. Let's wrestle."

He clapped hands with one of the other wrestlers. "Hell, yeah."

"In the pool," I added.

"I'll wrestle you anywhere you like, you little pussy."

Sam put his hand on my shoulder. "Easy, Dylan…"

"You gonna let your mom talk you out of a contest?"

Taylor got in front of me. "Let it go."

"Look, his friends are scared for him. They know what's what."

I pushed Taylor back softly. Just enough so he'd know he couldn't stop me. Taylor tried to catch my eye, but I was focused.

I left the locker room, walked straight to the pool, and jumped in. "Let's go."

The wrestlers and swimmers all gathered around the deck. My guys were motioning for me to get out of the pool, but the wrestlers were all hyped up. Some were yelling jeers at me.

My eyes hurt from crying the day before. They felt dry and scratchy like they'd been rubbed down with sandpaper. So when I looked at my audience, they were blurry. In some way, this whole scene didn't seem real, like we were in one of those cheesy high-schooler-being-bullied movies.

Sam and Taylor stood at the side of the pool. Sam's arms were crossed over his chest. Taylor had his hands on his hips. I knew both of them well enough to realize they were pissed at me. They didn't know about Max, and if they had known they probably would have tried to stop me. It wouldn't have mattered, though. Like the cancer that spread through my dog, I was being infected with anger. And Charlie was just begging for me to erupt on him.

"We'll start in the shallow end," I said and pointed.

"Whatever you say, Chief." Charlie jumped in the pool right in his wrestling clothes as if that made him all badass.

He put his hands in the air, and his teammates cheered for him. The swim team didn't, because Sam and Taylor would've beat their asses if they had. My team stood silently on the pool deck. Sam and Taylor and Gabe and Derek. Even Eddie was there. Sam shook his head, and Taylor looked around. I couldn't tell if they were hoping someone would stop this or if they were just really nervous. A vein in Sam's neck stood out and Taylor's jaw was clenched. They looked like they were ready to jump in and help me if it came to that.

There was still time to call this off, but my heart and mind were set on this course of action. I nodded to the little weasel.

Someone on deck blew a whistle, the one Coach usually used, the one he left on a hook on the side of the pool. It started us off. I pretended to let him take me down into the water. His hand around my neck, the other around my waist. We both went under.

He pushed up to get a breath, but as he did, I pulled him from the three-foot to the four-foot depth. His feet scrambled for the bottom of the pool, but I kicked them out from under him and pushed him back under the water. He wrapped himself up with me again in one of his wrestling moves, but I dragged him into the deeper part of the pool. I wrapped my legs around his chest and held his head under water. He was struggling really hard, but I held him down.

I started counting, or at least I thought I had. I hadn't even gotten to thirty, I was sure it was only twenty or twenty-five, but I must have gotten sort of lost, spaced out, because before I knew it, there was a lot of splashing behind me. Sam and Taylor and half the wrestling team were swimming around me, pulling me off him.

It was like my eyes weren't even seeing anymore. I held my hands over my head and walked around the pool like an Olympic champion, oblivious to the coaches who were now on the pool deck. The wrestling coaches, the swimming coaches, and the principal were all screaming at me. Charlie was on the side of the pool coughing and gasping for breath.

Obviously, I was kicked off the team. I was also suspended for ten days. Ten days of staying home without Max was the worst punishment of all.

CHAPTER 8

I've only seen a few hikers this morning, which means following the advice to leave after April 1 to avoid crowds was a good idea. I'm in a groove and doing at least ten miles a day. Could maybe do more, but I figure I've got no reason to push myself. No real place to go. Part of me wonders where that hiker—the one who saved me from the bear—is currently, but if I can't force myself to use socially expected behaviors around her (like not spying on her and not digging up her secret notes), it's probably good that we're not on the same stretch of trail.

The weather catches up to me today, though. I race for cover under one of the shelters that the guidebooks mentioned. The Tray Mountain shelter is painted this blend-into-the-background green, making it look less sheltering than it would if it didn't look like part of its surroundings, but it does have a roof. That alone makes it worth investigating. As the rain pours down and lightning and thunder explode all around me, I sit, knees pulled up into my chest, my pack stowed on the floor, protected from the mud by its elevation. The shelter itself is this slanted wooden thing that doesn't exactly seem sound or well designed. As I listen intently, if not obsessively, for sounds that indicate rodent infestation, I'm surprised to hear footsteps.

Definitely human. Sharing a small space with someone, especially someone I don't know, is not exactly exciting times for me, but I'm not about to give up protection from the storm, no matter how random the person is.

I look up as a face appears in the doorway, lightning flashes behind him. *Him.* My disappointment registers in my gut.

The man gives a stiff wave, kind of like I do. "Hey. I'm Rain Man."

I am stunned by this fortyish man. His face is covered with gray hair, which matches the gray mop on the top of his head. Creases paint his face, but they're soft, and even the scraggly gray-and-black eyebrows that would normally be scary to me look soft and nice because he smiles the kind of smile that lights up his eyes. I'm sort of at a loss for what to say in this situation and I wonder what my social skills teacher would say about my how to work myself into a conversation with a total stranger on the Appalachian Trail.

The guy doesn't wait for me to figure it all out. He throws his pack onto the floor next to me. "They call me Rain Man, because I'm always bringing the rain."

I look outside. "Apparently."

"Yeah."

Awkward silence. I figure now's the time to come up with my trail name before someone gives me a doozy. A good trail name, not that girl's suggestions. "Wild Thing."

"What?"

"My trail name."

"As good a name as any, I guess. You hungry, Wild Thing?"

"Guess so."

"Well, you are in for a treat. I happen to be known for my gourmet meals."

My stomach growls just hearing that news.

Rain Man puts down his pack. "I use two stoves. In this case, mine and yours, And I dehydrate the meals myself. That's the secret."

I nod.

"You like shrimp and grits or chili?"

"I've never had shrimp and grits. So maybe chili."

"You've never had shrimp and grits? That settles it. We'll make a little of both so that you can have a taste. No pressure if you don't like it. But you will. The trail makes you hungry. Especially a young guy like you."

I feel heat go through me with that remark. Not because I'm embarrassed, but because he's noticed I'm young. How young does he think I am? Can he tell I've gone AWOL? Is Rain Man a threat? Will he report me to the authorities?

I scour Rain Man's face for signs that he might betray me or turn me in. Rain Man, for his part, keeps unpacking. "I've been hiking the trail for over thirty years. It's how I get back to who I am inside. You know?" He points to his heart.

That gesture, along with its implication, makes me wince.

"You okay, Wild Thing?"

"Yeah."

"Too heavy for you, son?"

The word "son" also makes me almost flinch, but I force myself to keep my shoulders back and my head tall, the way Dad taught me. I force myself to fake smile. "Nah. It's fine."

"How's your water supply?"

I look at my almost depleted water bottle. "I'll go get more."

The lightning has stopped, so I'm feeling pretty lucky. Rain Man hands me his water bags. "Fill mine too? This one is where the stream water goes. Then we'll hang it and it'll filter into the clean water bag."

I'm staring at this contraption, which holds a crap ton of water, and wondering why I listened to Emily, who made a face when she saw this very system, the one the guy at the store recommended. She'd wrinkled her nose and said the bags reminded her of the urine bags from the catheter Grandpa Fred had at the nursing home. That did it for me. But now I'm wondering why the hell I'd let that ruin the easiest way to filter water in the world. "Sure thing."

He rubs his hands together. "Good. While you're doing that, I'll start our meal."

I hike down to the creek to fill his bag and my filter and bottle. Along the way, I actually pay attention to my surroundings—a little trick I picked up after the bear episode. It's stopped raining now, and the leaves are filled with water. Birds are out chirping. I can hear the water running down the rocks. I take my shoes off and wade into the water, letting the cool water calm my overworked feet. This is fast becoming my favorite part of each day.

A memory comes to me as I'm standing here in the stream.

Em and I were out with Dad at the movies. I was on one of Mom's incentive programs, where if I behaved at school, I'd get a reward. I'd had, like, seven good days at school in a row (translation: I didn't sleep in class), and we were seeing Godzilla. *When we got home from the movies, I roared like Godzilla, and Max got all excited and pranced around, barking back. Em and Dad and I laughed so much, and Mom popped her head in the room and called us her little monsters. Her little wild things.*

The memory weighs me down. I miss Max. I miss Em. I miss Dad. And also, I miss my mom.

A rustling to my left startles me. Is it a bear? My heart beats like mad. I peel a tree branch back and see it's the girl. She's about ten feet away. Her stare falls on me. I cast my eyes down, even though I wasn't doing anything wrong. Well. I'm guilty of watching her and digging up her notes the other day, but it's not like she knows that. This is just one example of how the body doesn't lie, how movements speak louder than words, if you can just learn to read them.

"You doing okay, Bear Bait?"

"Two points."

"Huh?"

"On Scattergories. That would be a two-point score. Letter B. Bear Bait. Both start with a B. So two points." There I go with my verbal impulsivity. Sure to impress.

She looks at me like she can't believe I'm still talking. I can tell because her shoulders are almost in a full shrug and her palms are facing up like *What the hell?* I don't dare look at her face, because she's got the kind of straightforward expressions I could probably read, and I'm not sure I want to see what she really thinks of me. "Okay… Well, enjoy your day."

"You're wet," I blurt. I have to force my finger not to point because my social skills teacher told me it wasn't cool to point at other people, it's accusatory, for sure, but I guess in this case, I am accusing her. I'm accusing her of wearing rule-breaking cotton clothes, because part of me is pissed that she gets to wear them even though she is soaking wet and I am dry, proving why the rule exists to begin with.

"Your powers of observation are improving daily," she says.

"You'll get sick."

"Not your problem, Bear Bait."

"It's Wild Thing, by the way."

"Wild Thing?"

"My trail name."

"You named yourself Wild Thing? Wow. I'm not sure if that's incredibly egotistical or just plain stupid."

I'm unprepared for criticism about my choice of nickname. So unprepared I find my hands on my hips like someone else put them there. "It doesn't mean I think I'm a wild animal or frat boy or something."

"It doesn't?"

"No. After the book."

Her head tilts a little. Her body leans toward me, and I take that as a win. "*Where the Wild Things Are?*" she asks.

"Yeah. It was my favorite book when I was a kid." I shake my head. "I guess it still is."

Her voice gets soft. "I know it by heart." She puts her hand over her heart, and I feel myself getting more and more interested in this girl who is so plainspoken with her gestures and all. The one who loves the same book I love.

"Hey, you want to come to dinner?" I ask. "I could lend you some clothes while yours dry."

"I'm good." She pats her pack. Places it on the ground and starts taking off her boots. She takes her water bottle and pump out and starts working on filling it.

"I mean, I'd have to ask, but I could chip in food if he needed. He didn't seem concerned over how much he had, and I could share my portion."

She stops. "Who are you talking about?"

"Rain Man. He's making shrimp and grits and chili."

"You met Rain Man?"

"Yeah, why? You know him?"

"My family does. We used to see him when we hiked sometimes. My parents really liked him." Her mouth droops a little, and I feel the sadness that memory cost her.

But once again, I wonder how this girl knows so much yet seems so ill prepared. I look at her half-ass water filter. Her soaking-wet clothes. It's cold. Not freezing, but cold enough to be concerning. I hand her my filter, which is definitely in better working condition. "Yeah. Fill your bottle and come up to the shelter."

Now she'll have to come, because she's got something of mine.

"I hate those shelters." The girl puts her arms around herself. "People are idiots. They leave crumbs that attract mice."

"We just ducked in to get out of the storm."

"I love storms." She looks up at the sky. "And after. It's like the air is cleared and everything smells so clean."

I actually hate storms, but I remember that guys are supposed to agree with what girls they like say. "Me too."

She smiles, and it seems my social skills training is finally paying off. *Booyah!*

"You don't think he'll mind?" she asks.

"I'm sure he won't. And if he does, I'll give you mine. I wasn't so sure about shrimp and grits anyway."

"You know he dehydrates all his food himself," she says.

I don't know why this is so important, but she seems really excited about it. So I say, "See you at the shelter."

"Thanks, Wild Thing."

Something about her using my trail name makes me feel warm inside, like I'm one of the gang.

"Sure."

I make it all the way back to the shelter before noticing that I left my boots and disgusting socks by the creek. So smooth (two points), which is sort of astounding anyway since now I've apparently walked over mud and sticks and pebbles, so far into my head that I didn't even notice. Me. Not noticing bare feet. On rocky and muddy ground. Wow.

Rain Man points to where my boots should be. "You lose your

mind? You never leave your boots. Never. What happened? You meet some hot, young thing?"

"I uhh… Yeah, this girl. She said she knows you."

"I hope you had the good manners to invite her for dinner."

This reminds me of Mom and Aunt Mary, how they always welcomed whoever we brought home. Sam and Taylor ate over whenever they wanted, but that's where it began and ended for me in terms of dinner guests. Aside from Emily, who doesn't count, because she's family. But I also know that Sam and Taylor's families weren't quite so open. Especially considering how much we swimmers eat. "You don't mind?"

"Three for shrimp and grits it is." He stirs the pot and goes into his backpack for another dehydrated pack.

"You can have some of my food if you want. You know, so you won't run out."

He holds up his hand. "I'm good. Always bring extra. Besides. Gonna do a zero day soon. I'll restock."

I nod like I know what he means. Only I've never done a zero day before. I have no idea what that even is.

"This girl. She the young blond one?"

"Yeah."

"She used to have a different name, but now they call her Ghost."

"That's her trail name?"

"Nah. It's a name hikers have given her. Used to hike with her family. She never talks to anyone anymore. So that means you must be special."

"You mean, she used to talk to people and just stopped?" It's not like me where I rarely talk to anyone anyway. But why talk and then stop? Something must have made that happen, and now I want to know what.

Rain Man stirs the pot and looks at me. "You must be special, Wild Thing, to get her to talk to you like that."

I've got no idea what that means. Nor do I care. I'm too distracted by the arrival of the girl who doesn't talk to anyone, the same girl who's carrying my boots and socks and water filter. Awesome.

CHAPTER 9

At first Ghost stays pretty silent. Then Rain Man tells her she needs to change her clothes. ASAP. She grabs her pack, with one hand, and it collapses inward, which makes me think she's got very little in there. She hustles into his tent and comes out in shorts and boots and a flannel shirt over a T-shirt. Her down vest is layered on top. She looks like she's freezing.

Rain Man shakes his head, hands her a sweatshirt and a blanket to wrap around her legs. "Thanks," she says.

"Your lips are blue." Rain Man stirs the food. "You could get hypothermia. That's no joke out here."

Visions of web pages with graphic images of people with hypothermia flood my brain. I see those words of warning and hope like hell that Ghost listens to Rain Man. This is serious.

Ghost nods and I breathe out. She takes a bite of her shrimp and grits and actually moans. "This is so good."

"It'll warm you up. Sleep with your wet clothes in your sleeping bag tonight. Your body heat will dry them."

She nods again. "I know that. I mean, I guess I forgot."

I take a bite of my food. I'm so hungry that shrimp and grits tastes like the most amazing thing I've ever eaten. Especially with a side of chili.

Rain Man tells us stories about the weirdest stuff he's seen on the trail, and Ghost and I exchange glances at the truly strange moments. A couple of times, Ghost actually bursts out laughing, and for some reason that makes me feel a bunch of different emotions at once. So far I've got angry and uncomfortable and this dread in my gut that must be jealousy. So weird. But honestly, I wish I could make her laugh like that.

Then Ghost jumps up. "Wait! I have dessert." She opens her pack and shoves her arm all the way down to the bottom. She roots around, balancing the pack on her hip, which confirms my belief that her pack's pretty light for this part of the trail. She must not have a lot of food left. I tell myself not to take whatever she dishes out, because she needs it more than I do. But she pulls out oatmeal raisin cookies, which are my all-time favorite. "Not homemade," she apologizes as she doles them out. "But they are my favorite kind."

I look at the wrapper. "CM Cookies?"

"Yeah." She breaks off a tiny piece and pops it in her mouth. "They used to be called Cookie Monster Cookies, but I think they got sued or something. They're made by someone in Maine. A stay-at-home mom makes them or something."

"Don't make fun of stay-at-home moms," Rain Man warns, but he doesn't open his cookie. "I was married to one for forty-two years."

The finality of that statement makes me think Rain Man has a reason he's hiking the trail solo now, maybe he didn't before, and that knowledge hangs between us. For some reason, I care about this old guy even though we just met. I worry about him being alone. It's the way I should worry about Mom, which reminds me of all that's wrong with me.

Ghost looks at Rain Man, who still hasn't touched his cookie. Then she turns to me. Boy, do I wish I knew how to handle social situations, because I've got no clue what to do here. I try to think about what Emily would do. I imagine her breaking down the scene for me. On the one hand, it's rude not to take the cookie she's offering. On the other hand, she's obviously pretty low on food for her hike. I look at her face for answers, but that's not going to help me.

"You don't like oatmeal cookies?" Ghost asks.

The question is put out there for both Rain Man and me, but it pushes me to react. I rip open the wrapper. "They're my favorite," I say.

I guess that's the right answer, because she smiles, and even I'd have to be completely clueless to not understand what that means.

Rain Man hands his back to her. His big, beefy man-hands look really gentle—like a dad's or a grandpa's. Nurturing hands. "I'm diabetic, but thanks for the offer."

Is he really diabetic? Or has he found a way to make certain the girl can eat? Gracious, genius grandpa. Three points. Booyah.

"I'll clean up," Ghost offers.

"Go help," Rain Man points at me and I'm grateful to him, because he's given me a reason to have a conversation alone with her.

"It's cool. I got it." Ghost stands.

"There might be bears," I say with a fake seriousness, which does the trick, because she cracks up.

"Don't worry, I'll protect you," Ghost says.

Soon we're walking to the creek, shoulders almost bumping. We take turns washing the bowls and pots in the stream. When we're done, I wipe the inside with some paper towels and pack those out in a big Ziploc bag.

She nods at me like she's glad I'm following the Leave No Trace principles. Like I'm doing the right thing, which feels kind of good.

When we get back to the shelter, Rain Man is in his tent setting up to go to sleep.

The wind blows and Ghost shivers.

If I was smooth, I could offer to warm her up, but no way do I have the courage to do that.

"By the way," Rain Man says, "I wanted to ask you," he aims his voice at Ghost, "do your people know you're out here?"

She bends her head and looks at her feet. For a second, I wish Rain Man hadn't asked her that question more than I wish I knew the answer. Which is super weird for me, because usually what I want comes first. But Rain Man's question lands so close to my secret that it makes me a little dizzy.

She picks up a stick and draws a line in the dirt. "It's cool," she says finally. "It's not a big deal. Dad knows I know what I'm doing."

"Pardon me for saying so, but you don't look like you were planning for this hike."

"It was a pretty spur-of-the-moment decision." She pulls off the sweatshirt she borrowed, and for one giddy moment, I'm sure I'm going to get a peek at something amazing. But I turn away because, let's face it, I can't be that kind of guy. Not to her face anyway.

"Keep it," Rain Man says.

"I guess I just needed to go for a really long walk." Ghost holds the sweatshirt in front of Rain Man so he has to take it or it'll fall to the ground. "I'll sleep with my wet clothes in my sleeping bag like you said."

"Good. They'll be dry by morning." Rain Man nods. "The thing is, I happen to have some of my wife's clothes. She was a great hiker in her day. I can have them sent to the next drop for you. Wouldn't be a problem."

"I'm not really looking for hiking partners," she says. "I need some time on the trail to myself, you know?"

I get the feeling that she's taking it easy on Rain Man, and that if I'd suggested hiking together, I would've gotten a much less careful reaction.

It's Rain Man's turn to nod. "Well, the offer's there if you need."

"Thanks. That's cool of you." She points to the darkness. "I'm gonna go pitch my tent. Thanks for the food, Rain Man. It was even better than people say."

"Aww." Rain Man waves away her compliment. "When you're hungry, anything tastes gourmet."

"Nah. You're the real deal."

His eyes well up, but he turns toward his tent, and she's gone as quickly as she got there. I watch her leave, memorize the trail she took, completely aware that I'm going to go try to find her next note graveyard. I know it's wrong, but that knowledge doesn't stop me from planning it.

Rain Man grabs his pack. Going to his tent I guess, and I'm standing here, all alone in the middle of the woods hanging on the silence like I would hang on someone's next word.

I stare at Ghost's tent without even meaning to. I stare at how the glow of her lantern lights the orange and blue flaps of her tent. Her tent is close, on the same flat area that is designated for camping. The land is set aside so that the woods along the trail can be preserved. I can see her silhouette. She's sitting, maybe cross-legged. Her back is bent and she's leaning forward. I imagine her notebook in her hand. The angle looks about right. Ghost is writing in that book of hers, I'm sure of it.

"Give her a blanket," Rain Man says, startling me because I hadn't heard him approach.

"Huh?"

He points to her tent. "You saw how blue her lips were. She's freezing, and she doesn't have the right gear, but she's too proud or stubborn to ask. But do it."

I jog to Ghost's tent. I hold the blanket in my outstretched hand. "Hey," I whisper.

"What do you want?" She holds the flap closed and her voice sounds a little shaky. Did I scare her?

"It's just me," I whisper. "I'm leaving this for you."

Her hand grabs the blanket and then retreats inside again. I run back to my tent and get inside, turning on the light, so she can see that I'm not anywhere near her. She opens the flap of her tent and her arm pokes out and waves to me. I turn out my light so she'll think I'm going to sleep and not watching her.

I stare at her light and her shadow, how she is hunched over, writing. I think about doing some of my own writing. My fingers find the notebook Emily gave me before I left for the trail. She always said I had a story in me dying to get out. I used to joke, "No wonder my head hurts."

I reach into my pack for my phone. 8:30 p.m. and I'm exhausted. I spray the area under my sleeping bag, then get out my insecticide wipes and start wiping down the outside. I climb in and watch until Ghost's light goes off. Then I roll over and put on my headphones and am asleep before the first song is over.

CHAPTER 10

The next morning, I hear Rain Man zip up his pack. "Morning," he says as I poke my head out of my tent. "She's gone already." He lifts a mug of whatever he's drinking and points in the direction where Ghost's tent should be.

I figured she would leave early, but I'm annoyed with myself for sleeping through her departure. I stand, wrap my arms around my back, and scratch like a bear. I reach into my pack for my camp shovel.

My trek into the woods complete, and actually a minor success, I wind back to where her tent was. Rain Man's blanket is folded, with a note pinned to it.

Thanks. My clothes are dry now and I'm fine.

Something about the *I'm fine* irritates me. Like a burr in my skin. I'm not sure if it's because it's presumptuous of her to believe I care, or if it's because I do care and that's not always easy for me. I'm only trying to be a nice guy. I walk back to my tent and find Rain Man still drinking his coffee. Time to make mine.

"You gonna get moving soon?" Rain Man asks.

"I might hang here for a while."

He looks at me like he's trying to figure out why I'd do that, but he doesn't ask. It's part of life on the trail I can totally get behind. The privacy thing.

"Okay. See you around, Wild Thing."

"Yeah. See ya."

He starts to leave, but stops. He hands me a yellow walkie-talkie-looking device. "I'm giving away all of my wife's gear. It's a waste to keep it in a closet. This is a satellite phone. Call this number if you need anything. It can get and receive text messages too."

I stare at the phone in my hand.

"Nobody can track you with that, if that's what concerns you. Not unless you want them to. But it's good in case of an emergency. You and Ghost look like you need someone to look out for you, if you don't mind my saying."

I don't mind, which is weird for me, because that kind of thing usually gets to me, but Rain Man feels different. Like a person version of Max. Or maybe it's just his Dad vibe? And maybe, just maybe I'm jonesing so much for some Dad-ness in any form I can find it. Which makes me feel a little bad for Mom, to tell the truth.

Rain Man hits the trail and I watch him go, a little sad to be alone again, but that feeling is very fleeting and almost immediately replaced with the strong desire to search for Ghost's notes. How hard can that be?

———o———

By noon I'm kicking myself for thinking that finding Ghost's little burial sites would be easy. I've gridded the forest floor in my mind. Searched each possible square of land within two hundred yards of where she pitched her tent.

Nothing.

Well, not nothing. I did find one actual cathole, which is not what I wanted to discover while digging, but maybe that's what I deserved.

I'm drinking some water by the brook when it occurs to me that maybe she didn't bury any more notes. A panicky feeling comes over me. What if it was a *one-and-done* situation? I'll never know what she was burying and why.

I picture my social skills teacher telling me I can't control life, as burning regret grows inside me like a volcano ready to erupt. The feeling is too much to contain. I think of all the times I screwed up. How I didn't know about Max. How I didn't say anything about Dad's heart. How I continue to create this wake of destruction around me that is now affecting Mom. Shame infects me, and I've got to get it out.

I stand on top of a rock and let the scream erupt. Then I scream again and again. No one rushes in to wrap me in a blanket, even though I can almost feel Dad's arms holding me to his chest. Rocking me like he used to during one of my legendary freak-outs or meltdowns when I was little. He'd press me to him, and I'd listen to his heartbeat. Dum dum. Dum dum. Dum dum.

Dum. Dumb. Dumb. Dumb. I was so dumb. How could I not know there was something wrong with his heart? The pattern was there, screaming at me to fucking pay attention.

I scream some more. Scream about Max. About Dad. About not knowing how to save either of them. And then I sit on the rock, shaking. My cheeks are wet, and I realize that I've got no more fire in me. I splash my face with water from the creek, careful not to swallow any. The thought of giardia makes me wipe my mouth out with the bandanna I've got tied to my shorts. The same one that will theoretically be purified by the UV rays of the sun. The sun that bakes me and makes me feel warmed and loved and liked, maybe. Dad is looking down on me. That he's sending me his love.

That's when I decide the trail is making me a total idiot. Making me believe in things that aren't true. Can't be. Then I see it. A small area of disturbed dirt to my left with boot marks the size of Ghost's feet. *Of course.* She wouldn't have to bury her notes away from the water. It's not pee.

I scramble down from my rock and dig up the note. This one is torn in three parts. I hold it to the sun. I can make out three words. *He.* And then *knew it.* Ghost is writing about some guy who did her wrong. Perfect.

That nasty sensation of jealousy worms its way into my stomach and I want to catch up to Ghost to make certain she's not with that guy she's writing about, even though I've only seen her hiking alone. I know that's probably not a normal reaction, but I also know she's miles ahead of me. By the time I reach her, I'd be too tired to do much but stiffly wave at her. So, I head back to my camp, pack up my tent, and start walking.

———○———

I hike at a very brisk pace. The sun is strong today. The tree canopy protects me from most of the glare, and it's not like I've got to start using sunscreen yet, but I definitely wish the trees were closer together or that the sun was behind a cloud. Too much of a good thing is still too much. Em and I used to say that all the time. Usually after our gorge fests on Oreos or Doritos or both. She'd look me in the eye and say, "Regret is a terrible thing." She'd say it with a really serious, Mom-like face and then we'd both lose it, cracking up so much it'd make our stomachs hurt even more.

I suddenly decide I want to be around people, so I scan the guide for a popular trail point. Neels Gap is doable and has lodging, so there would definitely be people there. I could resupply, recharge my phone, and maybe, if I'm going to be honest with myself, maybe I'll get another sighting of Ghost. She's got to be needing supplies, her pack being so light and all.

Today's hike feels really hard. It's not only all the downed trees in this area of the woods, but the trail is also muddy and water is pooled in places. The mud makes each step slippery, but it sucks my feet into the soft ground too, cementing them with each step. Water seeps into my boots. I can't stand the feeling of walking in wet socks. My cell phone, even with the spotty coverage, is still helpful. Like now, it tells me there's more rain predicted tonight, lighter than last night, but I'm thinking it's going to make tomorrow's hike even worse.

When I make it to Neels Gap, my legs are exhausted. The trail leads up to this big stone building where I've read there are laundry facilities, a resupply store, and a hostel. I want to stay here so bad but I don't know where Ghost is and I want to catch up to her.

My eyes are drawn to the pairs of boots hanging in the surrounding trees. As I tilt my head back to see them, I actually stop walking. My mind itches to count them, label them, sort them. Each pair must mean something, and it's maddening not to know what. This is the kind of thing I could usually get lost in, but now I've got more than quirky obsessions on my mind. I want to find the girl. Weird.

I walk through the breezeway. The stone walkway gives me this strong nostalgic feeling, like I'm supposed to be here. Like here is safe and homelike. There are rooms for rent with green trimmed windows in the stone-faced building. I'm tired and it would be nice to shower. There's something about this place that calls to me.

I enter the hostel, and the clerk at the desk is a woman, older than Mom, with strawberry blond hair. She's got freckles on her face and patches of her skin are super white. Soft wrinkles and creases form around her mouth. She reminds me of my grandmother who lives in California, who we see once a year. *Twice this year though, with the funeral and the unveiling.* That thought sneaks up on me, and I feel like I could fall over backward from the impact, but the woman speaks to me. "You want a bunk or a single, sweetie? We only have one of those left. You're lucky to get anything with the weather getting bad."

"Single, please."

I hand her money, and she gives me a key. It's almost like summer camp. The fun kind. Not the miserable one Mom made me go to. I know everyone has these amazing summer camp memories, but I never did. Mom was convinced Emily and I had to go to separate summer camps. That was the first mistake. Then the food sucked. The bugs sucked. No electronics. No books. Just outside "fun." All the freakin' time. The director called Dad when she found me in the library, which was this tiny room with damp books, their pages gone warped like when your fingers prune for being in the water too much. I was hidden in the closet trying to read *The Adventures of Tom Sawyer,* but the books kept making me sneeze. When she tried to get me to come out, I screamed at her and threw books. I kicked and tried to burrow deeper into the closet. Eventually she gave up and went away. Two hours later, Dad showed up. He didn't look upset. He just asked, "Should we get fries on the way home?"

That's how Dad was.

"Hey, Dylan," a voice I don't recognize calls to me. It's my friends from that first night.

I raise my hand to them.

Drew and Lenny jog over. Drew claps me on the shoulder. "Good to see you, man."

"Yeah," I say. I'm obviously a brilliant conversationalist.

"We're staying here for a few days. There's a nasty storm predicted for tonight," Drew says. "Best to listen to Mother Nature and take a break from the trail when the weather gets like that."

I look around. There are a lot of hikers gathering. Boots sit outside of rooms, airing out. Socks also. I think about finding the Laundromat, but I want to catch up to Ghost. Does she know about the bad weather?

"Trail's already flooded in parts," Drew says. "We're waiting for Emerson to get himself human enough to go eat. Pirate's cooking sloppy joes tonight. They're supposed to be his specialty."

Lenny scowls as usual, but this time it feels like it's directed at me, and honestly maybe he has a right. I'm rank from the trail, "ripe" as Mom used to say. He doesn't say that, instead he says, "You better go clean your swassy ass up too. Pirate doesn't serve scrubs."

"See you in a few," I say and just like that, I'm back in my room getting ready to shower. I figure the faster I get ready, the faster I eat, and the more likely I'll find Ghost or Rain Man. There's this panicky feeling in my stomach when I think of her empty bag and her wrong clothes. It's weird for me to care about other people so intensely. I mean, of course, I care for my family, but I almost never put their needs ahead of mine.

Mostly because they are all older and wiser than I am, and they tell me that all the time. Also, there's this birth order hierarchy in my family.

All of the cousins are named in alphabetical order, so we all remember our place. First came Abby, then Brad (my brother), Christian, Dylan, and Emily. That's why, Em and I, the cabooses of each family, only recognize the alphabet if it's done backward. Dad was the one who showed us how the back of the train, the caboose, was the best car. He called us his cabooses, and I freaking loved that. I plug in my phone to charge and grab my wallet. Then, I'm out the door.

I'm glad for the single room, but I'm wishing I had a reason to walk through the bunk areas to see if Ghost is there. I make my way outside where music is playing and the sweet smell of food is delivered by the cool mountain air. I shiver and pull my down vest closed. Is Ghost cold, wherever she is?

It's not hard to find the food, you just have to follow the smell. And the people, all shuffling toward this covered outdoor area with a big grill manned by some guy named Pirate. I'm handed a plate by a tan girl with straight blond hair. She's got chapped lips with some kind of cream slathered on it. Lip gloss, I guess? It's kind of distracting in a bad way. Still, I take the food because it looks and smells amazing. Drew gestures for me to come over, and I find a seat by them. He hands me a cold beer. "You probably could use this."

I take it, grateful for something to numb my mind, not to

mention make me pay less attention to my aching feet, which are so happy to be in sandals and breathing.

The first and last time I had a beer was with Dad. It was after one of the best swim meets I'd ever had. Sam and Taylor, their dads, and Dad and I sat out in our backyard, and Dad made us all hot dogs and hamburgers.

"I don't think one beer will hurt these elite athletes, do you, Stan?" Dad said to Taylor's dad.

"Nah. I'd say they've earned it."

Pride bloomed inside me. Or maybe it was the alcohol.

This time I drink a second. Then a third.

I reach into my pocket and hand Drew money for my share. He waves it off. "My version of trail magic, dude."

We walk by tents that are set up outside, and I look for Ghost, but I don't see her orange and blue tent. I breathe out. My eyes roam the campground, but she's not here.

Emerson smacks me on my arm. "Dude. Dylan's pink blazing."

They all crack up, making me feel like I'm in middle school again, a pack of idiots making fun of me.

Instead of just standing here feeling like a weirdo and getting mad, I ask, "What?"

"You're trying to meet up with a lady."

"Or a guy. That's cool too."

"Oh. Yeah. No," I say.

"Ha. Which one is it?" Emerson asks.

"Neither. I'm just worried about someone."

"Is this someone a girl or a guy?"

"A girl."

Drew raises his beer to his mouth, drains the bottle. Throws it in a recycle bin we pass.

Then I spot Rain Man. He's sitting outside his navy blue tent, looking through a book.

"I'll be back," I say. "Gonna go ask Rain Man something."

I'm not two feet in front of him before Rain Man looks up. His smile spreads wide. "Hey, Wild Thing!"

"You know Rain Man?" Drew asks catching up with me. Then he stares at me. "Wild Thing?"

"My trail name."

"Introduce me to your friends, Wild Thing."

I freeze. Names are the worst. I can never remember them. But I don't have to worry, because Drew puts out his hand, "Gator."

I did not know that.

Lenny says, "Pepsi."

Emerson says, "Emerson."

Rain Man nods. "Nice to meet you all." He motions to the area in front of his tent. "Pop a squat."

We do.

"You restocking?" I ask Rain Man.

"Yeah. Sort of."

"Hey, have you seen…"

"She was here earlier. I made her take some of my wife's clothes. I think she went back to the trail, though."

"But it's supposed to be bad with the storm. You didn't tell her?"

"I did. But you can't stop someone who doesn't want to be stopped. That girl's on some kind of mission, Wild Thing."

I nod, but the worry has made its way past the beer, into my gut. "I have a really bad feeling about this."

"So, look for her tomorrow."

My eyes go in the direction of the trail.

"No. Just no," Drew, a.k.a. Gator, says. "Night hiking in these conditions, flooding on the trail, and a new storm descending is a bad idea. Under any conditions, it's really only for experienced hikers."

"She'll be fine, son," Rain Man says.

There's that word again. It's supposed to calm me, but it has the opposite effect. I start pacing. Rolling my neck to keep from getting too stiff. "I gotta go."

Back in my room, I'm throwing my things in my pack when my phone rings. Emily.

"Hey," I say out of breath. "Everything okay?"

"No. I mean yes. Mostly. But needed to talk to you. Hey, how cool is this? I can talk to you!"

Emily's voice is a wonderful gift. A sign or reward for doing things right. For once.

"I can't talk for long," I say, "Going back to the trail in a minute."

"You can't."

"What? Why?"

"You have to come home."

"What's wrong?"

"Your mom is going to sell your boat."

The news is like a punch to the gut. I have to sit. "What?"

"She said you must not want it since you left it behind."

"She's trying to force me out of hiding."

"Maybe."

"She's bluffing. She wants you to tell me that so I'll come back."

"Maybe you should."

Disappointment coats me. Emily never takes their side over mine. Never. "Dad gave me that boat. She has no right…"

"After everything your mom's been through, after all we've all been through, you should come home and talk it out."

The thoughts bounce around in my brain. I picture Mom's face when we found out Dad was gone. How I wanted to help her. How I felt like I fell down a well and was trapped there. But then I remember when I found out how Dad died. And I know that no matter what she says, it's not a good idea for me to come home.

"Em. I can't come back. But not for those reasons."

"Then what reasons?"

"There's a girl."

"A girl?"

"Yeah. She needs me."

"*I* need you. *We* need you. More than some girl you met on the trail. We are your family, and we are mourning. Come home, Dylan. Please."

"I can't."

Emily sighs. Sighing means she's frustrated. Sighing means I'm losing my only ally in the family. "Dylan, I never ask you for anything. I'm asking you for this."

"Em, come on. That's not fair. I'm caring about other people who I have no blood relation to. That should mean something."

She stays silent.

"And I feel like I'm getting better. I mean, I feel less angry. More, I don't know, more clear." I add quietly.

"Really?"

"Yes. I keep thinking I see Dad on the trail. But not hallucinations. Like he's here with me."

"Brad is never going to forgive you for leaving your mom right now. You know that, don't you?"

"You're right. But I can't come home yet." I think about the last time I saw my brother. How we both were so angry and sad that we couldn't even make eye contact. How in a better family with better people in it, we'd probably hug it out and be there for each other, except we can't, and I can't blame him. To Brad, I was always the pain-in-the-ass little brother who made trouble.

"Why is this so important to you?"

I know she doesn't understand, and I can't bring myself to tell her. The words burn inside me like a brand on my heart. I should have known Dad was sick, like Max. And now I feel like this is maybe a chance to make it up to myself. Maybe if I help this girl, it'll somehow balance it all out. "I don't know exactly. I just feel like I've got to do this. I have to help this girl."

"How do I know this girl isn't one of your weird obsessions?"

I stop. Try to find a way to explain it so she'll understand. "I find myself worrying about what she wants more than what I want."

"I don't believe it."

"Serious as a heart attack."

"Don't say that. It's not funny anymore."

"It never was. It was ironic. Remember?"

"Dylan, come on."

There's a knock on the door.

"Em. I gotta go."

"Who's knocking on your door?"

I do one of my nervous laughs. "I don't know. One of my friends, I guess."

"Your friends? Dylan?"

"I have trail friends. See what I mean? I'm connecting with people. *Finally.* Mom always wanted that. I know you did too."

"Dylan." Her voice is shaky now and so far away. I want to reach out to her, be there for her. I want her to understand that I've got no other choice. But when you weigh emotions and actions and consequences, at this point, Emily's needs have to take a back seat. Ghost is out there and she's alone. I've got to find her, and each second I am not going after her is time where she could be getting hurt…or worse.

"I'm sorry, Em. I really am. But I've got to go." I hang up. And I know this time, those two words won't fix anything. But I can't go home. I've got to find Ghost. I've learned that not doing something is sometimes worse than doing something wrong.

I open the door to find Rain Man, his backpack in his hands. I almost knock him over on my way out. "I'm not going to try to stop you," he says.

"Good. You were the one who said she needs watching over."

"She may not welcome someone doing that."

"I know. I'll keep my distance."

"Did you restock?" Rain Man asks.

"No. But I'm a few meals ahead."

He thrusts two packs of dehydrated chili in my hand, along with two other packets I don't recognize. "Homemade ramen," he says. "If she's cold and sick, she'll need that." He also hands me a small bag with Advil Liqui-Gels. "Some vitamin I," he says. "You take two when you find her, and save the rest for her. Oh, and here," he gives me a pair of new wool socks. "These will help."

"What about you?"

"I'm heading out tomorrow. I'll restock before I leave. She's got four hours on you. You won't make up that much time tonight. Only go as far as you feel safe and then camp. You can catch up to her tomorrow."

I nod.

"Use the sat phone if you need it. You have a headlight?"

I nod again, even though I have no idea how to use it. I haven't taken it out of the packaging yet, haven't read the instructions.

"Let me see," he says.

And because he's Rain Man, I feel like I have to give in to him even though I feel like there's no time for this.

He opens the box and sets the whole thing up for me in seconds flat. "You got a good one." He adjusts the straps around my head and switches it on.

The fact that the man set this up without reading the instructions would usually totally get to me. But I'm in a rush, so I tell myself he already had this particular type and read those instructions. He digs in his pack and takes out a garbage bag. "Put this around your pack. Keep it dry."

I must hesitate or something because he grabs my pack right out of my hands and starts wrapping it up. "You need to keep this dry, or when you find her, your stuff won't be worth anything."

I nod. He's right. I feel like I should pay him back somehow and then it comes to me. So, I hand him the key to my room. "You want to bunk here? I paid for the night."

"Might take you up on that, Wild Thing. My aching bones could use a break. Last night in a real bed." He pauses as if that's supposed to mean something more, but "time is a-wasting," something Dad used to always say, and I've got to go.

I look at Rain Man as he sits on my bed. He looks tired. I hope he stays longer than a day and rests up. I almost tell him that, but I'm busy putting on my new socks. "Thanks, Rain Man, you've been really great."

"It's not hard to be great to a great kid. I could tell you were special the moment I saw you."

For a second, with the low light in the room, and Rain Man tired and not trailsy, he reminds me even more of my dad. "See you on the trail, Rain Man," I say.

"Yeah. See you, son."

This time I don't flinch when he says that. This time I let

myself feel his fatherly concern. Maybe Dad can reach out to me in small ways.

The rain has already started, and I pull my hood up, tying it tight. As my feet hit the path on the way to the trail, I hear Emerson screech after me, "Go get her, Wild Thing!"

Gator and Pepsi chime in with their cheers.

If I was the kind of person who blushed, I'd blush now, but I'm not, so I don't. I pick up the pace, counting my steps as a way to drive myself forward.

I know if Emily were here, she'd tell me I was being an idiot for hiking at night like this, when I'm not even great at hiking during the day, when you can actually see stuff. And being able to see the downed trees and the roots and the rocks and the mud makes the hiking part so much easier. If Emily were here, she'd have made me stay and wait to look for Ghost in the morning. But she's not here, and I *am* here, on the trail at night, doing my best to aim the light on my head at the ground in front of me, but it keeps slipping and I keep tripping. Emily would say something smartass about how I'm no poet. And I'd laugh right with her.

I can almost feel her with me, Emily, and that makes me feel like I'm doing the right thing. Am I really pink-blazing? Or am I just being a concerned citizen? Ha. Even I can't be that dense.

My feet are pissed at being shoved back into boots, but I'm grateful as hell for Rain Man's socks. That man must have some kind of major stash of supplies the way he's doling them out all the time. Something about that makes me worry a little. I mean, is it normal to give people stuff all the time? But maybe that's what trail magic is all about. Anyway, I don't have time to worry about Rain Man. I've got to find Ghost.

CHAPTER 11

The trail is even more slippery than I remember. I have to go really slow because it's dark, which I'm not used to, and because the trail is climbing and dipping. I'm terrified that I'll miss the white blazes that mark the trail and get lost in the woods.

The fear of getting lost lodges under my rib cage, making my breath come out ragged. The squish of my boots getting stuck in the mud, the thick sucking sound as I pull them out, and the steady rain are the only sounds I hear as I trudge forward.

My path is blocked by a massive downed tree. I have to stop to climb over the trunk that feels way too big to have fallen by itself, but the light shows a charred mark and my hands feel where it split, so it must have been struck by lightning. This adds another fear to my list. In order to fight the panic that's building, I fill my head with the imaginary sound of my drums. I've listened to that track so often that my head can replicate it at will. I keep those drums going as I walk through the woods, getting hit in the face with small leafy twigs that hurt like hell each time they make contact, but something tells me that Ghost is near and needs help, so I keep going.

I make it to the top of the incline and shine my headlamp into the gap below. I think this one is called a bull gap. Water moves below me, and it sounds like more of a threat than a soothing welcome. Every ascending part of the trail feels treacherous, and for once, I wish I was hiking with those poles that the older guys use. Especially on this sloggy trail.

I reach down and grab a long branch from the ground, break off some of the limbs, and use that as a staff to propel me forward. I'm making my way across what I'm sure is supposed to be a small creek, but it has become a rushing stream. I'm very glad for the extra stability of the staff, and I am almost across when I see a dark mass about a hundred feet ahead of me. It doesn't have the same shape as a tree or a rock, but it's hard to see in my light and the rain.

As I get closer, my pulse quickens. The shape is definitely human. A lying-in-a-lump-on-the-ground human. I race up the slope, not even caring about the stray branches that wallop me in the face, closing my eyes to avoid being blinded. It's Ghost. She's laying on the trail, her leg pinned under a tree. Her breath fills my ears as I bend down and the rain falls in heavy drops around us, my headlamp aimed straight at her face.

She puts her hand up to shield her eyes. "Are you trying to blind me?"

I shake my head. "Are you okay?"

"Sure. I'm fine. Just thought I'd lie under this tree for a while."

"Right."

I take off my pack and put it on the ground under a tree, still encased in the garbage bag Rain Man gave me. I look for a branch to use as leverage so I can get that tree off her. Somehow, despite all of the surrounding trees, there seem to be no suitable branches. Ghost's teeth are chattering, and I can hear her breath sticking in her chest. I untie the garbage bag and open my backpack, pulling out my tarp and a blanket. I throw the blanket on top of her and the tarp on top of the blanket while I keep searching the forest floor. I finally find a useful branch, and when I circle back to her, she's got the blanket up around her neck and she's breathing into it, maybe even crying, it's hard to know for sure with the competing sound of the rain.

"It's okay, we'll get you out of here in no time."

Her head bobs up and down, and I go to work getting that tree off of her. It starts to lift. I hold my breath while silently thanking Dad for making me a swimmer. It's made me strong enough to prop up the tree while she grabs her leg with both hands and pulls it out of the way.

I drop the tree, let out a breath, and then kneel next to her. "Hey, let me check that out."

She looks back at the tree. "Who are you, Superman? Maybe we should give you a new trail name." Her hands run up and down her foot. "I don't think it's broken."

The rain slows a little and I feel like it's a gift. "You think you can stand?"

She gives me her hands, and I pull her up. She balances on her good foot, then carefully puts the injured one on the ground. Her face contorts with a groan and she lifts it again.

"Here." I hand her the stick I was using. "Let me get on my pack and then we can get yours."

With our gear collected, I sling her arm around my neck and put my hand around her waist so she's got the stick on one side for support and me on the other. We hobble forward, almost trip, and have to stop. She laughs a little, but it's a tiny sound, like her lungs are too tired to exhale. I start to worry that maybe she hurt a rib or punctured a lung. First-aid pictures and descriptions float through my brain, because, yeah, I read up on issues you could encounter being alone on the trail. I can see all of them laid out in front of me. I try not to focus on everything bad that might happen, but on easing us forward, listening carefully as I do to be sure she's still breathing. I hear her little whimpers as her injured foot inevitably touches the ground and her teeth chattering. I try to pull her closer to keep her warm.

"There's a campsite up ahead," I say.

"How do you know, newbie?" Her voice is so worn, the insult is barely formed.

"I looked at the map before coming after you."

She stops. I almost fall.

"You came after me?"

"Well, everyone was saying it was dangerous to hike in this rain. There's been flooding. And Rain Man said you'd gone anyway."

"And you just had to—"

"I was worried. It's a trail thing. My own version of being a trail angel, you know, like paying it forward. Or actually paying you back, since you saved my ass from a bear, in case you forgot."

"How could I forget that?" She points. "Let's set up here."

It's definitely a campsite, but there are no other campers here tonight. The rain slows to a drizzle.

"You want to find a shelter?"

She shakes her head. "Hate those." She drops her pack and almost falls back with it. I reach for it and she pulls it away.

"Take it easy. I'm going to set up your tent for you, okay?"

She doesn't answer. Just sits on a log, hanging her head.

I spread her tarp on the ground, then set up her tent. When I'm done, I reach into her pack and grab her sleeping bag, noting that her pack is still so damn light. Did she not restock? I leave the tent flap open and throw in new clothes. "You need to change, okay? You're freezing."

Then, I set up my tarp between two trees and put her pack and mine under it. I set up my tent next, and then get out my stove. I light it and start cooking the ramen under the tarp. I want to make her coffee too. I read somewhere that coffee helps open up the lungs. It's the theophylline or something. It's also supposed to speed up pain relievers. She needs both right now. So I reach into her pack and grab her stove. There's almost nothing else in there. What the hell is she thinking? Why didn't she resupply when she had the chance?

But this is not the time to ask questions. This is the time to assess her injuries and ailments. I start up her stove and grab my coffee supply, which I'm sad to say is dwindling. I could have used a restock myself, but I'll think about that later.

"Hey, how are you doing?" I call into her tent.

"Uh."

"Is that a good *uh* or a bad one?" I listen outside the door of her tent. "Hey, can I come in? I've got soup, and I'm starting some coffee."

"Okay."

I stick my head in. She's buried under the covers and still shivering in her dry clothes.

"We need to check your ankle."

"It's okay. It hurts like crap, but it's not broken."

"How do you know?"

"I just know, okay?" She shivers some more.

"What about your ribs? Your lungs? Let me check."

She pulls the covers up higher. "No. I'm fine."

I put out my hand, palm up like surrender. "Look, I'm not trying anything. I promise. We have to be sure you didn't break a rib or anything."

I'm holding the soup, and there's really no room to put it down, so I'm hovering, my butt hanging out of the tent, which makes me almost laugh. If Emily was here, she'd definitely laugh at how ridiculous I must look, but laughing for no apparent reason in this difficult moment might piss off Ghost. It would probably piss off most normal people, so I don't.

"I'm sure I didn't break a rib. And I'm starved. So the soup sounds good."

"It's from Rain Man. Homemade ramen."

She rolls her eyes. "That sounds amazing. And not only because I spent the last four hours stuck under a tree." She pushes herself up, and I watch her face and listen carefully. She makes noises like she's sore, like Dad did after running or working out too hard at the gym. But I don't hear any acute pain noises.

I hand her the soup. "I'm going to get you some ibuprofen, also sent by Rain Man."

I leave her tent and open my backpack. I grab the bag of Liqui-Gels and bring the coffee with two packs of sugar, because I've got no idea how she takes her coffee. She's sipping the soup. "Rain Man is the best."

"Agreed. Here." I hand her two Liqui-Gels.

She nods. "Thanks. Really." Some color has returned to her cheeks.

I hand her the coffee. "This too, if you can."

She holds up her hand when I try to hand her the sugars. "I take it black."

Like my heart. Dad's laughter comes to me.

I must have made a face because she asks, "Did I say something wrong?"

I shake my head. "Nah. My dad did also, but then he'd say, 'I take it black. Like my heart.' Which was a stupid joke because my dad was the nicest person on the planet." This is the most I've talked about Dad, especially to a stranger, since he died. I wouldn't even speak with that counselor. Or the guidance counselor. Or my behavior therapist. Nobody. Just this girl.

"That's sweet. Your dad sounds great." She brings the cup to her lips. "God, I love coffee."

I put my hand over my heart like she did when I talked about the *Where the Wild Things Are*.

She laughs. After a couple of sips she says, "I'm really tired."

"You need anything else?"

She waves me away. "Nah. I'm good."

"Okay. Good night…" I almost call her Ghost, but I'm not sure she'll like that.

"Sophie."

I smile. "That's a nice name. Good night, Sophie."

"Good night, Wild…"

"Dylan."

"Wild Dylan?"

"Just Dylan."

She hands me the cup and her soup bowl and rolls over.

Before I even make it all the way outside, I can hear her breaths shift into sleep breathing. The woods are quiet with no one else here. Only Ghost and me and the sound of the drizzling rain. I heat another packet of food, this time the chili, and drink the rest of Sophie's coffee. It's weird that drinking out of the same cup and using the same bowl doesn't freak me out. Instead it makes me feel sort of warm inside.

I rinse the dishes and pack out our trash, and then get ready for bed myself.

By the time my body hits my sleeping bag, I'm this weird combination of exhausted but too hyped to sleep. I look at the ceiling of my tent, listen for sounds outside that seem alarming. I hear none. My eyes shift toward Sophie's tent, which is still dark. Should I go check on her? Should I go see if she's okay? I roll over, face her tent full on.

Then this weird thought comes out of nowhere but hits me hard. I could go through her backpack while she's sleeping. I can almost hear Emily's voice urging me on. We rummaged through Brad, Abby, and Christian's stuff all the time. But they sort of asked for it, lording over us with their earlier-in-the-alphabet birthright and all. What a weird family. But this time, those battles and Emily and my tiny mutinies feel fun and sweet and make me miss them all more. Even the older cousins.

Back to Sophie's backpack. My curious nature sort of demands I act, but she trusted me with her real name. It seems like she doesn't do that very often, so I don't want to break her trust. Instead, I stare at the ceiling of my tent, thinking about the girl sleeping in the tent next to me. About how I'm changing my ways, even though leopards aren't supposed to be able to change their spots. I think about Dad and how he'd be proud of what I did tonight, and that I'm glad that, wherever he is, he knows that. And all of that makes not breaking into her backpack and reading her secrets feel like the right choice. Mostly.

CHAPTER 12

The sound of sobbing outside my tent wakes me. I sit up and listen hard. I'm in the dark, there's crying. I hear crying. But that doesn't make sense. Does it? My eyes strain to see past the thick darkness. I try to force my vision to make out details, but none surface. I push on my head, which feels like it's stubbornly guarding secrets, like where the hell I am, what I'm doing, and who could be crying. Then I realize. I'm in my tent. On the Appalachian Trail. With Sophie. Oh crap. *She's* the one crying.

I race to unzip my tent, and go to hers.

"Sophie. Are you okay?"

She's mumbling and crying. I can't make out what she's trying to say, if she's even using words.

"I'm coming in." I don't wait for her answer before pushing open the flap of the tent.

Sophie doesn't look up. She's curled, the sleeping bag, blanket wrapped around her. "Sophie?"

She shivers and mumbles some more, and I know that's not good. I put my hand on her forehead. She's freezing. I should have made her put on a hat. "Sophie, do you have on socks?"

She doesn't answer, just curls up tighter.

"Hey, Sophie. We've got to warm you up, or I'm going to have call for help on that sat phone Rain Man gave me. Okay?"

She nods, at least I think she nods. I take it as a nod, so I press a little further. "I'm going to my tent to get you a hat and my sleeping bag. I'm going to hold you. I won't try anything, and I don't want to make you uncomfortable, but you've got to warm up. This is dangerous."

Sophie whimpers and I don't know if she understands what I'm saying, but I get going, because all of those websites I read discussed hypothermia. This is serious.

It takes me five seconds to get the stuff I need and return to her tent. I bend down and put the hat on her head. She doesn't fight me, and I'm glad for that. Next I unzip my sleeping bag. "I'm going to lie down next to you, Sophie. I'm going to warm you up. Okay?"

She says something I don't understand, but I hold open her sleeping bag, and cram my body in next to hers, trying really hard not to hurt her ankle. I reach behind me and throw my sleeping bag over me, wrapping my arms around her shivering body. Emily always said I was unnaturally warm, like my body temperature ran higher than everyone else's. Sam said it's because of my swimmer's metabolism. I don't care why I've got this fire in me, I'm just glad I can use it to warm Sophie.

My body wrapped around hers, I put my hands over hers. They're so cold. She shakes and shakes. "You want me to tell you a story?"

She nods.

"We'll start with *Where the Wild Things Are* and go from there." I start to recite the book. I'm not sure if I'm imagining it, but her body relaxes. I go all the way through that story and half of *The Death of Yorik Mortwell*, before she stops shivering. "That's it, Sophie, you're warming up. Good job."

We stay like this, me telling her the stories that are cataloged in my brain for no good reason except that I read them so many times, the words are now imprinted in my mind. I never thought my memory was so useful before, but now I'm glad I have it.

I'm not sure what time it is, but almost three quarters of the way through *Yorik Mortwell*, Sophie's hands are warm and she's breathing easy, sleepy breaths. I hold her and finish the story, not that I think she's listening, but because I like to finish what I start.

I guess I must fall asleep, because when I open my eyes, the sun is out. I'm not sure I should move, because I don't want to wake Sophie, but she says, "I'm awake."

"Oh. Okay." I unwrap and extract myself from the sleeping bag. "How are you feeling?"

"Better. Definitely. Not sure about the ankle though."

"I hope you're not mad I stayed with you last night. You were so cold…"

"You saved my life. Thank you."

"Do you think you need a hospital? Rain Man gave me a sat phone. I could call for help."

"No. I think I just need to rest."

"And to eat. Rain Man sent meals."

Sophie covers her stomach. "I'm starved."

"I'll go make breakfast. Oatmeal or chili?"

She laughs. "Better start with oatmeal. But I don't have…"

"I've got tons. I picked up a resupply package in Neels Gap."

"I'll pay you back."

"Don't worry, I'm sure you'll save me from a snake or a bobcat or something."

"Dylan? Thanks."

I nod. "That oatmeal is not going to make itself."

She smiles and wraps herself tight in the blankets.

Outside, it's barely drizzling, but it's cold and the moisture hangs in the air. It's nice to have something to do. Make oatmeal. That's pretty easy.

I fire up the stove and pour the oatmeal and water into a pot. I wait for it to cook while I warm up some coffee. Enough for both of us. Sophie peeks out of the tent. "You need help?"

"Nah. I'm almost done."

"Okay. I'm gonna…" she points to the woods, shovel in hand.

Is she going to bury another note? I focus on the task at hand, trying not to watch where she's heading. She's back in a couple of minutes. Her face looks skinny and pale. Her eyes are sunken. All of which makes me worried. "You need to eat." I hand her the oatmeal and a mug of coffee.

She sits on a rock. "Thanks. What about you?"

Has she eaten enough to have to dig a hole to poop in? Or did she just bury another note?

"Dylan?"

I must be staring off into space. I do that sometimes. "Oh, right. I have to wait for the bowl and mug."

"You can use mine." She points to her pack. "It's in the front part."

"I didn't want to go into your pack without asking."

She nods. "Oatmeal's good. Coffee's better."

"It's instant." I return with her dishes. I stir the sugar and fake creamer in mine and start to eat my oatmeal while my coffee mixes. "I would kill for a mug of fresh brewed."

"So, Wild Thing…"

"We're back to trail names?"

"No. But do you realize told me your entire story with that name?"

I scrape my spoon along the right side of the bowl, take a bite of oatmeal, scrape the left side, take another bite.

She watches, slightly amused, like Emily would. "First of all, most people are given a trail name. Did you know that?"

I laugh. "Nope. I guess I screwed it up already then." For whatever reason that feels so funny, how I could screw up the simplest things.

"Wait. I don't mean everyone does it that way. Most people are given trail names based on a habit or something."

I take another spoonful of oatmeal and listen to the sound of Ghost reminding me of my failings, only I don't mind at all. It's almost like being with Emily. Almost.

"Some people *do* give themselves a trail name. Like you did." She salutes me with her spoon.

"Yes. I'm very much in command of my trail name-ness."

"Back to what I was saying. If you named yourself after that book, you're essentially saying you've run away from home because you're mad at your mother."

She's uncomfortably close to the truth. Scraping my spoon along the side of the bowl, I reply, "Not necessarily."

"I'm pretty certain about this. When you choose your trail name, it's about your mission, why you're hiking."

"Always?"

"Pretty much."

"Then I'd be Max, not Wild Thing."

She smiles and raises her spoon in protest this time, and I'm struck with the number of different ways the same gesture can be interpreted. The smallest nuance, this time the emphatic stature of her hand, indicating firmness of feeling. "Nice try, but Max is a wild thing. He's the original wild thing. His mother calls him that. Remember?"

I take a sip of coffee. "I remember."

"So?"

"So… I could also be paying tribute to the song."

She has to cover her mouth not to spray oatmeal with her laugh. "Yeah. No."

"Maybe I'm the exception to the rule," I offer.

"Everybody thinks they are, but most people aren't. Or there would be no rules."

I wrap my arms around my stomach. "Shudder."

She laughs again.

"So what about your trail name?" I ask, then wish I could take the words back. I'm not sure she likes that people call her Ghost.

She shrugs. "It's as good a name as any. I *am* a ghost."

I get chills when she says that. "Why?"

She rests her cheek in her hand. Her gaze goes to the treetops. "Because I've disappeared from my life."

I think about the notes she's buried. I wish I could ask her about them. I wish I could find an excuse to slip away and find her most recent graveyard. Instead I simply ask, "Why?"

She looks at me. "You tell me *your* story first."

"Yeah, maybe not." I stare at the ground.

So she says, "I know. Let's analyze other people."

I perk up a bit. "My friend Gator."

"Okay. Gator wants others to think he is strong and fearless, like the reptile."

"Pepsi."

"Someone who doesn't want to grow up. Pepsi is hiding from responsibility, for sure."

I smile and poke at my oatmeal.

"What?" she asks.

"You might be right."

"*Might*? I was right about the bear, wasn't I?"

"And I was right about following you."

I think maybe I've gone too far, then a slow smile forms on her face and she says, "Touché."

"Do Rain Man."

Sophie takes a drink of her coffee, and looks at her hands, quiet for a moment. "Don't know. I think his name may not be trail specific."

"He's the exception?"

"Maybe."

"How long have you known him?"

"My mom and Dad and I used to hike together all the time. Since I was little. Rain Man and his wife always hiked too."

"His wife? What happened to her?"

"She died last year."

"What happened to her?"

Sophie shakes her head. She wipes a tear, and I figure this is a conversation that can wait. So instead I ask, "What was she like?"

"She was tough. Sweet. Funny. Everything he deserved."

It's weird to be feeling so sad for this man I've just met. I think of Mom. About how hard it must be for her without Dad. I never really thought about it that way before. My phone is in my backpack. I could take it out right now and call her. Sophie's eyes trail mine and she must figure out that I'm thinking about someone back home because she says, "I can give you privacy."

Privacy. The word rolls around in my brain. I think about calling Mom. Should I? Would she listen to me? Or just be so angry she'd simply demand to know my whereabouts and send the police?

Sophie says, "I'm really tired."

"You need to sleep. You look kind of gray."

"Gee, thanks."

"Your lips don't have a lot of color. That sounds creepy, but I mean…"

"I know what you mean. Do you mind if we don't hike today? Can we do a zero day here at the campsite?"

"It'll be my first zero day," I say. The concept sort of surprises me, and I know without Sophie asking for us to stay here, I would have just gotten going like every other day. Not because I like hiking that much, just because it seems like on an Appalachian hike, you should hike. And now that we are going to rest and stay here, even though it's completely against my nature, I'm kind of looking forward to it.

"You have more books? I liked when you read to me last night."

I blush. "I always have books."

"Aren't they too heavy to pack?"

I laugh. "Nah. What do you feel like?"

She points to her tent. "Can we go in there so I can lay down?"

"Sure."

She gives me a wary look.

"You don't have to worry. I swear."

"Good. Thanks." She opens her tent and crawls in.

I wait until she's settled before following her in. "What kind of book do you want to hear?"

"Don't you have to get your pack?"

"Nah."

She looks at me.

I point to my brain. "They're in here."

She pushes herself up on her elbow. "Really?"

"Yeah."

"That's amazing."

I blush again, which is weird, but in a strange way wonderful, because her opinion of me matters. "So what'll it be? Pick your poison. Comedy. Fantasy. Dark. Whatever."

"I like dark. Dark is real. Dark can be beautiful."

I start to talk. "I love this book because it's about a son who's run away from his life."

"A grown-up Wild Thing?"

"I never thought of it that way, but yes."

I'm sure she's going to give me a hard time about all of that, but instead she settles into the sleeping bag and with a worn out sounding voice asks, "What's the title?"

"*The Catcher in the Rye.*"

"Why do you love it?"

"Because it's beautiful. And sad. And I don't always understand emotions the way other people do. So books help." It's a stupid thing to admit, and as soon as I say it, I want to take it back. But then Sophie says, "That's so nice."

I start to read, picturing Mom the first time she took me to the library. I was four and I'd taught myself to read. She brought me to the children's section and sat down while I spent hours looking through the books. She kissed my head as I carried a stack of books home. "These books," she said, "are going to teach you everything you need to know about life."

Sophie's asleep before I get to the second chapter, but I replay most of the book I've read over twenty times in my head anyway. The entire time I think of Mom.

CHAPTER 13

Two days with Sophie and she's still not strong enough to leave camp. Plus we are running out of food…and coffee. I make us both breakfast, using our last two bags of oatmeal, and she limps out of her tent to sit on a downed tree log across from mine. Her hands go over the ACE bandage wrapped around her ankle. She's got her little notebook with her and it's all I can do not to stare at it.

She puts her notebook on the ground and takes the cup of coffee I hand her. We sit like this, the birdsong around us making this feel more dreamy and less precarious.

"I thought we'd see more people on the trail since the weather let up."

"You must have slept through most of them."

"Really?"

"Yeah you missed super-beefy guy and his skinny wife."

"Jack Sprat was here?"

"Apparently."

"Oh, and there were the fighting women. Four of them. All in bad moods."

Sophie nods. "Trail does that to you."

"I guess."

She laughs. "This is good," she says, and because she lifts her bowl as she says it, I know she's talking about the oatmeal, but I wonder if she also means this. Us.

"We've got to get some food." I hold up my mostly empty pack. Shake it. "The cupboard is bare."

"I'll go change. I think I'm okay to walk now," she says.

"No."

"No?"

"Your ankle is still not good enough to hike."

"I think I should be the judge of that."

I raise an eyebrow at her. "You'd think you should, but…"

She picks up a pinecone and throws it at me. She misses.

"Man, you're getting mean like those women on the trail who came through while you were sleeping."

This makes her throw a stick that is easy to duck, but I let it hit me so she can feel accomplished. "I need to make some phone calls anyway, so I was thinking I'd go back to Neels Gap and resupply."

Her eyes go to her backpack. "I don't have much… I was going to find a job…"

"It's okay. I'm pretty sure I've got a box coming anyway."

Her face looks like she doesn't understand what I've said.

"Ha! You're reconsidering your theory about me running away from home, huh?"

She eats around the smirk that's popped up on her face. "A box *does* put a dent in it."

I finish scraping the sides of the oatmeal bowl, and put it on the ground. "I'll be back later today."

"Leave the bowl. I'll clean it." She picks up her notebook and starts writing.

So, now I'm torn. Is she going to bury another note? A note I won't be able to dig up. I pull my shirt down over my wrist, and tug at the rubber bracelet Em gave me. I need to stop obsessing about her notes and start doing the right thing and go get food since we are almost out.

"I'm going to leave you with this, just in case." I hand her the sat phone Rain Man gave me.

"What if you meet up with a bear on the way?"

"You just can't help yourself, can you?"

"Nope."

I try to look cool by saluting her as I walk away, but like most gestures with me, it comes across as stiff and weird. She laughs and salutes back. I adjust my pack and set out southbound instead of northbound, which feels weird, since it's back tracking. That's the kind of thing that I usually can't let go of. But this time, it's necessary. Sophie needs me.

———○———

As I get closer to the mountain crossing, my phone vibrates in my pack. I stop and take it out. Messages from Emily.

You need to check in!

Everyone's worried.

You have to start thinking of others.

And by others, I mean your mother.

This is wrong.

I shouldn't have agreed to cover for you.

Call me as soon as you get these messages.

I'm instantly filled with anger. It grows and grows and I have to sit down. Then get up. Then pace.

Then I get another text.

I'm coming to find you.

She's got to be kidding. The worst part is I've got no idea when she sent this text. Was it after I hung up on her and left to go after Sophie? My reception has been nonexistent, and now that I'm back in reach of phone service, I can't tell when these texts were sent—they're all time stamped when they came through on my phone.

I jab at the screen, my aim affected by my mood, and I almost end up dialing some random number. At the last second, I cancel the call. I make myself breathe for ten seconds. Then try again. I find Emily's contact and hit call.

She doesn't answer. Great. Does that mean she's in class? Asleep? I can't even remember what day it is. Where could Emily be? *Please* not here. I don't want her to come looking for me.

I try not to think about Emily and why she isn't answering her phone and if she's already left to come find me, but it's got me kind of rattled. I walk in circles around and around. Me circling. Like a dog chasing its tail. I crouch. Put my head in my hands. This is ridiculous. What are the odds that Emily's actually here?

I push on toward town, going back through the rocky section of trail. Remembering what it felt like to chase after Sophie, the memory of that fear growing along with my current anger. I'm so busy racing ahead, I almost run into someone. That someone calls out.

"Hey, Dylan."

I startle. The voice is familiar, like a punch to the gut. Not Emily, but her boyfriend, John, which means she's not far behind.

"Emily had a location from your last call. She figured we'd start looking for you here."

"We?" My stomach contracts hard.

"Just Em and me. Nobody else knows."

"Yet," Emily's voice comes from behind John.

John moves aside, and I face her, and even though I don't normally read facial expressions well, I can see hers are angry. Every muscle in her face is tight. Her unflinching stare knifes into me. I hold up my hands. "I get it, Em. You're mad."

She shakes her head. She can't even look at me. This is bad. She starts to walk away. John stands there, letting this crappy scene play out. Letting us work it out.

I jog to catch up with her. "Come on, Emily Rose."

"No fair using that." She scoots around me.

I jog in front again. Even if we all-out raced, she'd never keep up the pace with my long legs. "I'm sorry."

She stares at me, her face getting all scrunched, and she starts to cry. She punches me in both arms. "You can't keep saying that and think it makes your actions okay." She swipes at her tears like she's more pissed at them than she is at me, which is probably not the case.

"Emily, you don't understand. No one does."

"So make me understand."

I think about telling her about Dad's heartbeat. I think about telling her how I should have known it was irregular. I should have said something, but the words are cemented inside of me, and there is no way they are ever coming out.

"What do you want me to do?" I ask.

"Come home."

"I can't."

"Then at least write to your mom. Tell her you're okay. She'll listen to you."

"You think?"

Emily is quiet for a moment. "Even if she doesn't, this is not fair."

"Did she sell my boat?"

Emily looks down. And just like that, anger builds inside me again. I know it's not fair to be mad at her, but it's my go-to emotion, and that was my boat. *My* boat. From Dad.

I've got ten different responses lined up in my head, all artillery I know better than to use on Emily. But she must think my staring at her is worse than yelling, because she throws her hands in the air and shouts, "What did you expect me to do?"

"Stop her! Dad gave me that boat. It was my private boat, like in the story!"

"Don't you think I know that?"

I push past her toward the resupply store. I pass people on the way in, but don't pay attention to them. I grab some oatmeal, more beef jerky, some noodles in a bag, and ibuprofen. I'm throwing stuff in my basket when Emily appears in front of me again.

"You write to her now. Or…" Her voice is low and growly, but I'm too focused on the supplies I need, how my boat is gone, how she let it happen, and how she's here threatening me.

"Or what?" I snap.

"Or I'm done with you."

"Then be done. I'm done with you."

I grab bags of cookies. Candy bars.

I don't even pay attention as Emily storms out of the store. I grab a jar of instant coffee and am considering a second when Emily returns. Her face is red and there are tears staining her cheeks. "Be done with me all you like, but I'm telling everyone where you are. You are being selfish."

John comes into the store and puts his arm around Emily. He leads her out.

There's a guy working in the shop who tries to act like he wasn't listening to our outburst. I take my things to the register and pay. I'm usually careful about how I pack supplies in my pack, but I just shove it all in.

Emily can't mean what she said. But I'm pretty mad also. My boat is gone, and Emily and I are broken. The only person, other than Dad, who was always on my side isn't anymore. I barrel out of the store and break into a jog. The rhythm of the run should calm me, but I've got to get to Sophie. I've got to tell her they're coming for me. My family is going to drag me out of the woods and back to my life. Back to all of their expectations. Back to that horrible school they've picked out for me. Back to Brad shaking his head like I'm some curse on the family. Back to all of the yelling. Back to everything I ran away from. Back. Back. Back. Suddenly I'm calm. Backward. We should hike backward. A person could lose themselves on the trail if they wanted. Maybe forever.

CHAPTER 14

Sophie's sitting on a log drinking water when I arrive at our campsite. She must read my mood, because she asks, "What's wrong?"

The furious words continue to circle in my brain. I think about what I can tell her. What wouldn't sound nuts or mean or ungrateful, but every phrase that comes to mind seems awful, so I do the only calming thing I can, given the circumstances: I sit down.

"What's up?" she asks again.

"I... My cousin was at Neels Gap."

"I'm guessing that's not good?"

I put my head in my hands. *My boat. Gone.* My life is a mess. But maybe I deserve that. Hell, I know I do. I screwed up. "My dad died."

"What? Just now? I'm so sorry."

"No. I'm telling it out of order. I always do that." I slide out of my pack and push the heels of my hands into my eye sockets.

"So when?"

"Last April. April 16. It was always a big day for us. He'd always say, 'We made it, Dylan. We made it another year.'" I stop talking because it's too hard to keep talking. Sophie reaches across the space between our logs and puts her hand on my leg. It feels soft and comforting, so I keep going. "It was sudden. His heart." I look up at her. "That's why I left. I couldn't be at home anymore. My dad was everything to me. He always took my side. Even when that was hard to do. I mean, I'm not always easy to get along with. I messed up a lot. I still do. But he always got why I did the things I did. He always knew I wasn't trying to be bad."

Sophie comes and sits directly next to me. She's got this outdoor smell, like her soap is the wind and the dirt, which sounds gross but it isn't. It's honest.

"Everyone was sad when he died, of course. Dad was an awesome guy, but they went on with their lives, you know? They did normal life stuff like go to school or work. Like buy groceries. Nail polish. Mom got her hair cut differently, and that made me so mad. Maybe that doesn't make sense, but I'm not exactly... I don't process my feelings like other people do. I'm not normal."

Sophie pulls her shirt down over her wrist, then holds onto the edges with her fingers, stretching her sleeve. It's the same fidget I have. She straightens the necklace that's tight to her neck. She clears her throat. "I know what you mean."

"Most people say they know what I mean, but they don't. They can't."

"My mom died six months ago."

I sit there not knowing what to say, knowing firsthand that nothing you say is good enough. So I keep eye contact with her, and this time I put my hand on her leg, keeping my palm flat and the pressure even so that it comforts her and doesn't annoy her.

"I used to watch people buy coffee and chew gum and treat themselves to lollipops and candy, and it would make me sick. Physically ill." She puts her arms around her stomach.

I think about the notes Sophie writes. Are they to her mother?

"So when you saw your cousin…" she prompts.

"Emily and I never fight. Only once, over who had to clean up my dog's messes at the Cape. That was stupid. And one time she was dating one of my friends on the swim team, and I knew the guy was cheating on her and I told her and she got mad. But that was for her own good. You know?"

Sophie nods.

"But this time, this time she's really pissed. She wants me to go home. She said Mom's been through enough. She shouldn't have to worry about me too."

"That makes sense," Sophie says gently.

"I know." I drop my head in my hands. "But I can't."

Sophie puts her shoulder against mine and it's weird because I hate being touched. I mean, I hate, hate, hate it, but I don't with her. "I get it. If you can't, you can't."

"I know that it's not right. I know I should.…" My voice catches.

She looks up at me. "Some things happen that are unfathomable. And they can make us all do unfathomable things. It's a cycle, and it can't be stopped. Until it stops itself."

"Yes." It's like Sophie understands everything I feel, like she reached inside my mind and plucked out my thoughts. The feeling is at once violating and liberating. I'm overwhelmed by the urge to rock back and forth. My hands itch to cover my ears. It would calm me down, but I can't do that in front of this girl. Please, not in front of her.

Sophie bumps my shoulder with hers again, and soon my body and hers are doing this rhythmic movement that feels enough like rocking that my body and mind start to calm.

"What if you wrote to your mom? You could send her a letter." She reaches for her notebook.

I shake my head. "No. It's too late. Emily said she was going to tell my mom where I am. She'll come get me."

Sophie gets quiet. Rubs her hands on her legs. "You think she means it?"

"Yeah. I was thinking maybe I hike the trail backward. Except we aren't that far along, so there's not that much to hike if I go backward."

"Have you ever heard of a flip-flop hike?"

"Some guy said something about it when I started…"

"Traditionally, it means hiking halfway, taking a ride to the top of the trail, then hiking back to the halfway point."

I sit there miserable and depleted. In addition to feeling like an awful human being, I am picturing myself without Emily and without Sophie. Then Sophie says, "But we could just get a ride to the halfway point and hike south from there. It would throw them off."

"We?" That word shines and I feel a little bit of hope. "You'll come with me?"

"Yes."

"Why?"

She sits up straight, looks around like she's just decided something and has to get going on it. "Why not?" She hands me her notebook. "But in the meantime, if you'd like to write to your mom, you can use this."

My hand closes around the notebook I'm dying to look in, but I can't right now, with her sitting here watching me. I think about giving it back because I know if left to my own devices, I'd try to analyze the blank pages and look for indentation marks from her previous notes to try to see what she'd written. And that would be wrong.

"Thanks. Maybe I'll write her later." I hand her back the notebook. "Are you able to hike?" I ask.

"Can we leave tomorrow morning?"

"Sure."

"Then I'll be ready." She points to my pack. "So what did you bring me?"

I start picking through the bag, naming items as I take them out, like I freakin' foraged (two points) in the forest and made all of our supplies appear. "I found oatmeal raisin cookies, but not the ones you like."

She puts her hands out like a little kid doing a "gimme, gimme." "Wild Thing," she says, "this is the beginning of a beautiful friendship."

—————◦—————

The next morning, I'm up before Sophie, packing my stuff, when she unzips her tent. "Oh, sorry. I'll get ready."

"It's early. I couldn't sleep."

"I'll get the water," she slips off before I can stop her.

I watch her go. Her foot is better, but she's still got a limp. Flip-flopping will definitely buy us time, but she's going to slow us down, for sure.

We eat the peaches-and-cream oatmeal I got yesterday. It's really sweet, and I picture Emily loving it. Of all the flavors, it would definitely be her favorite. That thought sits in my stomach, and I wish I could talk to her again, but she said we were done. So that's it.

"We'll go back the way we came," I say. "It's the shortest route to a town."

"No. You'll get caught. We keep going north." She points. "It's only five miles to the next town." She shows me on the map. "Tesnatee Gap. This is where we go."

"No. We go back past Neels Gap to Blood Mountain. It's half the distance. And it's the other direction."

"It'll be harder to find a ride up north from farther south."

"We'll do the best we can."

Sophie shrugs. "Up to you." Then she goes into her tent to change. When she comes out, she's got on shorts and a different shirt, one of those half shirts with a flannel over top and boots. The look is startlingly sexy. I stare at her a little too long.

She looks past me. "It'll help us get a ride if I don't smell all nasty."

Before I can stop myself, I throw my hands in the air and say, "Preach it."

For two terrifying seconds, she stares at me, and I feel like I've totally blown it. But instead of yelling or backing away, Sophie punches me in the arm. "Don't be a pig."

"Can't help it."

I take the lead as we start to hike. Sophie is making these soft grunts, and I wonder if she should have rested another day. Or two. We come to a big incline so I stop. "Put your hand on my back."

She does and I can smell the lotion she put on to cover her hiker smell. It smells like a peach. Like that Kiss My Face brand Em used to use. I concentrate on the scent and not on the sounds that make me worry about Sophie.

"You okay?"

She breathes out. "Yeah. Fine."

I know she's lying even without seeing how her body braces. Her voice says it all. We go like this for as long as we can, then I hear her grunt, and I sit on a log and take out my map. I pat the log next to me.

"Nah. I'll stand."

"Your leg is hurting. We need to stop."

She wipes her brow and looks away. She can't look me in the eyes. "I'm fine. Just gotta keep moving. Stopping makes it worse."

"Okay."

She puts out her hand. Lifts me. I let her. Before I start walking, I shrug out from under my pack.

"What are you doing?" she asks.

"I've got something for you."

"I don't want to take Advil until we stop hiking."

"No. It's not that. Wait." I dig through my pack to get to the bottom. My phone. In the front pocket, the wire is all wound up with my headphones. I cue up sacred drums.

She stands in front of me, her arms by her side like a child. So trusting and sweet. I don't think she trusts many people, gauging by what Rain Man said about her and what I've noticed myself. So it feels really nice to have her trust me. I lean forward, my hands so close to her cheeks. She holds her breath while I put in the headphones for her. I hand her the phone. I watch her face.

I can hear the percussion leaking out of the headphones, and her eyes go from wide open with surprise to slits, like Dad's did when he was pleased. She nods to the beat, and I pick up my pack and we start hiking again.

It's midday and we're almost to Mountain Crossing/Neels Gap, which means alarms are firing in my mind. Will my mother be there with the National Guard? Maybe that's too extreme. Did Emily actually betray me? Is turning me in a betrayal? Maybe I've asked too much of Em to keep my secret. And then it hits me. The credit card with the money on it. Em can trace that shit. *Damn. Damn. Damn.*

I ball up my hands into fists and hit my leg hard, over and over again. I should have known.

Sophie gets in front of me. Her face is tight. "Hey, take it easy. What's wrong?"

I put my hands over my ears and pace. "I'm so stupid. Stupid. So effing stupid."

"What?" She stands there, her hands in the air, then lowers them, like she's trying to get me to calm down. She balances on one foot, so I know the other one is hurting her. She looks around. "I can't get us a ride if you're acting like this."

Tears stream down my face. "I screwed up. Emily has the info for my credit card. We have no money. And my phone. She knows this number."

"It's okay. We don't need money. Trail angels will help us find a way."

"I have like, fifty bucks. Maybe a little less. Those cookies cost a fortune."

She laughs.

I do too.

"We'll be fine," she says.

There's that word again. *We.* But I still feel like an idiot. Like I keep making these big mistakes, and they are starting to hurt people I care about.

"Why don't you stand over here? I'll work on getting us a ride."

"Sure. But I've got to ditch the phone."

"Aww. I was really loving those tracks."

"No worries. We can keep those going. Just have to ditch the SIM card."

I stick my finger nail in the slot on the side and remove the card, then I smash it with my foot. I pick up the garbage and pack it out. Leave no trace. I'm still shaking my head, annoyed at myself for being so reckless.

She smiles at me, and I didn't really think she was watching. "We'll be fine, Wild Thing. Just fine."

A feeling of warmth fills me, like it used to when Emily and I were working on something together. It's good to have someone with me. A partner in crime, so to speak.

She hikes her pack high on her shoulder, then aims herself at the road. She twists around one last time and shines a smile on me that makes me know that she's just as happy with our new partnership as I am.

CHAPTER 15

It takes less than half an hour until we're snuggled into the cab of a big-ass pickup truck. Sophie sits next to one of the Trail Angels, Nicholas Granger, who will give us a ride up to Wilmington, North Carolina.

"We were planning to do the whole trail, but then I hurt my leg," Sophie explains. "I told him to go without me, but Wild Thing wouldn't hear of it."

"Good man, Wild Thing."

"What's your trail name?" Sophie asks.

Nicholas turns a slight shade of pink. "Don't have one."

"We should call you Saint Nick then."

The guy chuckles and she shoots me a smile, like she knows Nick is putty in her hands, which surprises me because Sophie doesn't seem like a flirty girl, but I guess it's cool to give this guy some props for helping us.

"What do you guys like to listen to?"

"Anything's fine," Sophie answers for both of us.

"Then rock it is." Nicholas switches the station and Nickelback is finishing *How You Remind Me*, which is definitely not rock enough for my taste and has me wishing I had my chants or my drums or could reach my Dramamine, because riding with a stranger makes me anxious. Led Zeppelin's "Kashmir" comes on next and I lean back a little, my breathing settling.

"I hiked part of the trail, years ago," Nicholas says.

"Really?"

"Yeah. There's this guy in my hometown who's an old trail legend. He and his wife used to hike the whole thing every year."

The droning of their conversation and the sound of the highway make me sleepy. I lean my head against the window.

"Gary and Mary Lunsford. We always laughed at that. Gary and Mary."

"They still hike?"

"I think he does. She died last year."

We drive for a while with Rascal Flatts blaring in the background. I shove my tongue to the roof of my mouth, pressing the tip there. It makes me less nauseous. Country music is not my thing. It's too twangy and without a reliable drum beat or guitar riff for me to attach my mind to, The motion of the truck makes me sick. I think about what Nicholas said about the old couple. There's something weird about the story that makes me want to focus super hard on it. Either that or my car sickness is now making me paranoid in addition to queasy.

Saint Nick continues, "Gary had a strange trail name, which didn't make sense to me, but trail names don't always. Hey, do you have trail names?"

"They call me Ghost." It surprises me that Sophie shares that with him, given how private she is.

He slaps the steering wheel, which makes me jump. "Rain Man. That's what they called him."

My head snaps to attention. "Rain Man?"

"He hiked the trail for years. Sometimes his wife came with him for parts of it. Once she did the entire thing with him. But not usually. Then, apparently out of nowhere, she decided to hike alone last year. Got lost on the trail. They never did find her. Until it was too late."

"Wow," I say. Understatement of the year.

"Yeah. Gary searched and searched. We all did. It was almost about the same time last year as a matter of fact. The beginning of May, it was. May 5. There were all of those Cinco de Mayo parties. I was at one when I heard the news. Weird how time flies."

For some reason, everything Nick says produces pictures in my mind. I hadn't heard Rain Man's wife's story before, but now I imagine newspaper headlines. Photos of people on the mountain carrying someone in a stretcher. Mom is always telling me I have to start thinking about how other people would react to things. So now I try. Rain Man's wife died a year ago, almost to this day. That means something. It has to. But what?

I think about how I feel it's my fault that my dad died. Does Rain Man feel the same kind of guilt? I think of Rain Man giving away his wife's things. Maybe that's what you do, but I don't see it. Not the way he's doing it. It's like he over-packed his pack to give away her trail things. That doesn't make sense. Unless…

"Oh my God. Rain Man. We have to go back. *Now.* Can you get us to the trail?"

"Huh? Sure. I mean, I guess. I can drop you anywhere you want."

"What's going on?" Sophie asks.

"I have to go back." I scramble through my pack, looking for my map, despite how dizzy reading in a moving car makes me. My eyes are blurry and the map shakes in my hand. Sophie puts her hand over mine.

"Why do we have to get back?"

"We just do." I look to the side of the road for mile markers. "Where are we?" The disorientation that comes with riding in a truck, trying to read, and building panic makes it even harder to read the map.

"We're about ten minutes from the Albert Mountain bypass. I can drop you there. That's as close to the trail as I can get you by car."

I stare at the map. *Where would Rain Man be?*

"Where did Rain Man's wife disappear?" I ask.

"She went off trail. Got lost a few miles from it. Very sad."

"But where?" I thrust the map toward him even though he can't possibly look at it while driving.

Sophie intercepts the map. "Take it easy, Wild Thing."

Nick scratches his head. "I think it was around…Sassafras Gap."

"That's like forty miles from here," Sophie says.

"Four days," I say mostly to myself.

Sophie folds the map. She looks at me. "I can't hike that fast."

"Seven days, then."

"Dylan, we don't have enough food for that."

"We'll figure it out."

Sophie sits, hands fisted, so I'm guessing she's pissed. I have no idea why she's pissed at me, but for once, I don't care. I have to find Rain Man. This is not a want or an arbitrary fixation. This is a must. I recognized the pattern. This time I recognized the pattern. He spoke of his wife like he was still with her, said how much he missed her, and didn't care that he was running out of food. He was giving away her things—and his own belongings.

Nick pulls into a parking lot where a bunch of people have gathered. "You guys sure about this?"

I'm already out of the truck. Sophie shoots me an annoyed look, so I double back. "Thanks, Nick," I yell into the cab of the truck.

Sophie turns to him. "Thanks for everything." Then she slides out. I catch her so she doesn't land on her hurt ankle. She pulls away.

We watch as Nick drives away. She sits on a bench next to the path leading to the trail. "What are you thinking?"

"I think Rain Man is going to hurt himself. I have to stop him."

Sophie looks at me like I've got two heads. "You don't know that. You don't even know him. You only know what you think you know."

"That doesn't even make sense." I put my hands to my head to block out the sounds of people around me. "It's his movements. I'm looking at what he's doing. It's a pattern. He's giving his things away."

"His wife's things. She's dead. Maybe he doesn't want them around anymore."

"His things too." I lift the hem of my pants to show her my socks and realize it doesn't make as compelling an argument as I think it will. "He stayed in my bunk at Neels Gap. He said it would be the last time he slept in a bed."

"He probably meant until he got back from the trail."

"He didn't. I knew it was weird the way he said it, but I was trying to get to you, so I let it go."

"It doesn't have to mean…"

"It does. I know."

"Okay. So we call ahead. Anonymously. We put in a call and tell the police what we think."

"They won't listen." I turn around. And around again. I realize I look like I'm losing it. I guess I am.

"Dylan, you're scaring me."

I'm scaring her. *I'm. Scaring. Her.* I force myself to stop. I face her. "You know how I came after you? How I knew something was wrong with you? That you needed help?"

She nods.

"It's like that. But this time it's Rain Man."

Her eyes focus and she reaches into her pack. "Okay," she says. She pulls out the map and opens it. "Okay. So we find Rain Man…" Sophie points to an area on the map. "We are here, right?"

"Right."

"So we have to hike back to get to Rain Man, assuming you are even right about this."

"I am."

"I said assuming." She points to Neels Gap on the map. "This is where your family is going to start looking for you. And here is where you think Rain Man is."

"Yeah."

"You don't see the problem? We are going to be hiking toward your family." She points on the map, "There might be forest rangers at any of these points." She bats at the map again.

"We'll find a way."

"Don't you think the forest rangers would be looking for us in those places? Your cousin knows about me now too, so if they are looking for you, they'll be looking for both of us. Neither of us can safely go into town now. You get that, right?"

I do. I'm still making mistakes. For all of her talk of "we," I can't drag Sophie through the woods with her foot like this. Not with people looking for us, because of me. I can't make her chase after Rain Man.

"Me, they'll be looking for me." I throw my pack on the ground and rifle through it until I get to my wallet. "Here." I hand her twenty dollars and my credit card. "Use this and go north. It'll throw them off."

She shakes her head. "They won't let me use your credit card."

"The code is 2625. Use it as a debit card. They won't check ID that way."

"You've thought of everything, huh?"

"There's almost eight hundred dollars left on the card. You'll be fine."

"And what do I do when your family shows up, and I am arrested for stealing your card?"

I hadn't thought of that. *Damn.* I *am* getting sloppy. I think of all of those phony missions with Emily. All those pretend capers. Those sure didn't get me ready for real life on the run. Even the time I hid away in the city, I never screwed up like this. "Only use it in places where they don't have cameras over the ATM. Withdraw a hundred dollars, and then give it to someone hiking north. Tell them it's from a trail angel. So if they follow anyone, they'll follow them."

"Dylan, you can't decide my choices for me." Sophie says.

"On this, I do. I'm going without you. You won't keep up. And I won't have you getting found because of my family drama."

"What makes you think I don't want to be found? I told you my dad knows I'm here."

I want to reach out and touch her face. I want to be all comforting like I've seen boyfriends do with their girlfriends in movies, and even like I've seen with my swim team buddies. I can't do it, though. I can't figure a way to touch Sophie without it feeling bad for her. So, I just look at her really seriously and sweetly.

"Come on, Sophie. Your pack is always light. You don't have the right clothes. Or supplies. You know this trail, but you're not ready to be here. If you don't want to be found, you need to stay away from me. They are looking for me, and they won't stop. I know my family."

She looks down. Her face is tight looking, like she's trying to be brave, but she's failing.

"I know you're going to be mad. I know you're going to be pissed. But I'm going without you, Sophie. I'm going back to find Rain Man. And you can't come with me."

I don't even look back when I leave her. It's like when I left Emily a few days ago. I just keep walking.

Sophie shouts my name after me, my heartbeat drumming in my ears. I can't listen to her or anyone who would deter me from this path. Rain Man's movements tell me all I need to know. I've got to stop him. No matter if it's stupid or not. No matter if Sophie's pissed at me and I never see her again, or if I do and she refuses to deal with me. I have to do this. I can't not do this.

It's forty miles to where Rain Man's wife died. If I hike more than ten miles a day, I can get there three days before the anniversary of his wife's death. I've only got twenty dollars and a few rations of food, but I'm not going to let anything stop me. I can't change the past. I can't go back and tell Dad to get his heart checked. I can't warn Mom that there's something wrong with Dad's heart, but I can do this. I can find Rain Man. I can help him, even if it costs me Sophie.

———o———

There's only a few hours of light left, and I'm ahead of schedule, so I stop at Beech Gap and set up camp. I'm not going to night hike unless I need to. I go to the water source and refill my bottle. It's sad to be collecting for one person. I've gotten used to having company, but I only think about that for a second or two, because I want to eat, set up camp, go to sleep, and get up early and go again. I lay in my tent, exhausted from the day of hiking and fighting with every single person whom I like or love on this earth. My eyes don't even close. I stare at the ceiling of my tent. Listen to all of the bugs and the frogs and whatever is making noises. That's when I remember I didn't set up the bear bag.

I go outside and hoist my bag in the tree, thinking of Sophie, which is kind of constant these days. It is unsettling in and of itself, especially because I can't even speak with Emily about it. Also because after how I acted, I may never see her again. My mind is a mess when I crawl back into my tent. I have to get some rest. Hiking with little to no sleep is pretty stupid. Although not as stupid as so many other things I've done lately.

———o———

I hear rustling outside of my tent and immediately think it's a bear. I've got no phone and no real way to tell the time, but it's pitch black out. Should I look and see what's making the noise? Do bears scare as easily at night as they do during the day?

There's more rustling and then a zip. Bears don't use zippers. Or do they? I push open my tent door, and am grateful to the full moon and clear sky with stars that lights up my campsite. But I cannot believe what I see: Sophie is here, zipping up her tent.

All kinds of emotions swirl inside me. I need to sort them out before I blow, because blowing my top with this girl would not be okay. I know that much, at least.

She looks at me in a way that makes me think she's mad, but that sort of pisses me off. She should understand why I did what I did. She should be reasonable. Still, her stare is annoyed, and she's messing with her tent and limping really badly. I choose my first words carefully.

"What the hell do you think you're doing?" It comes out of my mouth before I can stop it. *Great.*

She holds up her hand and turns her body away from me.

She lowers herself onto a log by her tent and grimaces.

"What time is it?" I ask.

She looks at me like she can't believe I'd ask that. Like that is the stupidest thing to ask. Turns out she's wrong. I'm just getting started. Apparently, I have a barrage of stupid things lined up to say to a person who is clearly exhausted and in a ton of pain.

I move closer to her. "I asked you to do one thing. *One thing* and you couldn't even do that. 'Take my card,' I said. 'Take the money. Hand the card to someone on the trail after you take out money. Use it and draw the authorities away from me.' All you had to do was stay away and here you are." I turn away, try to smack my brain into submission. At least that's what I tell myself I'm doing as I hit myself in the head repeatedly.

"I didn't ask for your money."

I whirl back to face her. "I know you didn't."

"I don't want your help."

"That's stupid. You need help. I mean obviously..." I point to her leg.

"I've been hiking long before I met you. I know what I'm doing. And you don't have to be mean. I don't owe you anything. I don't have to follow your instructions like your assistant."

I'm stunned. Her words dive-bomb my brain and freeze inside of me. A weak "What?" is all I can manage.

"I said, I'm not working for you, pal, and I can do what I like." She rifles through her bag, even though I can tell she's tired and hurting and should probably chill out, eat, and get some sleep. She takes out her wallet and holds out the Visa I gave her.

For some reason, her giving it back hurts like a kick in the stomach. I stand there dumbfounded and not able to function, because I don't want her to do this so much that I can't move. So she hops over to me and puts it in my hands. I stare at the card and consider how weird it is to be blown away by this simple action. Her returning my credit card shouldn't feel so sucky, but it does because I know behind the action is a really pissed-off girl. No, scratch that. A really hurt girl. Because of me. Now my words have been tamed by the sea of regret they have to swim through to make it out of my mind and into my mouth.

Dad used to tell me that whenever I get really mad, I should try to go outside my body and look down on the scene like I'm making a film. From the outside of myself, it's easier to see that being calm is the only way to fix a situation. So I try to do that. Try and fail, because the next thing I say is, "You are so infuriating. I can't believe you did this." My voice is calm, because I know I'm right. I am the king of right. Where's my crown?

"This trail is about more than hiking and camping. It's a way of life. You don't even stop to look at the scenery. It's a means to an end for you. What makes you think Rain Man would listen to someone like you anyway? You don't take time to get to know people or love the things he loves. You take and take and dictate. You aren't living."

It's not like I haven't heard that before. A lot of people think I'm arrogant. But I'm right about things when most people are wrong. It's not my fault I see clearly. And I hate when people act like it is. But accusing me of not living?

"Just because I don't relish the lookouts and the mountains and the views doesn't mean I don't live. I live plenty. And besides, who are you to talk? You're writing secret notes and burying them."

Okay, obviously my mouth should have shut the eff up already, because I did not mean to say that last bit.

Her eyes get wide, and her mouth opens like she can't believe I just said that. Then she covers her mouth, and her face looks like it's collapsed. Like after you puke.

And then my stomach drops. "I'm sorry, I shouldn't have…"

"You've seen me.… How could you.…"

"It just happened. I saw you. I couldn't help it. I only dug them up once…"

Her mouth drops open. She closes it and opens it again, until she looks like a guppy gasping for breath. "You *what*?"

"Okay, okay, it's…" I've got nothing to say anymore. I've done it now. I've killed any chance I have with this girl. Obviously I *am* a danger to myself and others like that school counselor said.

She puts her head in her hand and starts to cry. Huge sobs. I think maybe I should talk to her, so I try to do that, but instead of being happy that I'm trying to make things right and comfort her, she starts throwing stuff at me. Pinecones. Rocks. Dirt. You name it. If God put it on the forest floor, I'm now dodging it.

I drop to the ground to take cover. Sure she's going to bonk me over the head, but the moon is shining, and I've already scanned the area by her feet, grateful she threw most of the heavy stuff already.

"I'm not normal," I say.

"Obviously."

"I have issues."

She crosses her arms over her chest and bends over like she's doing a sitting version of the Cheerio stretch, the one where you lie on your back and try to touch your head with your toes. I have no problem reading that body language, but I guess she wants to make sure I pick up on her mood, because she answers me with a sniffly. "Clearly."

"I know I do. I'm being serious, not flippant or sarcastic. I have problems, Sophie."

"Go away and leave me alone. You can't stop me from looking for Rain Man. So don't try."

She reaches down and grabs her ankle and for some reason, that small motion makes me feel so bad for her that I remember to make myself look down on the scene we're in. When I do that, I see that how I feel about any of this doesn't matter. All that matters is that she's hurt. I've got to stop fighting with this girl. I've got to do what's right. So I make my voice come out all soft and sweet. "You're hurt, Sophie."

"Don't call me that. I am nothing to you, and you are nothing to me."

That's exactly the kind of verbal hand grenade that should inflict damage. But since I'm outside of my feelings now, since I'm busy worrying about her, I don't let that get to me. I only care that Sophie is hurt and needs to rest. And for once, it's my ability to distance myself from emotion that helps me do the right thing. So I say, "I understand that. I get it if you hate me. But your foot is hurt, and you need help."

"I don't need anything from you."

"I know you don't. But when's the last time you ate anything?"

"Not your problem."

"Look. I know you bury notes. I don't know what they say, because when I dug them up, I couldn't read them. I don't even know why I did that, except I wanted to know more about you. And I don't like getting to know new people, so in a totally messed up way, that means I care about you."

"Great."

"You're changing me. Making me care about other people and making me listen more. You are making me behave better. Well, except for the digging up your secret notes thing. But in general, you are making me a more caring person, at least. And now I'm going to tell you something about me that no one knows. Not even Emily."

"There's nothing you can say that will change anything."

"I killed my father."

Her eyes go wide. She must think I shot him or bludgeoned him, and here we are in the forest, alone, and she's hurt. I put my hands up like I'm surrendering. "No. I don't mean it like that." She relaxes a little, and that frees me to say, "He died of a heart attack, but it was my fault."

"People always think stuff like that is their fault, and it never is."

"Well, I have proof. And if you let me take care of you tonight, and hike with me tomorrow, I'll tell you the whole story. Then we'll each have a secret that no one else knows, okay?"

She's still crying, and her shoulders are shaking a little. Mom used to cry like this when she was mad at Dad. She'd shake, and he'd tell her he was sorry and put his arm around her. I don't think I can put my arm around Sophie, so I stay where I am and wait. Eventually her cries become sniffles. When the sniffles slow, I try again. "Sophie?"

She sniffles again and looks down at her hands. "Okay."

"You are wet and cold, and I'm worried about you. I have rain pants that will be way too long on you, but we can cut them. I want you to wear them, okay?"

She wraps her arms around herself and shivers.

"And then I'm going to make you some coffee and some food. You need to get warm. You know how easy it is to get hypothermia out here."

"It's late."

"What time?"

"Midnight."

"For real?"

"Yeah. Why?"

"I've been going to sleep so early, this will be my first midnight meal in the forest."

She smiles. "I love this time of night."

Even though I want to spring into action, I force myself to look around and smile. It's not even fake. I smile big. "It's beautiful. It really is. It's so quiet. And the stars are beautiful, when you can see past the trees, that is."

She cranes her neck until she can see through the canopy. "Yeah. My dad knew all of the constellations and their names."

I do also, but boasting isn't going to help her feel better, so instead I say, "I'm going to get the pants from my tent, and then I'm going to start cooking. Okay?"

She nods.

"I'm sorry for everything, Sophie."

She nods again.

I'm amazed how often I've said those two words lately, especially when it wasn't already too late. And it makes me feel good that I can do it now when it matters. When it can actually help that person. Sophie in this case, but then maybe eventually Mom too.

CHAPTER 16

Eating rice and beans out of a bag next to Sophie is much
better than eating alone. Not only because it's nice to have
company, but because that company is her. She's wearing my
rain paints (Emily was right about my needing them!) and a
sweatshirt I hadn't worn yet. She looks adorable.

She takes a spoonful of food while I quiz her on our favorite
books. Luckily, she passed a few of the must-haves without
hesitation. All of the Harry Potters, C. S. Lewis's books, *Eragon*,
and she's added a few of her own favorites to the mix.

She stops eating to ask, "Edgar Allen Poe?"

"Yes."

"And you loved his stories?"

"Yes."

She feigns wiping sweat from her brow. "That would be a
deal-breaker."

"Well, I haven't read all of his poems and stories. I hope that's
not too upsetting."

"Not if you're willing to rectify that as soon as possible."

I hold my spoon in the air. "I swear I will."

"Shakespeare?"

"He's okay."

"Okay? Just okay?"

"Douglas Adams?"

"Have never read him."

"I'll trade one Shakespeare for one Douglas Adams."

"Deal."

Sophie yawns. "I should probably…"

"Yeah."

Sophie looks better, but her lips are still a little beige. "Don't take this the wrong way, but you don't look so good."

Sophie looks down at my clothes, which are too big on her, and says, "Hey, my designer says this outfit is the shit. Also, that's a hell of a thing to say to a girl."

"I meant you look like you're not feeling so well."

"Hiking all night without eating and my foot hurting was probably not the best idea."

"Well, you did have to chase the jerk who annoyed you, so…"

"Yeah. So?"

"I think I should stay with you tonight. Keep you warm."

She cocks her head. "That sounds like a line."

"A line?"

"A pickup line, a play. To get me to… you know…"

I blush again, and it's such a weird feeling. Of course I want to stay with her, but I'm not going to admit to that, because that would not be cool. "Oh no! Not at all!"

She makes a face like she's annoyed, then smiles, so I'm so confused. "You don't have to act like that would be the worst thing in the world…"

"So you want me to act like an oversexed, hormonally driven asshole who only cares about, you know…"

She raises her eyebrows.

"Look I'm not exactly good at this stuff."

"I noticed. It's kind of sweet."

I stand up. I can't take being made fun of, not by this girl. "I better go clean the dishes."

"Don't make me chase you," she says. "I wasn't trying to insult you."

I look back at her. "I told you I'm not good at this stuff. I never cared about that before, but you make me care about it, and now I feel like an idiot because…"

"Shh. You're not an idiot. You're very cute and I care about you too."

Those words. *I care about you.* They dive into my heart, making it pump harder and faster and stronger. I almost reach to hold it in place, but that would make me look like a total dork, which I already do since my mouth can't seem to shut up.

"One day, it might be nice to be together in that way, tonight I think you need the extra warmth. I'm worried about you."

"Okay."

"Yeah?"

"But I don't spray bug spray under my sleeping bag. It's not good for you, with all of those chemicals. So if you're going to stay with me, you will have to deal with that."

"Okay."

"I have some eucalyptus oil that you can put on instead."

"I'm not worried about the bugs tonight. I only want you to be okay."

She smiles. "It's been a long time since someone's said that to me. Why don't you leave the dishes. Pack them up and I'll help you clean them in the morning."

I don't know much about girls or dating, but I figure when a girl tells you to hurry up and come to bed, you do what she says.

It's such a bizarre chain of events that led to my body being pressed up against a girl's, especially this girl in particular, who I've spent an inordinate amount of time trying not to alarm or disgust. As a result, sleep doesn't exactly come easily. Pressing a woody into a girl's body could go badly, or so I've heard from Sam and Taylor, so I'm careful to keep myself far enough away that my body's reaction to my thought of *What the fuck? There's a girl next to me!* won't be an issue. But somehow, when I wake up, I find myself nuzzled against her. My arm is actually draped over her and her hand is on top of mine, which must mean she doesn't hate me holding her. Weird. For the hundredth time, I wish I could talk to Emily. Hell, I wish I could talk to Brad or Christian. Not that they would believe me without a picture (if I hadn't already smashed my sim card). They would flip out, for sure.

Instead, I lay here, wondering if my basic early-morning

hard-on will go down enough so I can take a piss, or if I'm destined to walk the earth with this part of my body pledging allegiance to Sophie.

The light outside the tent is still weak, but there's enough to let me know it's actually morning. I don't want to wake Sophie, so I carefully pull myself away from her, bit by bit, so I can go take care of business.

After that, I grab the dishes and take them to the creek to clean. I filter and fill two water bottles and bring everything back to camp. I get down the bear bag and dive into it, checking to see what's left. Which is pretty frightening because, among other things, we are getting super low on coffee.

Gah. I finally get a girl to pay attention to me, and now I'm going to totally zone out when she talks and she's going to ditch my ass the first chance she gets. I cannot focus without coffee. I can't hike without coffee. I can't think without coffee. Without coffee, I am all muscle and bones and no brain.

For a second, my mind conjures images of coffee grounds, chocolate-covered espresso beans, real coffee made in an actual coffeepot. Oh my God. The first package Emily sent, before we had our fight, is waiting for me at Hiawassee, which, by my calculations is about twenty-one miles ahead of us, but I'm also not sure if she can track when I pick it up, so there's no way I'm going to chance that.

I check my supplies. Four bags of oatmeal, three bags of rice and beans, two bags of beef jerky, three bags of pasta sides. It's not enough food for two people for three days of hiking. I'm going to have to make a supply run. Soon. Money is pretty dismal. If we don't use the charge card, I've got $18.50, and I'm not sure what cash Sophie has. The only supply I have enough of is ibuprofen, which won't last long either.

Sophie starts making noise in the tent, so I peek in. She must be having a nightmare. "Shh, Sophie. It's okay." I pat her leg. She's mumbling and thrashing and doesn't wake up. I climb inside the tent and start to shake her gently when I hear rustling outside the tent. Then some banging. I pop my head out in time to catch a bear eating my oatmeal.

All I can think of is that we need that food and that we don't have enough, so I charge at the bear. Desperation must make me seem intimidating, because he takes off. The beef jerky and most of the bagged food is already eaten or in his mouth as he leaves the scene of the crime. I fall onto the ground, trying to pick up what's left of our food. Some rice, a few beans mixed with a little dirt. Awesome.

That's when I see the rest of the damage. The coffee is scattered on the ground. Panic starts to pump my heart. Tears spring to my eyes. I realize it's ridiculous to cry over spilled coffee, especially when I can't always cry over normal reasons, but these are anger tears. I need caffeine, or I'm going to lose my shit on so many levels. I bend down, face close to the ground and wet my fingers to pick up coffee grounds, and yes, I eat them. I don't realize I'm mumbling to myself until Sophie asks, "What will be okay? And what will be enough?"

I turn to see her poking her head out of the tent, looking rather puzzled.

Awesome. Just how I wanted her to see me. *Life. Is. Good.*

———°———

I don't have to explain that a bear stole almost all of our food, because that's painfully obvious. My cheeks are heated and I'm sure I'm blushing again. Sophie must know I left the food unattended.

Her eyes drift to the tree where the bear canister was. Then to the ground.

"You were having a nightmare. I... I... I know I shouldn't have..."

"No, I get why you... But... Wow."

"Do you have any food in your stuff?"

She shakes her head. "But I have the money you gave me..., except there's really no place to resupply for, like, twenty miles."

Damn. I look at the remains of the food. Slim pickings for sure. One bag of noodles, one bag of oatmeal, a bag of pasta that has spilled open. I scoop up some of that and pour it into the torn bag. "I guess this will be our last supper."

"People can live for twenty-one days without food," Sophie notes.

"Yeah, but do they *want* to?" I shoot her a smirk.

"Good point."

"We better clean up the rest of this and get going."

I feel the rage fill me. How could I have been so stupid? I start drumming my hands on my legs, then open my palm. The need to smack my thighs or my head is building, building.

Sophie's busy picking more noodles out of the dirt. Some coffee gets more scattered and I have to bite the inside of my cheek so I don't say anything mean that I'll regret. Sophie collects a pile of food, but I know it won't be enough. This is all because of me. Bear Bait Taggart. Dipshit Dylan. Stupid Space Cadet.

She must pick up on my mood. "Don't beat yourself up."

Funny she should say that.

She continues. "It could've happened to anyone. Besides, you were trying to help me."

Some of the pressure within me releases, like a balloon being deflated.

"Hey, can I ask you something?" she says. "What were you doing on the ground?"

"Oh." My face heats. I've become a blushing fiend. "I'm sort of addicted to coffee, but not the way most people are. If I don't have coffee, my brain gets foggy and I zone out and stop caring about everything around me."

"Okay…"

"I mean, if I don't have coffee, I could sit in the woods and not hike or eat or… It's extreme."

"Then we better get you coffee. Stat."

"Yes. Stat." I rub my hands together, like Lady Macbeth wiping off that damned spot.

Sophie points to her tent. "I'm going to change, then we can go." She holds the flap back, but then swivels her head to face me. "Oh, and you don't have to confess any more of your dark secrets. Your coffee addiction was enough." She's laughing now.

I should be annoyed because she's laughing at me, but it feels good to share a joke with someone. Like when Sam and Taylor used to kid around with me. Or when Emily did, and suddenly it feels kind of good, like even though we are going to go through tough times, at least we'll have each other. And that makes me think about when I get home. Sam. Taylor. Emily. Maybe there's a way to fix all that? I don't know, but it's something to think about. And thinking about that might make the next twenty miles go by faster.

CHAPTER 17

As we hike slowly to accommodate Sophie's foot, I think about how long we'll have to go without food. And coffee. The hike is mostly uphill at this point, gradual, but climbing nonetheless. Before setting out on the Appalachian Trail, I would have thought hiking uphill would be harder than going downhill, having to lean into your slope, lugging your pack, but it's the opposite, so I'm glad Sophie has less of a strain.

The landscape shifts and we have to start a downhill climb. I worry that the ACE bandage we wrapped Sophie's foot in won't be enough, that she'll lose footing and slip, and that I won't be able to keep her from getting hurt. So, I pay special attention to how Sophie sounds, not just her breathing, but the sound the walking stick makes as she places it before each step. The funny thing is that with her, I could think of a million conversations to have, just like with Emily, but I keep the silence going, careful to listen for any sign of alarm, but I'm also comfortable to hike with her and let the setting and our continued progress keep me going.

A little clearing at the bottom of the small hill we descended feels like a good place to stop. "Hold up," I say.

She reaches for her water bottle and I do the same.

"You need any ibuprofen?"

She finishes a big swig and wipes her mouth with the back of her hand. Closes her bottle. "Nah. I'm going to wait."

It's a really pretty day. One of those sort of gray ones with a small breeze and the sound of birds all around us. The kind of day I'd usually not pay attention to, but with Sophie's accusation the other day, saying that I don't pay attention to the beauty of the trail, I tell myself to do just that. To pay attention.

We get to one of those Appalachian Trail signs, one of those moments I've come to look for. As soon as we see the wooden sign with block print, capital-letter writing, I am reminded that I am on track for this hike. The one I've chosen, something I don't get to do for my school or my classes, something Mom has always done for me since, even though my brain is designed for big thinking, it's not mature enough to make long-term decisions.

I remember one of the meetings at school to discuss my inattention and inappropriate behaviors in class. We were in a conference room. Mom, Dad, and my teachers were there along with the school's ESE contact, Mrs. Winters. Mom explained that Mrs. Winters would be helping us make good decisions about what we need to do to make this year a successful one. Those were Mrs. Winters's words, and because I was sort of pissed at having to be sitting there, discussing this, with a group of teachers who didn't like me, and Mom, who was always pissed at me, and Dad, who was quietly supporting me, I chose to focus just on those words. *Successful year. Good decisions.*

Mom touched my arm. "Come on, Dylan. Help us out here."

But they didn't want my help. They wanted to berate me for being who I was. And just like that Mr. Stephens spoke up. "He's daydreaming in class. Doodling. Never has his materials for class…"

Dad leaned forward, but he stayed silent.

Mom asked, "Do you hear what your teachers are saying, Dylan? You need to be more involved in your classes."

I wanted to talk back. Give Mr. Stephens a zinger, but the truth is, that wouldn't help anyone. So I stayed silent as Mom finished. "Every class matters in high school. You don't see that now, but it does."

She meant my grades matter and that my doing the best I could in each class would create the kind of resume and GPA that would give me options for the future. But my future came to me in bits and pieces. One long-ass second at a time, at least in Mr. Stephens's class. That's the way my attention worked. It wasn't something I could always control. She never understood that. But now, on this trail, free to make my own decisions, I also see what she was saying. Every choice matters. I wish Emily was here more than ever, because this kind of moment is one she'd understand, having been through all of my school crap with me. I wish I could tell Mom I understand what she was trying to do for me.

Sophie's hand snapping in front of my eyes draws me out of my daydream. "Hey, you still with me?"

"Yeah, I was just remembering something."

"About your cousin or your dad?"

I wiped the hair out of my face. "Wow. I'm so predictable."

"You asked me about my notes? I write them for myself. Maybe you should too. It could help you square things in your mind."

I nod. "Maybe I will."

Sophie rewards me with a strong smile despite her worn-out look. She points to the Standing Indian campsite. "Hey." She nudges me in the arm, which reminds me of Emily. "I think there's a little store here. One time, when I was hiking the trail with my parents, I got really sick and Mom got me stuff there. I hope it's still here."

"You think they have an ATM?"

"Probably not. It's tiny. They run out of almost everything worthwhile after the first few weeks of hiking season. I think they get trucks in once a week to resupply during peak hiking season, but at other times, it's much less and we are not at peak season yet. I can try to get money if they have a working ATM and if you think that's safe."

Safe. Safe to withdraw my money from the account I set up and told the only person in the world who is supposed to be completely trustworthy: Emily. The thought of forest rangers looking for me pisses me off. All because I was stupid to trust Emily with this. She's always been behind me, but maybe this time it was too much. Obviously it was. Emily is hard to rattle, something I put to the test often, but I guess this time I went too far. "You're right. I guess I better stay here," I say. "So get the supplies and maybe some money and meet me back in the woods by this sign. Say, in forty-five minutes?"

"You won't go far while I'm gone?"

"I'll find the water supply. Refill. Then I'll come back here."

She looks at me like she's not so sure about that, but she doesn't have a choice. I hand her the debit card and the rest of my money.

My stomach knots as I watch Sophie limp away. Sophie's hurt and she's got to deal with this on her own. I watch her figure disappear out of my sight, and I know I'm letting her down. As a hiking partner, I suck.

Feelings swirl inside me, all of them vying for my attention. Sadness. Regret. Anger. I settle on the last, because it's the easiest to pinpoint, and it feels the best to unleash. I'm pissed. Really pissed at Emily. This is all her fault. Like an attorney in a courtroom, my arguments become a trial in my brain as I start to remember everything she's ever done wrong in our friendship. Line up the evidence like I'm conducting an indictment.

Sam and Emily dated for a while, and there were times I lied for her so she could stay out with him. I was always covering for them. Sure, after Dad died, I ran away to New York and she came to find me to make sure I was all right. That got her grounded, and she almost missed one of John's big events at school. But for the most part, *I* covered for *her*. She owes me.

But more than that, we were always supposed to be there for each other. And she ruined that with her "I'm telling."

It wasn't only Mom she said she was telling. It was the police. If they catch me, they'll force me to go to that awful school. Because of her. And they could keep me from saving Rain Man. Because of her. People's lives could be ruined. His kids, assuming he has kids. I mean, don't most people? And if he has kids, then maybe also they have kids, his grandkids? And pets. They might have pets. And I know this is too much and too big, and I know I'm making it all too much, but this is how I get sometimes. Emily knows this. And still she got mad and betrayed me.

That's what hurts the most. It's like Ron or Hermione turning in Harry. It's plain wrong. *And* she let Mom sell my boat. If she were here, I'd tell her I hated her.

I storm back into the woods, not looking for white blazes, not looking for anything, just walking, my face hot with tears, my throat swelling with the rage that wants to pour out of me.

Dad is dead. *Dead*. And now that Emily and I are broken, I am alone in the family. No one will want me back because I am the reason Dad died, and even if they don't know I am to blame, I do, and I'm sure on some level, they suspect it.

Agony fuels my climb to a lookout, where I scream down into the abyss, "I hate you, Emily. I hate you. I hate you." But I know it's not Emily I hate. It's myself. I hate myself for not recognizing the pattern. The stupid fucking pattern. *Dum dum blip. Dum dum blip.*

"I should have known. I should have known. I should have…" All of a sudden it's like I'm in the auditorium that day. There were tons of kids there. Bodies bumping into each other. All of the sounds echoed off the wall. Kids were laughing, and there was a drumbeat in the background, building and building, and it sounded just like Dad's heartbeat, and it felt like everyone knew. They knew and I couldn't stop myself. Like I can't stop myself now. I strike out, like I did that day, my hands hitting the walls of the auditorium. Right before they emptied it. The sound surrounded me: laughter, screams, jeers. I should have known.

I punch the tree I'm standing next to, the rough bark scraping my knuckles. I punch the tree, again and again. I know I'm on the trail and not in the auditorium. I know this because the auditorium walls were smooth, but here on the trail, now, the tree fights back, the bark assaults my hands. I don't care. I punch and punch and soon I hear Sophie yelling, "Stop, Dylan! Stop!"

I look up and she's standing there, staring at my hands. They are a mess and there's all of this blood. Slowly, I start to feel the pain in my hands. Horrible pain. *What did I do? What did I do?*

"Oh, Dylan. I think you're going to have to tell me about your dad."

I'm crying. "I'm sorry. I've ruined everything."

"We need to get you to a stream and clean these hands."

"I know," I say. "I did this. I know."

She doesn't answer. It's like she understands the medicine I need is quiet support and leadership. Like that day at school when Emily led me to the courtyard while all of the kids were forced to evacuate. How the administration shouted for her to get away from me, but she yelled back, "He's my cousin! He won't hurt me."

Then Emily said to me, "Dylan, tell them you're okay. Tell them you won't hurt me." She was crying, and I guess maybe I was too, because I knew I could never go back to that school after how I acted. They'd told me this was my last chance there, and I knew they wouldn't let me stay. And I was embarrassed that they saw me cry, which is so fucked up because I should have been embarrassed that I acted like that to begin with, but the heartbeat was the thing that did me in, and I wanted to explain that, but I knew that no one would understand that. Mostly because I'd never admit it was my fault.

I hear the stream and another sound that gives me the tiniest bit of hope. It's the sound of a soda can top being popped.

"Here, drink this. They only had one. Can you believe it?"

Even through my eyesight is blurry I can see it's a Mountain Dew. Mountain Dew is the best kind of soda, because it has a ton of sugar and the most caffeine you can get in a can. I gulp it down and imagine the caffeine clearing the fog in my brain. I believe I can actually feel it get zingy and tingly, even though it can't work that fast. But then the effect spreads. My focus sharpens. I can see the blood on the tree I hit. The blood on my hands. I follow Sophie, and I don't even try to talk. I'm too damned worn out for that.

She helps me lean into the stream, the water turning red and my aching hands screaming at me. I watch the blood swirl away along with my regrets.

"I'm sorry. I don't know what happened. I don't know…"

"It's okay, Dylan. We all feel like going a little wild sometimes. And after what you've been through, it makes sense."

"What have I been through?" I ask, confused. It was my father who died. Not me.

"You lost your dad, Dylan. I know how hard that is."

I nod, and then I start to cry again. She says softly, "The notes I write are to my mom."

Something passes between us, a kind of softening of barriers. I want to lean in to her. It's what any other guy would do in this situation. Kiss the girl. Right? But I'm not any ordinary guy, so I let the moment pass and simply ask, "What do the notes say?"

"A lot of different things, but mostly that I'm sorry."

"About what?"

"The day she was diagnosed, I was pissed that Dad wouldn't let me go to blink-182. I was a total bitch, and I didn't even notice that she'd been crying. I yelled at her, which was never okay in my house, but it was definitely not okay that day. So, in one of the notes, I told her I was sorry that I made that awful day even worse. Stuff like that."

I nod like I understand, but really I'm imagining what I'd say to Dad in speech bubbles now if I could tell him I'm sorry for not saving him. And now I'm also remembering all of the things I overheard Dad say, trying to reassure Mom that I'd be okay. All the times I made her cry, because I was difficult or rigid. The times I knew I was making her life harder, but I didn't care, because I was mad or stubborn, or just plain right. And I think about writing to Mom like Emily said before and like Sophie told me too.

But then, because I'm me, I focus on the one thing that really gets to me about what Sophie just said. Nobody in her house yelled. I can't even imagine that. My general noisiness aside, everyone in my house had an opinion, which they happily espoused as soon as it came to them. My father. My mother. My brother. My cousins. My aunt. All of us were a noisy swirl of chaos. And part of me loved that. "You'd never survive in my house. We are a very loud and opinionated family."

"Sounds wonderful."

Is she teasing me? I search her face, but it looks sort of dreamy, so I guess she's being sincere.

"Did you want to tell me about your dad?" Sophie asks.

"He was super cool."

"No, I mean about…"

"Oh." I stare out into the forest and back at my hands. "Is it okay if I save that for another day? I've already humiliated myself enough for today."

She nods. "Sure. It'll give me something to look forward to."

I laugh. To be out-snarked by a girl is awesome. "Did everything go okay in town?" I ask.

"Mostly. I didn't get money though, because I thought that was a bad decision."

"Why?"

She pulls out a piece of paper from her pocket. It's a missing child poster with my picture on it.

———○———

Sophie gets the ibuprofen out of my bag and gives each of us two. I figure at some point, we are going to have to take out more money. But we'll do it after we find Rain Man, because that is more important than finishing the trail or hiding out until my eighteenth birthday. Sophie puts some antibiotic ointment on my knuckles and then ties a bandanna over each of my hands. The Mountain Dew is wearing off. Caffeine from soda doesn't work as long or as well as coffee. Plus the sugar gives me a big crash, which makes the caffeine pointless. But right now, my limbs feel all loose and my veins feel like my blood is cold. It's weird, but that's the way my body processes manufactured adrenaline.

"I couldn't find many supplies," she apologizes. "They were out of almost everything."

She hands me some oatmeal and a few bags of peanuts that look like they are really old, based on how wrecked the wrappers are. I don't check for an expiration date, something I would have done in my old life, but we are desperate, and the worst thing old peanuts will do to a person is taste stale and oily. Which we just won't eat if they do.

"They didn't have coffee. I asked. But they did have hot chocolate."

She holds up packets with a little flourish, so I clap, even though it's not a viable substitute.

"I wish they had more," she says. And then. "Oh, wait, they had these." She reaches into her back pocket and takes out two Tootsie Pops. "Grape or cherry?"

"You choose." I'm such a gentleman.

"Okay, then I choose cherry."

And of course, my mind goes back to the hundreds of times Emily and I fought over the last cherry Life Saver. Scheming, smirking, then all out warfare, pushing and running and grasping for it. All in good fun, but enough to make Mom or Aunt Mary shriek at us. One time, Mom brought home a pack of all cherry Life Savers thinking that would make us happy, but it had the opposite effect. Emily and I just rolled our eyes. The fight was half the fun. Mom didn't get it.

Sophie hands me the grape, and I unwrap it and pop it in my mouth, wanting so much to be able to tell Emily about how flexible I'm being, how I let the girl choose the lollipop flavor. If she were here, I'm sure she'd roll her eyes and make a huge thing out of it. But deep down, I'd know she was proud of me. After loading my pack with the new supplies, we walk the trail, my attention somewhat restored, which sucks, because that means I feel every cut on my hands.

Sophie clears her throat. "Some guys hanging around the store were talking about Rain Man."

"What'd they say?"

"Just that they think he's camping in the area where his wife died."

"Sassafras Gap?"

"Yeah."

"What are we? Like thirty some miles away?"

"A little less."

"Great."

"If we do ten miles a day, we'll be fine."

I watch Sophie limp along and flex my hands. Boy, we make a great team. Her ankle. My hands. Both of us winged by our stubbornness. It makes me want to laugh, but I'm not sure Sophie would be up for it after having to take care of me. Plus, I think about how she's used to quiet and I'm used to noise.

"I think we need to rest," I say.

"We need to hike a little more today, put some distance between us and town. The forest rangers and all…"

"Yeah."

We keep moving. We're silent about our individual suffering, but we move forward, and just because I'm doing something physical, my mind is able to start making connections, which I know sounds weird, but it's how my brain works best. Maybe moving forward is what my family has been doing this whole time. That's what they were doing when I got mad at them for getting their hair cut, for buying stuff for the house, or for going on with their lives in general. Going on with their lives like Dad would have wanted. So maybe the trail is teaching me something after all, or Sophie is. Maybe I'm just growing up. Finally. Either way, it's probably a good way for me to move. Forward.

CHAPTER 18

I spend a semi-miserable night sleeping in my own tent, because Sophie doesn't need me to keep her warm. I'm glad though, because I'm really restless (two points, baby… As in the rare Scattergories category: name an emotion you feel when you are camping next to an awesome girl and your hands throb because in a moment of heightened anxiety and upset you punched a tree repeatedly, and your family is so effing pissed at you that you may never be able to go home and there's this guy you know who is going to try to kill himself unless you get to him in time).

As I lay awake, knowing that sleep is the best way to heal my hands and my heart, I catalog the different types of insects that are probably waiting to walk on me and/or bite me at the slightest perceived provocation (also two points) since I didn't get a chance to spray my insecticide. Although, I'm running low anyway.

Then I start thinking about what actually provokes insects, which I can only think…nothing. Being an insect, you probably only think about eating and burrowing and finding more food to start the whole cycle again.

My fingers throb, and then I start to worry that, like sharks, blood attracts insects. That doesn't make it easier to fall asleep. I think about going for a walk, but I'm worried that will wake Sophie, and she definitely needs her sleep. So, I sneak very quietly out of my tent and sit on a log and look at the star-filled sky and think about Dad.

He used to show me the constellations, although sometimes he'd get the names wrong. He gave me a book about them when I was six, and I read it straight through. The sky became my own map. I read about pirates and sailors navigating by the stars, which seemed like the best and coolest way to know where you are in the world.

Looking at the sky, the stars appear to pulse. It makes me anxious like I got when I was little. It used to really bug Mom, and I never understood why.

"You worry more about stars than you do people," she'd say.

"Two hundred seventy-five million stars die each day, Mom. That's a lot."

"People die too, Dylan"

"Great. Now you want me to worry and obsess about everyone dying? People do horrible things every single day. Maybe the planet would be better off with less of them."

"Well, if someone you loved died, you'd care."

Dad would say, "We want the boy unhappy now?" and he'd wink at me. "Besides, stars are personal to some people."

Dad got it. If one of my constellations was compromised by star death, how would I navigate? How would I deal if my world was remapped? Recharted? I couldn't lose my stars. Sometimes, I'd sneak out in the middle of the night to check to make sure all my favorite stars were still there.

Dad would find me a street away, or at the park, or in our backyard, wherever I could get the best view.

One night I told him, "The thing is, Dad, we don't know if these stars are still alive. They could be dead already and we wouldn't know for forty thousand years."

"So, let's not worry that for the next 39,999 years, okay?" he said.

This would make me laugh and get me irked at the same time.

He'd gently put his hand on the back of my neck and walk me home. "Let's not tell Mom about tonight, okay? She wouldn't understand."

But maybe if I'd told her about why I was so worried, she would have understood my concern. Maybe I should have given her a chance.

I count my constellations one by one, and then I crawl back into my tent and go to sleep.

———o———

It was almost a year after Dad died that I ran away. I stayed in a lot of different places. I spent a few nights in a shelter. Then I spent a few nights with a guy I met at the gaming store. It all felt aimless and boring, but I figured it was better than going back home and to that awful school Mom and the teachers wanted to send me to. The one thing that no one tells you about running away is how boring it is to have to be nowhere and to have to do nothing. Maybe one day, I'll write a guide to running away and include crossword puzzles and sudoku puzzles in the back. Those would have helped. But as a runaway, I was so bored. To pass the time, I invented games and stories about people I'd see on the streets. This person buying coffee had just found out his wife was cheating on him, and he thought he'd get himself a little cup o' java to clear his mind. That girl over there totaled her car and is trying to figure out how to tell her boyfriend. Etcetera, etcetera.

I missed Emily. I missed Mom. I even missed Brad, although he had already gone back to Boston University, and my perfect cousin, Abby, was almost done with law school. Even Christian was touring with an acting company. Part of me was freaked the frick out, because I was scared I wasn't even going to make it through high school. And even if I did make it through high school, I had no idea where or what I was supposed to do after that.

I felt completely lost. If I hadn't heard about the Appalachian Trail, I probably would have gone back home to the tedium of existing without a purpose, because when I was home, I had no idea where I was heading. Or why. And being in my family, knowing I was the only one who had no plans in a family of planners, Dad included, was sort of crushing. Tedium is one hell of a word of the day, by the way. If only Emily was here to hear it. And just like that, my mood morphs to sour and rotten. I don't even celebrate the triple-word points I laid out.

Sophie peeks out of her tent, then unzips it and joins me on the log. She limps, her face tight.

"I'll make us breakfast," I say.

"How are your hands?"

"They're better," I answer, not because they are, but because I'm pretty sure that's what she needs to hear, considering how empathetic she is.

"I'm worried about the weather." Her eyes search the sky, which is overcast. The air smells like rain. I hand her my phone. "Yeah. I thought so. The weather looks iffy later. I'm not sure how far we'll get."

"Define iffy."

"It's going to rain all morning, and it looks like there might be some flooding on the mountain, so the trail will be slick, for sure. But the lightning is an issue too."

"I guess we should get going then."

I turn on the stoves and cook two packets of oatmeal and the two hot chocolate pouches. We eat our oatmeal out of the pot, sharing it between us, but we each have our own mug of hot chocolate. I consider starting a conversation about movies (best shark movie ever made or best female lead in a horror movie), because it amuses me, but Sophie doesn't seem interested. Honestly, I'm starting to get comfortable just breathing in the mountain air, which is starting to turn less cold and more humid.

I worry that Sophie doesn't like the quiet, that she's come out here to escape the heavy silence that has fallen on her house now that her mom is gone. But quiet has different moods and feelings. Sometimes quiet is about concentration. Or about being peaceful. Or about planning for the next goal. The in-the-zone kind of quiet might not bother her.

When we're done eating, I shake out our ibuprofen. There are less than half left, so I decide to skip mine. I figure if I act like I'm taking them, then Sophie won't know.

When we get on the trail, it's slick…like she said it would be. She's got on her shorts and boots, saving the rain pants for later. I wrap my tarp around our backpacks to keep our things dry.

It starts to drizzle. The rain usually chills me out, but I'm a little concerned that Sophie being wet for most of the day will be bad for her.

We've got to do at least eight miles today, I figure. Eight miles to Deep Gap. That sounds like a country song. I almost hum a melody and that cracks me up. Me being into country music? So weird. But this trail changes you apparently, and even I'm not immune to change. Apparently.

———∘———

The hike to Deep Gap is fairly uneventful if you don't count Sophie limping like mad, me worrying about her, and the effects of my caffeine withdrawal.

We get to a steep part of the trail, and I go first. "Hold on."

Her fingers go around my belt loop, and I reach back to stabilize her so she doesn't have to put all of her weight on her foot, but I'm going up the hill sideways. From this perspective, I notice the trees more. And Sophie's right, they are kind of amazing. They're like pieces of art, bent in different ways.

The different barks are brown, white, gray. Green ferns sprout around their roots, moss trails up the sides of the trunks. Even the rocks are covered with green.

My eyes take in the beauty like my body takes in caffeine. I can't believe I've spent all of this time in the forest and haven't noticed how freakin' awesome it is. The green fills me with this intense longing, sort of out of nowhere. I start to think of all of the green things I love. Green apples. Jolly Ranchers—sour green apple flavor. Green tomatoes, fried with tangy sauce. Green grass. A football field. That makes me think about how much Dad loved football. It was one of our things.

We'd play a family game of football every year at Thanksgiving at the Cape house when I was little. The lawn would be so green and plush and soft in the summer, but even when it was crackly from recent freeze or snow, I loved how it felt to roll in it. Emily and I would roll down this one hill, and Mom would frown at all of us, me especially, because I was usually the messiest. She'd say, "We were going to take a family picture."

And Dad would sling his arm around her, super cool and say, "Don't worry about it, Lily. It's only dirt. Besides, our pictures should look like us, right? Anyway, our game is about to start."

Brad, Christian, Abby, and Uncle Bill would all come out, and we'd run around like mad. I was good at catching the football. We played two-hand-touch, but I loved to tackle and be tackled. Part of my whole sensory deal. Touch me and I get enraged, but tackle me and I'm good. And rolling around on the ground? Heaven. So we'd do that, roll around, jeans stained at the knees. Mom would act like it was a huge deal, but there'd be a smile on her face, so I knew she didn't really mind. Dad and the older cousins got competitive, but Emily and I just liked to have fun. Every once in a while, I would come through on a key play, creating a lane by juking the blockers, and make it to the end zone. I'd throw my arms, up, yelling, "I'm open!"

Dad would see me, smile, and chuck the ball my way. When Mom and Aunt Mary called us all in for dinner, Dad would tell me, "That's my boy. Came through in the clutch, didn't you, Dylan?" And he'd ruffle my hair. Even though it was dorky and cliché, I'd eat it up. It was as if my chest was opening for an entire universe of good feelings to fill it. Mom would put her hand under my chin and kiss me on the cheek as she told me to clean up. I usually hated being kissed, but after that much contact in the game, and all my good feelings, I'd be totally fine with it. Emily would smile at me too, like she knew that moment of being the golden child happened so infrequently for us, but for me, especially. And the entire world would make sense and I'd feel like I was glowing.

"Dylan?"

I almost call her Emily. But it's not Emily's face that stares at me now. It's Sophie's. And she looks worried. At least I'm relatively sure that's why her eyebrows all scrunched together. Like an actual emoji.

"Dylan. Yoo hoo." She waves her hand in front of my face. "You in there?"

"Yeah, of course," I say, a little grumpy.

"You're so far away." She pokes her index finger into my forehead.

I stare. "Sorry. I was just remembering how I used to play football with my Dad and family."

"Tell me about your football games. They sound fun."

"Well, my family's super competitive, so they weren't *always* fun. Or more like they were fun for a while, then someone would get mad and there'd be an argument about a play and… We still had the best time."

"Did your family fight a lot?"

I think about that question for longer than I should, I guess, because she touches my arm. I shrug. "The normal amount. You know," I reply.

"I don't. My family was Mom, Dad, and me. They didn't fight that much, and I never had anything to fight about."

"That's good, right?"

"You would think so, but it was mostly lonely. Our house was quiet. Like living in a museum or library. Even before…"

I think about asking how her mother died, but even in this foggy state, I know that's not a cool question. She'll tell me if she wants me to know.

We keep walking, silence surrounding us like a mist, and I realize that if Emily saw me act so calm and comfortable with a girl, she wouldn't believe it at first, and then she would pester me and punch my arm and demand I tell her more. A hollow feeling in my stomach makes me stop walking. Sophie turns and calls for me to catch up, and I follow the up and down of her backpack as she leads me out of the forest. We go down this incline that reminds me of the hill on the Cape, but I don't let my mind go there.

"Hey, trail magic!" Sophie announces, and sure enough, there's a cooler with sodas and a basket of chips and chocolate bars sitting next to the trail.

I'm starved in addition to caffeine deprived, and for a second, a bubble of hope rises inside me. Caffeine! But then we get there, the only drinks left are some weak-ass shit like root beer and Sprite and Mello freakin' Yello.

"Aaaaagh." I actually feel like crying, so I'm pretty proud of myself for not outright sobbing.

"I know you were hoping for Mountain Dew. But look," she hands me a Snickers.

"Great," I sort of grumble, but start eating it anyway. There's five milligrams of caffeine in a Snickers bar.

"God, this tastes good," Sophie says as she chugs a root beer. Then she opens a bag of chips. When she's finished, she pours the crumbs into her mouth. It's so cute to see that huge smile on her face. She grabs a Hershey's bar and a bag of Doritos and points. "Take more. It's cool."

"I didn't know if it was a one-per-customer situation."

She laughs. "Maybe. Under normal circumstances."

"Our circumstances aren't normal?"

"Let's see," she holds up her fingers to make each point. "We have no food thanks to a rogue bear, I'm hurt, you're zoned out, and people are on the hunt for you."

I wonder if anyone is looking for her too. I think of her silent family and how weird it would be to live in a house with no mom and just a dad who doesn't talk. At least my house has the cozy sound of arguments and discussions, even with Brad away at school, Aunt Mary would come over or Mom would be on the phone with her. After Dad died, it was quiet for a while and that quiet made it so uncomfortable to be around that I turned on Brad's iHome and Mom's TV downstairs. I needed noise, and she seemed to get that even though she didn't do a whole lot of talking. She mostly just stared straight ahead, eyes fixed on nothing, as she sipped her tea. I felt so bad for her. And there were times that I did things to irritate her just to break the silence. Mad Mom was better than faraway-sad Mom. God, I'm an idiot.

But before Dad died, I remember negotiations and backroom brokered deals with Mom, who always said no at first but could be talked into almost anything as long as you could back it up with facts. Dad would intervene on my behalf with calm patience and tons of facts.

Standing here in the forest surrounded by the silence and Sophie, the knowledge that my family is totally pissed at me presses down on me from all sides. Maybe Mom would have relented if I'd just spoken with her. Emily was sure she would have, and honestly, that's how things usually happen in my family anyway. First, a lot of drama and even yelling and maybe tears, and then there's a slow understanding from both sides and a meeting in the middle.

Maybe running away was all a big mistake. Maybe I should have stayed and talked. "I'm…"

"We may change your trail name to Space Cadet."

I laugh, but I know it isn't convincing, because she's right. I am getting super spacey.

Sophie wipes Dorito dust on her shorts. That makes me wonder if her tongue is orange like her fingertips. Which makes me wonder what it would taste like to kiss her. Would she taste like root beer or potato chips or Doritos?

She says, "We better get going." Then she bends over and grabs the last two bags of chips and the remaining candy bar. I guess we *are* pretty desperate for food.

"How many more miles until Deep Gap?" I ask, watching how her body moves in little hops because of her injury. The other muscles in her back and hips will surely start to hurt soon since they are accommodating her injury. I'm not sure if that's the kind of information people want to be told, or if it's rude or insensitive to point out, so I don't say anything.

Dad broke his foot when I was thirteen. Mom got mad at him because she said he never went to the doctor. Even then he didn't want to go.

"Fit as a fiddle," he said, and he pounded his chest. He eventually went to a walk-in clinic and got an X-ray three days later, but by then the bone had already started resetting and it healed a little wonky. They gave him a crutch to use, but that didn't help much. He stopped running after that and stuck to the rowing machine in their bedroom. Mom was so annoyed with him for never taking care of himself. She was always after him to go to a doctor get a physical, but he always put it off. She said he made things harder on himself by being so stubborn, but I always thought he was

so cool, because he didn't listen to anybody, he just did what he thought best.

But remembering him on his one crutch reminds me I could get Sophie a walking stick to help her. And once again, I want to hit myself in the head. So I do. Like three times, which is okay, because Sophie is walking in front and can't see me. But she must hear me because she asks, "Dylan, what are you doing?"

I drop my pack and start searching the downed trees and tree limbs for a good walking stick. I must look frantic, because she shouts at me, "Dylan, stop! You have to get back on the trail!"

Finally, my eyes fall on a good candidate. I pick it up, bumping my hands, and the pain screams through my body. Pain is not as good as coffee, but it does give me some adrenaline clarity. The branch is a bit too tall, but I put it over a rock and stomp on it to make it the right size.

"Oh," Sophie says, apparently on board with my plan, "I should have thought of that."

She shouldn't feel bad. We are both making a slew of stupid decisions these days. I wonder if that's because life on the trail doesn't feel like the real world.

I drag my pack to me and pull out one of my rank sweatshirts, tie it over and around the top of the branch. All of this makes my hands ache like mad, but I say a cheerful, "Voilà," even though my mind is going to some of my prehike reading: *Trail mistakes can be more deadly, like running out of food, losing a water bottle, or not taking care of an injury properly.* I'm not just thinking of what happened with Dad's foot not healing properly, but I'm also thinking of the other complications of not treating a broken bone correctly. *Infection. Compartment syndrome. Death.*

Sophie's face lights up. "You're a genius. This is awesome."

This moment feels good, but it is followed by doubt. I feel like I have to decide between helping Rain Man and Sophie. My dad couldn't run after his improperly treated foot. What if Sophie's injury is more serious? It's only a hunch that Rain Man intends to hurt himself. What if, in the next town, we send someone to help him, and I take Sophie to the hospital?

Mom yelled at Dad after the doctor and said he had broken his foot. "You could have gotten a blood clot! A—"

Dad said, "Come on, Lily. You always think about the worst-case scenario. None of that happened. I'm fine. You don't have to worry about me." He pulled her into his arms and kissed her on the top of her head, but she pushed him away and went into the bedroom to cry. He looked at me with a wry smile, one I understood. "That's women for you, Dylan."

I laughed at the time. But Mom was right. If Dad had gone to the doctor regularly, they would have caught the arrhythmia. They could have done something to help his heart. Anger grows inside me, but this time I'm mad at my father. I've never felt that way before.

"Dylan?" Sophie injects herself into my fog. "You ready to start back up?"

"Yeah. Sorry. Let's stop here tonight. Deep Gap is just ahead."

"What about coffee for you?"

"I'll be fine for one more day."

"Okies dokies." Even though I hate sayings like that, it sounds cute coming from her, so I forgive it, the way Mom forgave Dad that night after their fight about his foot, when he made us all homemade pizza with the whole grain crust, the kind Dad and I hated, but Mom said was healthier for us.

CHAPTER 19

There isn't much to cook for dinner, since we've got almost no food left, but we arrange it all on a towel. Two bags of chips. A candy bar. One bag of noodles. One bag of oatmeal.

"So half a bag of noodles for dinner, with half a candy bar for dessert?"

"Sounds perfect." Sophie slips off her boot. Her face is all scrunched up and I see her ankle is swollen with purple marks all over it. "Oh, man. That looks bad."

"Yeah. I was thinking about soaking it in the creek."

"I'll help you."

"I can get there." She picks up the tree limb crutch I made her and limps down to the water.

I follow her.

She puts her foot in the rushing creek and moans a little. Last time I checked, there were six Advil. Thank God the bear didn't take those. I fill our water bags while Sophie sits on a rock and soaks her foot.

"So…does my crutch invention buy me a question?"

"What do you want to know?"

"What's your connection to Rain Man?"

Her face falls. She lifts her foot again to examine it, and I'm pretty sure she's going to ignore my question until she says, "He knew my parents."

Then she looks me square in the eyes. Her shoulders back, head high. This is a no-negotiation stance if I ever saw one. "Look, Dylan. I'm not ready to tell you my life story. Some things are just for me."

"I know."

She looks at the ground and picks at her sleeve the way I do.

"I want you to know you can write your notes again. I promise I won't dig them up anymore," I offer.

She laughs.

This totally annoys me and confuses me at the same time. "Why are you laughing?"

"Because you make us sound like dogs. All the burying and digging up things we cherish like dogs with their bones."

"Is that what your notes are?"

"Ha, I guess. Today I wrote to Mom about the trail things I remember. Like how she always fried eggs for us whenever we'd find a resupply and how I'd love waking up to the sound of the eggs in the pan and the smell of the coffee brewing."

"Does that make you sad? To remember that?"

Sophie picks at the bandage around her foot. "Not always. Sometimes I remember things like the birds Mom liked and that makes me feel like she's still with me."

I nod. I want to tell Sophie her Mom still is with her because people tell me that all the time about Dad. But I don't know if it's true. I want it to be though.

"What about your Dad?"

"I'd rather talk about my dog. I had a rottweiler once. His name was Max, and he was the best."

"Max. Like in the story."

"Exactly. He was the best."

"Was? What happened to him?"

"He had cancer. At the end, he hid in our laundry room. The vet said a lot of dogs find a quiet place to die when they're ready. To be alone."

"You think Rain Man…"

"Yeah. I do."

"Did you ever think maybe he's in too much pain to live?"

"Maybe. But it's hard to be left behind. How it's going to feel for his kids and grandkids and their dogs and their dogs' fleas…"

"Their fleas?"

I shrug. She smiles.

"It's all so much, you know? After they're gone, it feels so surreal. Like it can't be true. Like you're living some weird alternative universe." My hands go to my head. "I don't know."

"I know. Sometimes I think Mom is still alive. Actually I think it a lot."

I nod.

"Sometimes," Sophie adjusts her leg, moving it with her hand so her foot stays deep in the cold water, "Sometimes I wear Mom's things and stare in the mirror, and…Dad always said I looked just like her. My eyes especially…and I wonder…"

"What?"

Sophie stares at the water. "I'm just babbling. I just miss her."

I don't know if it's okay to touch Sophie, because I hate when people touch me, but I feel her sadness and want to help, so I shift over to the rock she's sitting on and sit next to her. I put my arm around her, and she rests her head on my shoulder and we sit like that for a while.

Then she says, "You should soak your hands also."

She's right, but I'm not looking forward to this. I unwrap my knuckles, thrust my hands in the water. It hurts like hell and I try to make my mind go elsewhere even as I hear myself scream.

I think of the time I fell out off of my bike on a dirt road and scraped my face and both of my knees pretty badly. Mom put me up on the counter in the kitchen. She wet some cotton balls and dabbed at the area. She held my leg still with one hand and picked the gravel out of the cut carefully with the other. As I tried to pull away, she looked me straight in the eye. "Dylan. I've got to clean this out so you've got to try to be somewhere else while I do it. Okay?"

I nodded but didn't know what she meant.

"So," she said, "first rule is you can't look at what I'm doing. Okay?"

"Yeah." I could do that.

"Second rule, keep talking. Name all the states and capitals. In alphabetical order. Go."

I didn't ask if she meant putting the states in alphabetical order or the capitals. I just went with the states, because that meant the most sense to my mind. By the time I'd reached Lincoln, Nebraska, she was done. And I barely felt it.

"That's my little warrior," she said. "Your mind is always going to be your best escape." And she kissed me on the forehead. I still remember how light that kiss felt. Light but good.

My skin feels uncomfortable. The muscles in my calves are tight and want to spring and recoil and spring again. I bounce on the balls of my feet like I'm getting ready to swim a big race. "Let's go back to the campsite."

"Help a girl out?" She lifts her hands, and I go to her side and bend down so she can slide her arm around my neck.

She starts to limp toward our campsite and my heart starts to feel as knotted as my calves. So I crouch down.

"Piggyback?"

I carry her on my back to our campsite. Her body is so small. She feels like a little bird, hurt and discarded. But her weight is enough to make me feel grounded, like when I wore that weighted vest and that helps to make my muscles feel less nervous.

I set her down as gently as I can in front of her tent. "We should probably get some sleep," I say.

"Yeah."

I push my hands into my eyes. The massive headache that has been building all day is now in full force.

"You okay?" Sophie asks.

"Yeah. Fine. Just a headache."

"Time to take your vitamin I." She points to my pack.

"Yeah." I pull the bottle from my pack, and I pretend to take the pills since there's no way I need them as much as she does. "How far are we from Rain Man? I can't keep it all straight."

"Well, we're at Deep Gap." She draws a line in the dirt. "Which is twenty-two miles to Sassafras Gap. His wife blue-blazed from there, so I'm not sure how much farther he'll be in the woods."

"So, about three days at eight miles a day," I say even though I know Sophie can't do that.

Sophie nods.

"Let's get some sleep. It always looks better in the morning," I say.

Mom used to tell me that. She'd say no matter how mad or sad you were, you'd feel better in the morning. Only that wasn't true after Dad died. That first day, it was like my body and mind forgot. For a second, I felt almost normal. But then what happened came back in a rush, and the pain felt ten times worse than when I first heard Dad died. It was screaming pain. Skin-on-fire pain. Heart-ripping-open pain. Mom said he died from a heart attack. Arrhythmia. Nobody could have known.

But I'd been listening to my dad's heart for years. I knew, or I should have known.

"Dylan?"

"Sorry. What?"

"I said, good night."

"Yeah. Good night, Sophie."

Sophie climbs into her tent and zips it closed. Suddenly, all I can picture is the body bag zipping closed over Rain Man's wife. Over Dad. Oh God. I start to sweat. Dizziness assaults me like a swarm of insects. I throw myself on top of my sleeping bag, wishing like mad that I had sprayed my bug spray, but Sophie's listening. I'm about to close my eyes and focus on the sounds of invading insects might make (two points, times two, Emily. Double play, girl!), when I hear Sophie.

"Hey, Dylan? You wanna share?"

Hell to the yeah, I do. I'm up and out of my tent and in hers in seconds flat.

"No playing around though, okay?"

"Okay."

"I just sleep better when you're here."

"Me too," I say. "Me too."

CHAPTER 20

I'm pretty sure Sophie's running a fever. She's shivering, even with me wrapped up around her. I put my hand on her forehead. She feels pretty hot.

"Hey," I shake her as she goes into full blown nightmare mode. "Hey, Soph. You're okay. You're okay."

She wakes up and turns over. "Ahhh."

"Your leg?"

"Yeah."

"Let me see."

I unzip the tent to let the light in. Sophie sits up and pulls her foot out of the sleeping bag, wincing. I scoot out of the tent to give her room and she pivots around, holding her calf.

Her foot is still really swollen and bruised.

"Can I touch it?"

"Just be careful."

I gently lay my hand on her foot. It's not hotter than the rest of her. "We should get you to a doctor."

"After we find Rain Man."

"You can't hike like this."

"You can help me."

I shake my head. "I don't know, Sophie."

"I've got to see Rain Man. I have to talk with him. I want to tell him…"

Sophie's got that look that means there's no way to talk her out of this. "I think your foot is too constrained in your boot. So maybe you wear a sock. I've got bigger ones than yours."

"That's a good idea. We have almost no food, so a bag of chips each and we can be on our way." She pauses. "Except I gotta go…"

"I can help you out there and prop you up, sort of…and…" I'm gesturing all over the place, which makes her laugh. "Come on. Before I fireman carry you out to the woods."

"You wouldn't dare."

"Never dare a Taggart!" I flip her onto my back and she squeals. Then she starts beating on my back.

I put her down and she crawls away, retching.

"Oh my God, Soph. I'm sorry."

I pat her on her back as she pukes. Then dry heaves. God, I'm an idiot.

When she's done, I hand her my water bottle and a bag of chips. "You need to eat. The salt will make you feel better."

She puts a chips in her mouth and chews slowly. My stomach growls.

"Aren't you going to eat?" She holds out the bag.

"Maybe later."

She doesn't argue. Just drinks some water. Chokes a little, then drinks again.

Water pours down her chin and tiny pieces of chips coat her

lips. I put my hand on her cheek. "I'm sorry. I'll take you easy this time."

"No, I've got it."

I pack up our stuff as she limps away. Then I make my own forest run. I listen for Sophie as she limps back to camp, and my gut falls when I see her. Face pale. Lips gray. She sees me and forces a smile. I smile back and give her my best stiff wave. There's no way that Sophie should be hiking, but I've got no idea how to stop her.

———o———

It's hot and muggy. and I'm amazed how much the weather can change in just a few weeks. Hunger gnaws at my insides and I feel like I could eat my fist. My caffeine depravation headache is a demonic heartbeat in my ears, which mixes with Sophie's little cries as she keeps hiking.

"Give me your pack."

She doesn't argue. I've got mine on my back and strap hers across my stomach. She balances with that homemade crutch. Each step feels elongated, like an extra blip on a heart monitor. I try to hear the drums in my head. I replace Sophie's little whimpers with the sounds of nature track, which neither of us can listen to because my cell battery is dead. It's the only way to get through this.

Up the hill. Down again. The only way through is forward. Part of me wonders if I should deal with Sophie first, just march her into town and make her go to the hospital, then go after Rain Man.

We stop in front of the sign for Sassafras Gap, but Sophie shakes her head. "That's not the right one. The one we need is in Georgia."

I make Sophie drink some water and feed her the chips. Her mouth doesn't move much, like it's stiff or something, and I worry about what that means.

"We should stop," I say. "It's getting late."

"No. We gotta get to the Georgia border at least."

"Why?"

"I don't know. I just…" she starts to cry. "I think I can make it all the way if we make it there."

I think about how I could stop her if I tried, but there's no way I can think of. Sophie is like me in that way. Once she makes her mind up, there's no deterring her.

"Okay. We'll keep going. But we camp right after."

She nods. I put her pack on the ground and roll it up as much as I can. Since we're pretty much out of food, I can squish her pack in mine. I slide on my pack and then put my arm around her. "Hold on."

"Okay."

"We can do this." I tell her this because she needs to hear it, and I need to say it. "Do you want to tell me about your mom?"

"She was always doing things."

"What kinds of things?"

"It didn't matter. Just things. Like cleaning or organizing or reading. She played the cello in an orchestra."

"That's pretty cool. Do you play?"

Sophie scoffs. "Nah. I was never very good at the cello. I play the piano a little."

"Can you sing me one of your favorite pieces?"

Sophie starts humming and it seems familiar, but I don't want to interrupt her to ask. My brain searches my vast musical inventory, and it lands on Bach's Cello Suite no. 1, which would make sense.

We limp along, as she hums and I keep my eyes ahead of us. The air chills, and I know sundown is coming. My neck is sore from supporting Sophie, and my heart and my head are thumping, and my stomach is growling, then I start hallucinating the smells of cooking, the sound of people talking and laughing, and of fire crackling.

Except Sophie must hear it too. Her face brightens. "Trail magic!"

"Wild Thing!" comes a call.

At first I think it is Rain Man and I'm so fucking elated, but as we get closer, I notice the long-ass beards, much longer than my own trail scruff, and the goofy smiles.

"Gator!" I yell back. "We need help! She's hurt."

"Hey guys, come on…it's Wild Thing and his friend is hurt." Gator calls. Chairs empty and guys start coming toward us. I've never been so happy to see people in my life.

Sophie's exhausted. I can tell by the way her body feels, limp and heavy. "Hey, Soph," I whisper. "Hey. We've got help. We're going to be okay."

She doesn't answer. Her body is draped over mine, all of it, and I wonder when she stopped participating. When she passed out. I hoist her body higher and lift her legs so I'm cradling her now. "It's okay, Sophie. You're going to be okay."

She barely stirs, and my stomach bottoms out. Is it too late?

CHAPTER 21

The boys come to help me. Gator. Emerson. Pepsi. Or whatever his trail name is. All I care about is helping Sophie.

Gator tries to take her from me, but I won't let her go, because I can't watch her limp body being carried off. "It's okay, Dylan. Bring her here."

Someone's pulled his sleeping bag out of his tent and opened it all the way. I lower Sophie onto it.

"What happened to her?"

"She hurt her foot. Then a bear ate all of our food."

Gator makes a face. Puts his ear to her chest. Listens. "How long have you been without food?"

Suddenly I can't remember what day it is. "I don't know. We've had some chips and peanuts, but that's it for a couple of days."

Emerson grabs a bottle of water and a bandanna. He wets it and starts wiping her face. "Sweetheart?" He taps her cheeks. "Hey. Sweetheart. Dylan says you might be hungry."

She sort of groans but any sound is music to my ears.

"Look. We've got to call this in. Get her help," Gator says to me. "You get that, right?"

"Yeah."

"Let's get Dylan some food," Gator says and Emerson jumps

up. "There's a guy here who used to be a medic, I think. He can look at Ghost."

"Sophie."

"Huh?"

"Her name is Sophie."

I lean down and put my face next to hers. "Soph. We're at the border, okay?"

She stirs. "Dylan?"

"Yeah. I'm here. You hungry?"

Two plates of food appear in front of us. Sloppy joes and hot dogs never smelled so good, but Sophie's not moving.

"Can I help you sit up?" I ask.

Her eyelids flitter. Then close. "Hmmm."

A guy pushes by me. "Hey. I'm a paramedic. How long since she hurt her foot? How long since she ate or drank?"

The plate of food sits in front of me. Flies land on it, and I don't pay attention to the buzzing or try to shoo them away. "I don't know. It's been a few days since she hurt her foot. We ran out of food the other day. We've had potato chips. Crackers. A candy bar. She drank. I made sure of that."

"You did good, Wild Thing," Gator pats me on the shoulder.

I watch, helpless as the paramedic lifts her eyelids and shines a light in her eyes. To me he asks, "What's her name?"

"Sophie. Her name's Sophie."

"Come on, Sophie. Wake up," he taps her cheek and I lean forward waiting for her to respond. She just murmurs again.

The man turns to me. "She's dehydrated and weak. It's a

THE SECRETS WE BURY

good thing you unwrapped her foot. We need to get her to a hospital. Immediately."

Hospital. Immediately. Those words loop in my head. I nod. She didn't want to stop going, but I had to do the right thing and let her go.

Gator pulls me aside. "I know this is hard, man, but you gotta get out of here."

"What?" It's not that I don't understand what he says. The words are simple. The syntax is easy. But my body sure doesn't seem to be understanding, because I press myself stubbornly against her side. "I'll wait with her," I say.

"You can't stay. The rangers will help her, but they're also looking for you." He thrusts a copy of the same missing child poster Sophie showed me in my hand. "They were asking about you in town too."

I hang my head. "It's my family. They're looking for me." I pause. "I'm not eighteen yet. I've got a few months." I run my hand across my scrappy beard. I sigh. "I'm a runaway."

Gator smacks Emerson on the arm. "We figured. You ready to go back?"

"Not yet. We. Sophie and me. We were looking for Rain Man."

"Why?" Emerson asks.

"We are worried about him. About it being..."

"The anniversary of his wife's death?"

"Yeah."

"We've been watching him. But when someone decides something like that..."

"So you think he's going to…"

Gator pipes in. "We don't know. Probably not. He's probably going to just punish himself a little. Go off into the woods and deprive himself of food and water. Make him feel what she felt."

"But why? What will that do?" I ask.

"Nothing. Not one thing," Emerson says.

"Look, Rain Man isn't talking to anyone right now. We've all tried," Gator says. "But he won't. Except, for some reason, you and Sophie. We'd go after him ourselves, but I don't think he'd listen. Maybe, whatever he's thinking, he'll talk to you."

Gator goes back to his tent. Grabs his pack. Starts taking things out at a frightening pace. His filter. His wallet. His food, which he puts in a pile. "Eat your hot dog and your sloppy joe, then hit the trail. Take this. I'll go to the hospital with Sophie and make sure she's okay."

"Why?"

"Trail magic, baby. I've been a recipient for years. Now it's time to give back."

I throw the LUNA Bars, pasta with sauce packets, and oatmeal bags into my pack. I sit next to Sophie and grab her hand, which is really cold, despite the blankets someone put on her. "Soph. You gotta listen to me, okay? You need help. These people are going to take you to the hospital. I am going to find Rain Man. I'll bring him to see you. Then you can ask him whatever you like. Okay?" I kiss her cheek.

Red lights flash from down the mountain.

"You gotta go, Wild Thing." Emerson throws me my pack.

Gator takes his headlamp off and puts it on my head. "Wait until you're on the trail for a bit before turning this on, okay?"

"Thanks."

Emerson hands me the hot dog. "Go, man. I'm serious. Don't get us in trouble for helping you."

I glom the hot dog and get it down in two bites, my stomach cramping as I barely chew and swallow, like a champion hot dog–eating challenger. Then I take off, looking over my shoulder at Sophie, whose eyes remain closed. My heart is falling and I'm tripping through the brush. The leaves blur in front of me. I have to get to Rain Man. The faster I get there, the faster I can get back to Sophie.

I'm walking at a fast clip, my hands aching, but my head and heart hurting more. When I'm a few yards onto the trail, and I can't hear the people at the campsite, I stop to rest on a log. I'm sobbing. How did I get here? So enamored with this girl I abandoned. So determined to save this man I barely know. I think of all the things they said about me. How I don't show compassion or interest in others. How's this misery for fucking interest? I think about Emily. God I miss her. I miss Dad too, but I miss her even more, because I could see her if I just went home.

I push off again. I pass signs for Rich Cove Gap, but I keep going. Uphill. Downhill. The headlamp illuminates the path before me, bobbing with each step. I can't stop. I don't want to.

My stride lengthens. I charge forward as if that will let me reverse time. I tell myself that if I just keep walking, I'll get to

Rain Man in time. I didn't with Max. I didn't with Dad. Maybe not even with Sophie. But I am going to get to Rain Man.

It starts to rain. The droplets stream down my face, but they can't wash away all of the hurt inside me. Despite how tired I am, I keep hiking. I lose myself in the repetition of one foot following the next. Time may not go backward, but it starts to fade with darkness. It gets completely dark. Then the sky lightens. I keep walking. Like I must have walked all night. Walking is the only way this gets better.

———o———

It's mostly downhill on this part of the trail, and I slip a few times. Panic makes my heart pump faster and I steady myself on a rock. I take a big drink of water and eat a trail bar. I don't feel like cranking up my stove to make one of the packets, and I'm fairly certain it's almost out of fuel anyway. I stop to drink and eat, then get back to walking. The sun is almost all the way up and it's gorgeous. Birds are all around, chattering from high in the trees. I wonder if any of these are the birds Sophie's mom liked. If it wasn't for all that's going on, I know I'd enjoy it a more. A little while later, I come to a big stone with Dicks Creek Gap on it and an arrow pointing north and south.

Without Sophie to navigate, I pull out my trail map to see where I am. I wipe my forehead with the bandanna Sophie wrapped around my hand. I put my finger on the entry for Dicks Creek Gap. Then scan for Sassafras Gap. Sweat pours off me, dripping onto the trail book, wetting the area I need to see.

My fingers are muddy and bloody and some of that smears on the page. I seem to be six miles from Sassafras Gap, six miles from where I hope to find Rain Man. I hear voices and back off the trail, hiding behind a big boulder, just like when I first spied on Sophie burying her notes.

Two guys and a girl I don't recognize approach. The sound of their shoes crunching the gravel path in synch is insanely beautiful. They talk in soft tones, and I wonder if they are sharing a word of the day or counting double-point answers. I wonder if they like the same books and love the same first lines or the same music. I close my scratchy eyes. Relief unwinds the tension in my jaw as I rest my heavy lids. I'm thinking about how funny it is that my eyes are connected to my jawbone, but all I can focus on is the cold smooth rock beneath my cheek.

———o———

"Hey. Hey, you okay?"

Someone shakes my shoulder.

"Dude, you fell asleep on a rock!" A guy with a scraggly red beard and red hair, a bandanna tied tight around his head and one of those CamelBak hydration systems tells me.

I blink up at him. The sun behind him makes a star-shaped light through the tree canopy. From the angle of the light, I'm guessing it is late afternoon. I've slept all day.

My neck is cramped from being in a weird position. Drool collects under my hand. That doesn't stop the red-haired dude from putting out his hand to pull me to my feet. "Thanks." I rub my neck.

"You okay? Must've been pretty tired to sleep on a rock."

"Yeah." I look around. *Where am I? How did I get here?* My gaze finally lands on the big rock at the foot of the hill marked Dicks Creek Gap.

The memories sift back slowly, and I hold my hand in front of my face to shield myself from the light. An urgency burns in my stomach. Rain Man. I was trying to get to Rain Man. Blue-blazing off of Sassafras Gap.

"What is the date?"

"May third. The trail will make you forget who you are and where you are and when it is. You need anything?"

"Nah. I'm good." I'm two days good. I start toward the trail.

"Hey, you're going the wrong way," unknown guy says.

I give him a wave of thanks as I reorient myself. Thinking about the old joke about one-way signs. "But officer, I was only going *one* way," I mumble as I head SOBO on the trail. I figure I can make it to Sassafras Gap in a couple of hours, easy. I take a drink and eat one of Gator's energy bars. It's sweet and crunchy. Both things I like. And the wrapper says it's got some coffee in it. I'm not sure I believe that, but it's better than nothing.

It's so stinking hot that the sweat drips in my eyes. I make my legs move forward.

The sun starts drawing toward the horizon, but the air has yet to cool. I wish I could talk to Emily. I wish I could talk to

Sophie. I'm so busy listing all of my wishes that I almost bypass Sassafras Gap.

There's a flat campsite where a few hikers have set up their tents. I look for Rain Man's navy tent and don't see it. There's a sign that points to water. It's off of a blue-blaze trail. I need water anyway, so I head down the incline. My legs are tired, despite the limited hiking I did today, and I skid on leaves and dirt. I stop myself from falling, but I have to spread my arms to balance myself.

"We could have called you Surfer instead of Wild Thing." Rain Man's voice snaps me to attention. "What are you doing here, son?"

In my mind I say, "I'm here to save you!" as superhero music plays the background. All I can think about is Sophie, and all I want to do is tell her I got here in time, that Rain Man is fine. That she'll get to see him again, that he wasn't like her mother, there for a while and then gone. I want to tell her I heard the birds her mom liked. That I found the trees that my dad liked. But here I am with Rain Man, and I've got to do what I came here to do. So instead, I say, "I was looking for you."

"I thought you and Ghost were northbound."

"Yeah. About that…"

"You hungry? I can make us dinner while you tell me all about it. My camp is about a quarter mile from here."

I look around and remember that Rain Man's wife went off the trail when she hiked that last time. That she died because she couldn't find her way back. We aren't far from the trail, but in the woods, it's easy to get lost, which is why they mark the trails. "You're blue-blazing?"

"Today I am."

I can hear and smell the water as we walk toward it. "Where's Ghost?" Rain Man asks.

I run my hand across my beard, which is filling respectably, even since the other day. "Sophie. Her name is Sophie, and it's a long story. Not a good one." I sit on the bank of the creek and take off my boots off.

He nods. "I've known Sophie since she was a kid. Before she had that trail nickname. She was always a serious little kid. Quiet and serious, but she loved the trail."

"You knew her parents?"

"Yeah. They hiked a little every year. Nice people. A shame about her mom." Rain Man kneels by the stream. "The trail is filled with the good and the bad. Trail magic is great, but trail magic can't heal everything." He puts one bag in the water to fill, but it pulls out of his hand and floats downstream, which is weird because the current isn't that fast or strong. I wade into the stream, letting the cold water trickle over my feet. Just before I overtake the bag, it washes out of reach. I can't help but laugh as I chase the damned thing down, but when I turn back, I can't see Rain Man. How far did I go? I get a little panicky. I look at the trees and try to place where I am while fighting the anxiety that crawls into my throat. This is how Rain Man's wife must have felt when she was lost.

"I got it," I call, my voice shaky.

"Over here, son." Rain Man waves from maybe two hundred feet away and I jog back, ignoring the hard stones under my bare feet as I do.

As I get closer, Rain Man's face looks weird. Like the muscle tone is gone out of it. I drag the bag through the water, then traipse back to him, holding the bag high like a big catch from the sea. He smiles, but his lips don't lift as high as they usually do.

"You okay, Rain Man?"

He stumbles a little, and then catches himself. "Just tired, son."

I follow him to his camp, wordless and worried (that might be a two-point score but, I'd have to defend it to Emily, because it would be hard to believe that the category would be how you felt on the Appalachian Trail or anything else that would make those two emotions make sense).

"You like rice and beans? I think that's all I've got." He starts a fire and I'm surprised, because he usually has dueling stoves, and because otherwise he uses a preapproved fire ring, so as not to needlessly burn the forest floor. I want to point that out to him. The asshole in me wants to shake my finger at him, tell him he's forever changing the way people will see this place for years to come. Except I'm here to save him. Only now that I'm here, he doesn't look sad. He looks tired and worn and sort of angry, but not depressed. But maybe I don't know what depressed looks like.

Rain Man interrupts my thoughts. "You said you were looking for me. What's up?"

How am I supposed to answer that? "We…I mean, Sophie and I.… We… I was worried about you. We both were."

Rain Man stirs the food. "You heard about my wife and wanted to check on me?"

I stare at the ground. "Kind of."

"Well, you can see that I'm all right."

"Yeah."

"So no need to worry."

"I'm sorry about your…" *Using a person's name is more personal*, I remind myself. "I'm sorry about Mary."

Rain Man doesn't answer, he simply goes back to tending the fire and the food. Fiery food. Two points. Category: name two things you find on the Appalachian Trail. Or a new category: what you use to avoid answering hard questions when camping on the Appalachian Trail.

"She got lost around here?" I ask.

"Two miles back that way." He gestures. "We were supposed to hike together, but we had a big fight and she left on her own. She was as stubborn as I am."

"When people die, everyone always says it's not your fault," I start but it's not coming out the way I want it to. It's coming out the way I see it though. For me, especially. "My father died. I feel like part of that was my fault."

"How could that be?"

"It's just what I feel. Do you feel that way about Mary's death?"

Rain Man stares at me, full on for almost five seconds. That's a long time to stare at someone. "You think it's my fault Mary died?"

"I don't know. I only know for me, how I feel. Or how I felt before I came on this trail."

Rain Man shakes his head. "And now?"

"Now I think we can't be responsible for someone else's life. Or someone else's death."

"That's probably true, Wild Thing."

"But there's still guilt. Isn't there?"

Rain Man stirs the beans and rice. "Probably."

"My dad died of a heart attack." I breathe in. Hold it. Breathe out. This is still so hard. "He had arrhythmia. That's what killed him."

"I can't see how that could be your fault in any way."

I clear my throat. Swallow. "See, I used to have a lot of these…meltdowns."

"Uh huh," Rain Man keeps stirring the food, but looks at me to keep me talking.

"Dad used to always hold me when I was freaking out. His heartbeat was the sound I'd focus on to calm myself. Dum dum. Dum dum. Dum dum dum." I tap the rhythm on my leg. "That extra blip was always there. I heard it. I knew."

"Wow. That's intense." Rain Man leans forward, both hands in front of him. "But it's not right to blame yourself. You didn't know it was a bad thing, and it doesn't change anything. Hell, most people wouldn't even pick up on something like that. You know that, right?"

"Yeah. But it's hard not to blame yourself, you know?"

Rain Man nods. Then it's his turn to clear his throat. He looks at me like he wants to change the subject. "You want some coffee, Wild Thing? I know you like that stuff. Mary sure did. Said she wasn't herself until she'd had her morning cup of joe."

"That would be awesome. And it's Dylan. My real name is Dylan."

Rain Man turns to inspect me. His look tells me that maybe it's weird I told him my real name?

"I don't want to lie to you anymore," I say. "My name is Dylan Taggart."

Rain Man's eyebrows rise. "Using a trail name isn't lying."

"It isn't telling the truth either."

"When you're on the trail, you get to be someone else for a while. You're holding yourself to a higher standard. Maybe too high."

"My being on the trail isn't about being someone else. I ran away. I am hiding. My mom wants to send me to a special school, you know for kids with emotional problems. But I don't want to go."

Rain Man nods.

"I have issues," I explain.

Rain Man makes a face. "We all have issues."

"Apparently, my issues make me 'a danger to myself and others.'"

He stirs the food. "I'm not sure I buy that."

"My teachers actually wrote that in my record. Whatever. The point is—"

"Were you pushed?" Rain Man asks.

"What do you mean?"

"A man will do things he normally wouldn't when he feels he has no choice."

I think back to that day in the auditorium. Then to a year before that. Dad and I were supposed to go to a lecture at Wesleyan University on star death. The talk included some time at the Van Vleck Observatory and an opportunity to join the astronomy club.

"That's what you call the trifecta," Dad had joked when he printed our tickets. I wanted to point out it was more eco-friendly to send the tickets to the app on his iPhone, but I didn't want to "harsh his mellow," as he called it. So I smiled. "Awesome, Dad."

But the day we were supposed to go, I came home from school and found the front door wide open. Mom was screaming. I raced inside. I saw Dad's legs on the floor first. His body was blocked from view by the couches. Mom was on the phone, screaming into the receiver. "Please hurry. He's not breathing."

I force my wandering attention back to the here and the now on the trail. With Rain Man. And I say, "The day I got in trouble at school, I was thinking about how I found my dad and…"

"You were the one who found your dad?"

"Well, first Mom did, but I walked in right after her. Last year. And my incident happened on the anniversary, which is something I just realized."

Rain Man nods. "Makes sense to me. Anniversaries are pretty tough."

Rain Man's face looks all serious and concerned, like my grandfather's face, Dad's dad, the one in California that we only see once a year usually. So, I keep talking, I tell him about the last straw for my school.

My social skills training has taught me not to monopolize the conversation. To check in with my listener. Rain Man stares off into the distance, nodding occasionally. I'm smart enough to know that means he's not listening to me. That he's got something else on his mind. But I'm on a roll, the smell of coffee igniting parts of my brain that have been sleeping for days. So I keep talking even though I should maybe shut up. Rain Man hands me the mug of coffee, and I take a sip. It's even better than I remembered, despite being instant. So I take another swallow, even though it's hot and burns the roof of my mouth and my throat. I drink and drink it and hope that this coffee will help me focus enough to do this next part.

Rain Man divides the food into two bowls. He hands me one and stares at his. The smell is amazing, but I'm not ready to eat yet. My mouth is still recovering from the coffee scalding. So I say, "The thing is, I never really thought anything could happen to my dad, you know? I thought he'd always be there. I worried about stars burning out and how bumblebees are dying. I never worried about what I should have."

Rain Man takes a bite of his food and swallows, then he waves his spoon around in the air. "Your parents are supposed to be your constant. You shouldn't have had to worry about your dad. He wouldn't have wanted you to."

I nod. But I tell him how Mom used to get so frustrated because she didn't think I showed enough interest in other people, that I didn't show that I cared enough about what other people cared about. He nods. Mom didn't get that I showed my emotion differently than she did. Like at the assembly. I tell Rain Man about how all I could hear was the sound of my dad's heartbeat.

"It grew louder and louder, until it thundered in my ears— but I couldn't make it stop. I squeezed my head, but the pounding got stronger." I feel my heartbeat matching that day. "I felt like I was suffocating, drowning. I had to breathe. But everything—my sadness, my clothes—was weighing me down. So I started stripping, right there in the auditorium. My skin needed air. People were laughing and pointing, but I didn't care. I had to breathe, had to make the pounding in my ears stop, to squeeze the sound out of my head." They wouldn't fault a drowning man for trying to save himself and gasping for air when the surface, but somehow my behavior was inappropriate.

The words take the wind out of me. I've made myself open and raw, but it's the right thing. I put Rain Man's safety before my own. It's hard and painful, but it will be worth it if it saves him.

"I'm sorry about your dad," Rain Man says.

I take a bite of my rice and beans. That's when I start to cry.

"It's hard, Dylan. It really is. Losing someone you love."

"It's not my dad. It's just... I love rice and beans."

He chuckles.

Through my tears I say, "There are moments in life that are as perfect as the first line in a good book. Or the last line. They're waiting for you to notice them. This is one of those moments."

Rain Man salutes me with his spoon.

"I'm serious. I'm tired and starving from the hike. And the food is good. After days without caffeine, there's coffee. It's perfect. But I had to go through all of that to get here to enjoy it. So in some sick twisted way, I'm glad it all happened, which would include my dad dying, How fucked up is that?"

Rain Man shakes his head. "Man, you think too much." Then he gets serious. "It's no sin to want to be happy, Dylan. Your father doesn't want you sad or moping or denying yourself happiness. Parents always want their kids to live. Especially the good parents, like your dad."

"Are you a good dad?" I ask.

"I used to be," he says.

"What changed?"

"Mary died."

"But you're still a dad. Their dad."

"They have their own lives. Plus I know they blame me for what happened to her. She and I were both really stubborn, but she was their mom and there's no messing with that."

"Yeah. Moms are the best. But dads…"

"So tell me, if you're so smart, why aren't you home right now with your mom?"

"As soon as I'm done here, I'm going home. And I'm going to tell her I'm sorry."

"Good."

"Well, I mean, after I go see Sophie. If she's even up to seeing me."

"Where is Sophie anyway?"

"She's in the hospital."

Rain Man's eyebrows raise. He waits for me to continue.

"You know how I went after her that night, when the trail was flooded?"

"Yeah."

"I found her pinned under a tree. Her ankle was hurt, but we took it easy and it seemed to be getting better."

"Then...."

"Then I decided I had to chase after you, and I sort of left her behind, which kind of pissed her off... She hiked all night to find me." I put my head in my hands. Retelling this story is as bad as retelling the other story. The auditorium one.

"And...."

"And she was hurt much worse than we thought. I think she's got some kind of infection or something, and a bear stole our food...and..."

Rain Man waves me away. "I get the picture."

"So she's in a hospital near the North Carolina–Georgia border, I think. And... I guess when you think about it, I really *am* a danger to myself and others..."

Rain Man laughs a hearty laugh and that sort of makes me smile even though it also confuses me.

"What's so funny?" I ask.

"You think too much, Dylan. Everything in the world is not your fault. You just have to do your best and hope for the best."

"Okay. But Sophie really wants to see you. So as I'm hoping for the best, I'm also hoping you'll come back with me."

Rain Man throws water on the fire. "You're a pretty smart kid, Dylan, and you've been through a lot, so you're probably more mature than most kids your age. But you're still a kid. And I'm staying here for a while. I'll tell you what. I'll write Sophie a note and you can take it to her."

"I know you're planning something."

"You do?"

"Yes. You're planning something that will likely make your kids really sad. You said you died after Mary died. But you're not dead. You're here, and I'd give anything for my dad to be here still."

Rain Man puts his hands on his thighs and pushes himself to standing with a big noise. "What I'm planning to do is get some sleep and then blue-blaze to the next town. Then I might catch a ride and flip-flop. All depends."

I want to ask, depends on what? But Rain Man has stopped looking me in the eye and I'm sure that means something. "I'm confused. I thought… I was sure…"

"You thought I was going to leap off that mountain? Shoot myself in my tent? What, Dylan, what did you think?"

"I thought…you didn't want to be here anymore."

"Maybe we don't get to choose that. I don't really want to be here anymore, and yet here I am, aren't I? I have kept going this entire year, even when I haven't wanted to." Rain Man's face gets those lines that mean he's angry. "It's almost the anniversary of her death, and I'm still fucking here."

"You should be with your family."

He raises an eyebrow. "Like you are with yours?"

"No. But I'm a kid. You're an adult. You should know better."

"Maybe my family doesn't want me around, you ever think of that?" He shakes his head. "You're too much." He holds up a hand. "Stop. Now. I mean it."

But I can't stop. I have to finish telling him the thoughts in my head, or I feel as if I'll explode. "After losing her the way you did, it makes sense that you'd want to…"

He grabs one of his pots and throws it into the forest, which freaks me the fuck out. "I'm still here, aren't I? And nothing about life makes sense. Not one bit of it does."

I stare at Rain Man's missile and its path of destruction caused by his anger. Leaves scattered. Branch bent. Bark banged on the tree trunk it hit. The air is completely changed. For the first time, I really get what it's like to be around someone who's out of control. My heart beats in my ears. Mine this time, not Dad's. "Come on, Rain Man. I'm not trying to piss you off. I'm trying to help you. I'm just really bad at it."

Rain Man cocks his head, which should warn me of what's coming. It doesn't. "You need to leave. Now."

His voice is commanding. But his words seem sort of idiotic. I mean, can he actually kick me off the Appalachian Trail? But the ludicrousness of throwing me off federal land eludes him and he continues, shaking his fist at me. "Get the fuck out of here."

As if by reflex, my hands go up in the international surrender position. No one can argue with internationally accepted gestures. "I can't. Not until you promise me you're not going to…"

"I don't have to promise you anything." He picks up his other pan and shakes it at me. "I don't fucking owe you *anything*."

It's not that I care about curse words, but it doesn't match with Rain Man's usual serenity. That serenity's gone now, and I wonder if that is a mask he wears on the trail. Or if when you are pushed to your limits, this is how you reveal your true nature? Do you become another person? However, I don't think Rain Man is up for that philosophical discussion.

His voice gets louder as he paces, gesturing with the pan. "I don't need you here. I don't want you here. I want you to leave me the fuck alone. Do you get that? It wasn't your fault about your dad. His doctors should have known about his heart. It was their fault. Not yours."

I watch this man break down in front of me. I know how he feels. And I know he just has to get out his feelings. I need to honor his wishes and leave him the fuck alone.

"I am fine." He smacks himself in the chest. "I am fine. I shouldn't be, but I am. I should have gone after Mary after our argument, but I didn't. We had a fight and we were both being stubborn and she died and I didn't. It's fucked up and stupid, but there it is. And now I'm done." He walks to his tent, then stops. "I'm going to sleep. I'm beat. Go home, Dylan. You want to save someone? Start with your mom. She needs you. I need my sleep."

The tent zips up and I'm standing there, completely unsure what to do next.

CHAPTER 22

Not once did I consider I could be wrong about Rain Man's intentions. I saw the signs, I came to find him, and I talked with him so he would change his mind. It was the only logical thing to do.

But here I stand, wondering what I was thinking. I am nothing to this man. He is nothing to me. But, he said he'd write to Sophie. He sort of promised. I stand in front of his tent and listen for settling-in noises, going to sleep noises. But it's silent, and I wonder if he is laying there, listening to his heartbeat, like I do when I'm worked up. So I soften my voice and say, "Rain Man, Gary, you said you were going to write to Sophie. Don't you at least want to do that?"

Rain Man opens the front of his tent. He takes a notebook and a pen out of his backpack. He scribbles a few lines and then thrusts it in my hand. "Now go, Dylan. Or things will get ugly. You don't want that. I don't want that."

But I can't. This can't be the end. "Rain Man—come on, man. I'm sorry. I know you're mad, but I was trying to help."

He puts one of his beefy, calloused hands on each side of my face. "Go, Dylan. I need to be alone now, but I will see you later. On the trail."

"I can't leave you. Not if I'm worried about you."

Rain Man face gets pissed looking. I can tell by the fire in his eyes and the way his hair is sticking straight up, but he doesn't bother to smooth it down. I can tell by the timbre of his voice. "What is *wrong* with you?"

He doesn't say, "What is wrong with you, *son*." And that omission, just one missing one-syllable word feels like a knife to the gut. So I strike back with sarcasm. "The doctors don't know, sir. The tests aren't back yet." I cross my arms over my chest.

Rain Man sort of staggers away, like a bear I've annoyed. He grabs for his backpack so aggressively that I'm forced to take a step back. He rifles through what looks like clothes until his hand closes around a sat phone, the twin to the one he gave me. "I will use this and turn you in. Leave me alone. I'm not kidding. I'll turn in you in without thinking anything of it. I'll tell them you kidnapped Sophie. I'll say you were the reason she got hurt, and that you forced her to hike with a hurt leg. I'm not fucking around, Dylan or Wild Thing or whatever you are called."

He's waving the sat phone. His eyes are kind of bugged out, and his face is bright red. He looks like I must have looked that day in the auditorium. And in this condition, he is definitely a danger to me and others. If he turns me in, I'll get sent home and will never see Sophie again. I need to tell her I'm sorry and give her the note Rain Man shoved into my hand for her. But mostly, the only way I can find her and see if she's okay is if I go back to where they took her to the hospital. I turn and walk away.

Rain Man yells at my back. "Get out of here and leave me be."

I can tell by his volume, the sheer force of his shriek, that this man isn't drugged or drunk. He's old and tired and angry. I should know. I've spent most of my life pissed at someone.

But it's his tone that seals the deal for me. He is not going to listen. He sounds like Emily did when she said that she was going to turn me in.

Or like the assistant principal at my last school, who'd clench his jaw and look at me like I was a piece of garbage. Or how Mom looked at me when she picked me up after my outburst at the assembly. She wouldn't talk to me on the way home. I wanted to tell her Dad's death was my fault, but I was too emotional to say anything.

Or how Sophie is going to look at me when I see her again.

Sophie. I put the note Rain Man gave me for her and throw my stuff in my pack. Then I turn away from Rain Man. I twist to take one last look at him, now lying in front of his tent, his head using his backpack as a pillow, his eyes searching the sky, not even looking at me.

I walk for close to an hour, until I'm back to white-blazing. I'm numb. I've got to get to Sophie. I've got to tell her we were wrong. They'll be plenty of time to talk with Rain Man. Not that he wants to speak with me, but he'll speak with her, I'm sure.

I'm NOBO now, just like when I started. I pass a cooler marked as trail magic with bottles of water, oranges, apples, and a box next to it with spiral notebooks and markers. I grab one of each of the fruits. My grubby fingers don't feel clean enough for

227

the pristine notebook pages, but I hesitate. Emily always said I should write my story. Sophie said that writing the notes to her Mom help her. That maybe I should try that also.

So I grab one of the notebooks and one of the black Sharpies (my favorite), and I keep moving. I walk another hour, then settle into camp because it's dark, and I'm not up for night hiking. My body aches and so does my heart. As I eat my orange, I stare at the notebook in front of me. I think it's going to be hard to start writing, but it isn't, and soon I'm pouring my thoughts out onto the page like it's something I do every day. Eventually, I turn off the lantern and roll over. I'm asleep before I know it.

———o———

A bird call wakes me, and suddenly I want to know the name of that bird. It's the same feeling I had when I learned the name of the stars. I know I'm a few miles from Dicks Creek Gap, where I could resupply and grab a book on birds. It never occurred to me that I could substitute birds for stars or stars for birds. It's the kind of revelation that seems important, and I consider writing about that when the desire to draw Rain Man's campsite hits me. I'm not a great artist, but I'm okay, so I start to sketch the fire he made, his tent nearby, the trees where he threw the pot, and finally, his backpack. I try to capture the feeling of it all, but my drawing ability is not at the level of my writing. So I switch to words and start labeling everything in the picture. I make arrows that point to Rain Man's tent and the scorched earth from the illegal fire. I make another arrow showing Rain Man's backpack, which I am proud to say I was able to capture in pretty good detail. Even how soft and slouchy it looked. That's when it hits me. His backpack was slouchy. Empty. Like Sophie's was when she was out of food.

No way Rain Man runs out of food. He said he was going to keep blue-blazing, then do a flip-flop hike, but he's got nothing left in his pack. And every hiker knows you need food on the trail to eat. No one goes hiking without food on purpose, unless they are trying to starve themselves…or do something worse.

Then I remember the note he wrote to Sophie, so I reach inside my pocket and root around for it. For a truly terrifying second, I think I've lost the note, that it has somehow fallen out of my pocket on the trail, but then I find it pressed up against the lining of my pants. I pull it out, unfold it, and stare at the words.

Live your life, Sophie. Parents always want their kids to go on after they've gone.

I try to extract meaning from those words. Context matters. They tell you that before you read any passage in English class, don't they? Out of context, this seems like an innocent note, but with Rain Man's wife… And how weird he was acting…

Drugs or sleeping pills could account for his erratic behavior like throwing the pots and cursing. He might have been able to counteract the effects just by sheer adrenaline. I'm a huge student of the adrenaline rush, I should've known.

I walk around my campsite. I walk around and around, and I'm sure I look wild, but I need to think, and moving helps me think. I could call the rangers, but would they believe me? And by the time they find him, would they be able to do anything for him.

I want to go find Sophie. Everything inside me is telling me to do that. To let whatever adults I can find handle the Rain Man thing. But the thing is, I'm on the run, so if I do tell people about what I think Rain Man is up to, they'll haul me away before I can go see Sophie. This is the only way I can both see her again and help Rain Man. I have to find Rain Man, call for help, if he needs it, hike my way out of there faster than they can find me, and then go back for Sophie.

I turn myself around and get back on the trail, hiking SOBO again. I go back to find him and stop him if it's not already too late, because sometimes people say they don't want help even when they need it. Just like I did all of those times at my school, the times I convinced Emily I was okay, and all the times I told Mom I didn't need to see a therapist or go to a special school.

CHAPTER 23

'm going as fast as I can, ignoring the snap of twigs against my shins and thighs as I race through the brush to get to Rain Man. My chest hurts as I attack the incline in a mad dash, and I have to stop to drink water. My chest spasms as I gulp. I think about Dad for the millionth time. Was this the way he felt when he died? Sweat pours down my face and fear pricks at me, but I know I'm not dying. My heartbeat is as sure as it has always been, and for a minute that feels colossally unfair, that Dad could have a defect worse than all of the things wrong with me. Not one that rendered him socially awkward like I am, but one that could and did kill him.

I replay Mom's voice on the phone that night, calling 911. Her face melted as we waited for the ambulance to come. She was terrified. Confused. Heartbroken. Scared. It's like all that I've been through on the trail, with Sophie and Rain Man, all of that finally breaks through the protective barrier my brain has placed over this memory. I feel everything like I did that day. I reexperience each emotion the same as that day. And I remember the weirdest thing. That for the first time in my life, everything made sense in real time, like everyone else experienced it. Agony did that for me. It made me process for real.

As I stop here trying to catch my breath, trying to let go of the memories that don't help me, I try to figure out why I care so much about this guy I just met on the trail. Or why Sophie matters to me more than my family. I just know I have to do this.

I push myself harder. The morning's cool air gives way to a blanket of humid disgustingness that wraps its fingers around my throat.

I remember when Emily asked me that time on the phone when I was in Neels Gap, before I went to find Sophie. "How do I know it isn't one of your obsessions?"

She's right, it could be. Sophie and Rain Man's whereabouts and welfare might be another thing I'm hyperfocused on, but I don't think so. My social skills teacher talked about that in group one day, and we actually role-played this thing. We learned a typical person would help a friend in danger. I know I'm right about this. I know. I get to the sign for Sassafras Gap. I start down the incline that leads to Rain Man's tent. I run the rest of the way to where it should be, only it's not. I look for signs verifying this is the place, and I see the dent in the tree where Rain Man threw the pot. My fingers trail over the damaged bark. Where is he? I bend over, spit on the ground. My sides ache from a severe cramp and my head pounds. My eyes blur. I need water. I take my water bottle out and swig the last remnants from it. I didn't refill it last night or this morning when I got up.

I head to the stream where I filled Rain Man's water bag. The water needs to be filtered before I drink it, but it's hard not to shove my face in the cool stream. I hold my chest, dip my water bottle into the water, and attach the filter. I can't get it to stay on. It slips. I swear at it, then try some again, but it keeps slipping and my hands are shaking. I climb out of the stream and grab one of those purifying pills I haven't used since my first few days on the trail. I drop it in the water and lie down next to the bank, waiting for it to purify, only I don't have a watch or a phone to time the half hour it takes to filter. I need to get to Rain Man, but I also need water. So I count one Mississippi, two Mississippi until I get to eighteen hundred Mississippi. My lips are chapped and my head pounds. The sun bakes on me, even through the trees, and I bring the bottle to my mouth and drink. I choke and have to lean over to regain my breath.

And then I return my attention to finding Rain Man. Where is he now? I look for signs of him. He said his wife died two miles from where we are. The question is which way did he go?

I close my eyes. Rain Man and I were at his campsite, about a quarter mile from here, when he talked about where his wife died. I hoist myself up and start to make my way across the trail. I stand where Rain Man had set that fire and remember how he had pointed behind him when he described his wife going off trail and getting lost. I make an arrow where he pointed out into the woods. That's where I'll find him. So I drink more water and get moving.

It takes another half hour to find Rain Man's tent, but the signs of his hiking light up the stretch of path I'm following. There are bent twigs from when he pushed through branches, some mud where he must have leaned against the trunk of a tree. I see one of the bandannas from his pack abandoned on the forest floor, and I wonder if he knows how many clues he's leaving for me.

I pause for more water, as his trail breaks off and the ground flattens. I see Rain Man's tent. I run. There is no movement or noise as I approach. That can't be good since I'm making a ton of noise as I run, the kind of noise that would wake the dead, as Mom used to say. My chest tightens from the exertion and fear. I unzip the tent without any sound or protest from inside. Inside, Rain Man is laying on his sleeping bag, completely still. Passed out. His muscles are slack in a really weird way. I shake him. No response. Pat his cheeks. Nothing. His skin is cool and clammy.

I reach for his wrist to find a pulse, but it's hard because my own heart is racing, making my whole body feel as if it's pulsing in synch. I lay my head on his chest and hear his heart. The rhythm is slow and weak, but it's there. There's a pill bottle lying next to him.

I don't know how many he took or how many it takes, and I don't care. What I need to do is laid out in exquisite clarity, like the perfect first line of a book. I pull out the sat phone he gave me and dial.

When the operator asks me what my emergency is, I tell them. The words come easily, because I've heard them before, when Mom called 911 for Dad. "We have an emergency. We need an ambulance." And when they ask my name, I tell them.

Because it's time for me to stop hiding behind my trail name. It's time for me to stop hiding, period. If I want to be the man Dad always said he saw me becoming, I need to stand tall.

CHAPTER 24

The morning is just starting to heat up, so I'm sure we're close to noonish, although my phone battery has been dead so long, it's just a guess. I stand outside Rain Man's tent waiting for the sound of help approaching. Part of me thinks I should leave and let them find him, but I'm worried that something would go wrong, and now that I'm here, with Rain Man, I feel the need to see it all the way through. Twenty minutes after I called on the sat phone, an onslaught of men and women converge on the sat phone's coordinates. It's utterly astounding. Some wear orange jumpsuits with yellow reflective tape and orange reflectors that have words on the back that say Search and Rescue Team. Some are in camo pants and black shirts and hats that identify them as forest rangers. Others are in dark sweatshirts, navy shorts, and black vests. They almost look like a gang in a movie, even if it's a helpful gang, carrying packs of medical supplies, a stretcher, and more sat phones. I stand back as they swarm Rain Man's tent. I back away as they carry him out of his tent and lie him on a yellow sling stretcher. They press stethoscopes to his chest and listen. These are practiced movements… They insert an IV. Then strap him down, six strong guys surround him, lift him, and start to walk Rain Man out of this bleak gap. Helicopter blades sound overhead. I'm glad he'll be going to the hospital.

"Are you the one who called it in?" one of the guys who isn't carrying Rain Man asks.

I want to laugh, because, there's no one else around, so who the eff does he think called it in? It is exactly the kind of comment Emily and I would bust a gut over, but I straighten myself and hide my smirk. "Yes," I say, soberly.

"Do you understand where you are? What's happening?"

"Yes."

"Sit here," hands lower me to a rock.

"I'm fine. I'm fine," I repeat, but another guy wraps a blanket around me. I want to complain about it being too hot, but I'm shivering. The guys in black and navy are taking pictures of Rain Man's stuff. Do they always do that? Is he dead?

"Is he…going to be all right?"

"They have IVs in him. His vitals are stable."

One of the guys in a navy shirt and black vest ventures over. He's got a badge on his belt and a walk to match. It's his talisman, for sure. He extends his hand. "Officer Oliver Stanton. Can I ask you a few questions?"

I shake his hand. He's got what Brad and Christian would call a "man's man hand," rough and callused with a tight grip. I return his handshake with one my father would be proud of. I hear him in my head. *Stand up straight, Dylan.*

"Your name?"

"Dylan Taggart." I'm sure he knows this already, but he seems like the kind of guy who checks his facts over and over again. There's nothing wrong with that, Dad did too.

He pulls a small spiral notebook with a pen pushed through the top out of his pocket and flips it open. Clicks the pen and starts to write. Officer Stanton's questions come at me fast and furious, and I try my best to answer with as much information as I can remember. It's important to get this next part right, so I take my time.

"I found him in his tent. No, sir, he wasn't awake."

"Do your parents know you're on the trail?"

"No sir. My father's dead. My mother doesn't know where I am." I'm surprised at how easy these questions are to answer, how good it actually feels knowing that after all of this, I'll be going home. No matter what that means.

"Did you know the man in the tent?"

"His trail name was Rain Man and his real name was Gary. I met him a few times on the trail, and he was always very nice. He cooked for me and Sophie."

"Who's Sophie?"

"She's a girl I met on the trail. She's in a hospital near the border. She got trapped under a tree and hurt her ankle. I'd like to see her and see Rain Man, if possible."

Officer Stanton stops writing to look me over. Like I'm a math equation that needs to be solved. I let him stare, not giving him my usual smart-ass attitude, hoping it'll help my case. He gives a slight nod, and I wonder if he's agreeing or it was just a twitch. He clears his throat and starts up again.

"Where was Gary from?"

"North Carolina. Near Wilmington, I think."

"Does he have any family?"

"His wife died on the trail last year. Right here." I point to Rain Man's tent. "He said he had kids, but I'm not sure who they are or where they are."

He flips his notebook closed. Looks at me. "Are you capable of hiking out of here?"

"Yes. I just need some more water. My filter…"

He hands me a bottle of water that I down in seconds flat.

"You okay to move?"

It's then that I remember I'm sitting. "Yeah. Fine."

"Where's your gear?"

"Oh." I turn around and around. "I must have left it by the creek."

He motions to some other guys who go after it.

"Follow me." I follow him up the incline, all the way out of the woods, to Dicks Creek Gap, where a squad car is waiting for us.

———o———

I sit in the back of the one of those Jeeps with police markings on it. My gear is stashed in the back. My head is pounding, and I wish I could get some Dramamine.

The front passenger door opens. A guy, not the one who interviewed me, a different one, hands me one of those disposable hot coffee cups.

"I guessed sugar and cream, that okay? We've got a big thermos full if you'd rather have it black."

"No. That's perfect."

He smiles. "I also brought you this." He hands me a glazed doughnut, still warm from being in the car. "How long have you been on the trail?" he asks.

"A few weeks, I think."

Someone calls over and he looks up, motions, then turns back to me. "Be right back."

I eat my doughnut, drink the coffee, and slowly feel my mind refocusing. I can see my memories of the trail. The boots hanging in the trees in Neels Gap. The creeks. Sophie.

I hear the first officer talking into a phone. "Dylan Taggart." He spells it, pauses. "Yes. Seventeen and a half." Pause. "Will do."

I put the empty cup in the cup holder in the back and lean back against the seat. I put the pad of my thumb on my forehead, as if that will erase my mistakes. I knew this would happen once I gave them my name. It's not like they wouldn't have found out anyway. The jig is up, I guess, and I deserve whatever repercussions come next. However it all goes down, I just wish I could see Sophie again.

Officer Stanton returns to the car. "We're going to take you to the hospital. It's protocol."

I nod. Rest my head on the headrest behind me. "Which hospital?"

"Smart boy," he says. "Did you know Rain Man is a legend around here? Damn shame about his wife."

I guess that means he's okay. A huge wave of relief floods me, but on the heels of that feeling is a growing fear of what comes next for me. The rhythmic movement of the police Jeep paired with my full belly and the warmth of the coffee, and the letdown response after the adrenaline rush from racing to get to Rain Man in time, drags me to a deep cavern of sleep. I go willingly.

CHAPTER 25

The jerk of the car transitioning into park wakes me. My head snaps to attention, even though my eyes are not yet processing what they see. Bit by bit, the image clears. We are parked at a hospital.

"Good morning, Sunshine," Officer Stanton's partner says. "We're here."

I don't ask where here is because it hardly matters. Here is where Mom will come collect me. Here is where my adventure ends.

Officer Stanton, the serious one, looks at me over his sunglasses, adjusts the rearview mirror so I can see his eyes. "You ready, Sport?"

God, I hate stupid nicknames, but telling him that isn't going to get me anywhere good. "I guess."

"We'll take you through the emergency room, and they'll process you."

"I'm not hurt."

"We have to do this. You're a runaway. We have to have you evaluated before…"

"Before my mom comes for me."

"Exactly."

"May as well go then. It's inevitable."

The second officer, the nice one who gave me the coffee and doughnut, opens my door while Officer Stanton takes off his sunglasses and puts them on a clip in his visor. It takes him a few seconds to catch up to us despite my lethargic stride, but he overtakes us as he pushes the button on the side of the door that makes the electric doors swing open. He cups my neck with his hand, loose enough to not feel threatening, but tight enough to let me know he means business. I will not escape on his watch. The two officers walk me to the intake desk, and a nurse asks me a slew of questions starting with my name, age, date of birth, and insurance.

I don't know how to answer that, but Officer Stanton says, "We're processing him," and she must get what that means because she types on the screen in front of her, nodding as she does it.

That done, she takes my vitals. I must be fine because she doesn't look too concerned. They show us into a room in the ER that has a hospital bed, another blood pressure machine, and a bunch of medical stuff on the walls, like those red, plastic containers for collecting needles. It's weird that none of this hospital stuff freaks me out with all of my other issues, but it just doesn't. I guess even God could only cram so much hysterical thinking into one person.

A guy comes in dressed in blue scrubs. "Come with me," he says.

My police guard raises his eyebrow, and the guy says, "We are going to have him shower before we deal with him."

"Good idea," Officer Stanton chuckles.

I follow the scrubs guy to a room that's marked as a patient bathroom. I figure there will be a sink and a toilet, but to my surprise, there's also a shower, and a bank of cabinets. The guy opens a cabinet and hands me a towel. I stare at the shower, and that's where my anxiety issues come in. The sounds reverberate in the tiled room. They build. Like that day in the auditorium. But also since this isn't my bathroom, I envision all of the other people who have used it. I poop in the woods? Okay. Take a shower in a hospital... Um, no? It might not make sense, but I can't help it.

"Do I have to?" I try to seem casual, but my heart is beating like mad, and the sound of it builds in my ears.

"Suit yourself, but I thought you'd like to look and smell better if they have to take you to court. It'll go way better for you if you don't look all nasty and woodsy. You wanna shave? Look a little less Unabomber?"

I run my hand over my scraggly beard. He's not wrong. Mom will probably be easier to deal with if I look like my normal self.

"Here's a shaving kit." He places it on the counter.

The guy peels back his sleeve to reveal a tattoo of the letters AT with 2015 going through it. "Did the entire thing in 2015. Never got to eat with Rain Man, though. Hope maybe next year I can. Heard he's doing okay, by the way."

I stare at the shower.

"Look. I know it's hard to reacclimate."

"It's not that. It's... I have issues."

He stares at me.

"Phobias, sort of." My eyes go to the ground. I know this makes no sense. I showered in the hostel. At camp, once, but that was awful. Somehow being a hospital makes it seem germier.

The guy opens a drawer and pulls out a clipboard and passes it to me. "It was just cleaned at three today. No one has used it since. Enjoy."

He leaves a towel for me and a wrapped bar of soap. Also a plastic bag with the instructions, "Put your clothes in here." He opens another cabinet and grabs a plastic bag with a pair of brand-new scrubs in it. "These should fit you."

I follow directions and get in the shower. At first, I'm totally grossed out by standing in this shower with my bare feet, no matter how recently it was cleaned. I imagine all sorts of nasty germs growing and wanting to attach themselves to me. I envision ants and spiders and roaches lying in wait to come up the drain. I tell myself that bugs and germs can't touch me in the water, so I turn on the shower, full strength and extra hot. The water feels so good. The smell of this soap, Dial, regular scent, fills my nostrils. I lather my body, and I wash myself like I always do. I start with my head, lathering the soap through my hair. Emily always said I should use actual shampoo, but Dial soap has always done the trick for me. I rinse my hair and then start my routine, lathering and lathering, cleaning the back of my ears, around the pinna, down my neck and shoulders. I clean myself, head to toe, using the same method I've used since I can remember. Ten seconds on each step. Ten seconds times all the parts of my body that need cleaning. The feeling of the hot water loosens up all of the emotions inside me, and soon I forget about not touching the walls of the shower, and lean against the tiles, crying like a baby.

I hear a knock on the door. "You doing okay in there? Dylan?"

I know if I don't answer, soon the door will open. So I say, "I'm okay."

I figure the shower thing should be coming to an end, but I don't want to get out. Eventually, I decide it's time and take one last rinse and wrap myself in a towel. The bathroom is steamy, and I breathe in the smell of clean. I haven't smelled anything this good in so long. My stomach growls, though I'm getting used to that being normal-ish. Normal people living in the real world shower. They shave. They eat. And they sleep, in actual beds. Suddenly, Mom coming to get me doesn't concern me so much. Because at some point, she'll have to stop being mad at me and let me sleep. I realize I am really looking forward to sleeping in my bed again. It's been way too long.

I stand at the counter, palms pressing down, and I stare through the steam at the mess in the mirror. It takes a while for the steam to clear, but I just wait and look. So, now it's just me and the mirror and my heartbeat and myself. I'm tired. I blow out a breath and it fogs the mirror, so I wipe at it. Now my reflection looks streaky and weird, which is how I feel, like a Picasso painting, the pieces of me not attached the way one would expect. I turn on the water and dispense the shaving cream onto my fingers. The menthol soothes my skin as

I carefully remove all of my facial hair, only cutting myself a little in one place. I smack my cheeks when I'm done like Dad taught me. *Stand up straight, Dylan.* I can almost feel the gentle reassurance of his hand on my shoulder.

I think about what I'm going to tell Mom when I see her, even though I have no idea how much longer that will take. Memories of my time on the trail and the people I met explode inside my head, and I know it'll be important to tell her the right details in the right order, so she'll understand that this was a good experience for me…even if she doesn't like how I went about it.

There's another knock on the door. "How's it coming, Dylan?"

"Good."

The scrubs he left me are clean and waiting. They're two pairs of pants, and I wonder if that's to make up for the lack of underwear, but I pull them up without too much worry. They are slightly scratchy on my skin, but I've missed the feeling of cotton, so it's nice in a way.

Another knock.

"Coming," I say. I pull the shirt over my head and stare at myself in the mirror. I look different than when I first ran away. More grown up maybe. My shoulders are back and my chest is high. I stand different when I breathe too. I breathe with my diaphragm, not with my shoulders, which was a bad habit that affected my swimming. I hope Mom notices. Dad definitely would have.

CHAPTER 26

The nurse and I walk back to my hospital room, and my feet are in these weird paper booties. I'm carrying my bag of nasty clothes that I'm sort of hoping Mom just wants to trash. When we arrive, a woman with a stethoscope is talking to Officer Stanton. She smiles at me and extends her hand.

"My name is Doctor Raul. I'm here to check you out."

I give her a noncommittal nod.

She starts by looking in my ears. My eyes. She taps my chin, and I open my mouth so she can look in there. I like that she's mostly movement, not talking. She lifts each of my hands and inspects the wounds on my knuckles. She arches her eyebrow but doesn't ask what happened, so I figure she's cool with my not filling in the details.

She warms the stethoscope on her hands which no one has done for me since I was five, but I appreciate it. "So how are you feeling?" She puts her face next to my chest and listens as she moves the stethoscope all over my chest.

"I'm fine, I guess."

"Cough," she says. "Big one." And then she moves the stethoscope to the small of my back. "Again." Moves the stethoscope. "Again."

I guess I pass muster, because she tells me to lie down on the table, but I truly hate this next part.

"Your first time on the trail?" she asks.

"Yeah." I hold my breath.

"Try to relax," she says as she presses on my stomach, rooting around for whatever is supposed to be there. That makes me think of the stars and the sky. If you have your kidney removed or your spleen and you go to the doctor and don't tell them, would they search for the parts of you that are gone? That makes me think about Dad again. Like how he's missing from my life and there's no amount of probing this doctor or anyone else could do to find that hole. But I know it's there. I must hold my breath, because she says, "That's it, we're done."

I sit up, the only one aware of this hole in my stomach where Dad's missing lives, the only one aware that it's expanding inside me.

"You look fit and healthy. I hiked the trail when I was twenty-one. Loved it." She stares at me. "Is there anything you want to tell me, Dylan?"

"No."

"Okay. Well, I'm not supposed to release any information about other patients, but I can tell you that the hiker that was brought in earlier is in stable condition, and his family has been notified and is on the way. I'll be telling the press that same information, without revealing names, of course, in an hour or two. So, I don't see why I can't tell you that much."

I don't say a thing because the words that are lined up trying to force themselves out are being kept at bay for this second, guarded by my throat that constricts and pushes them back down inside me.

"Also, your mother is on her way. She seemed very relieved that you were okay and is eager to get you home."

I stare at the scabs on my hands. They're almost healed.

"We can have a social worker help you through that meeting if you'd like."

I look her straight in the eye. Looking someone straight in the eye shows them you are serious. "No. I can deal with that myself. I need to apologize for worrying her. She's kind of used to me being a pain in the neck. I won't run away again."

"You seem like a nice kid."

I laugh. "That's because you don't know me."

She smiles, but looks back at my hands. "Seems like you might've already gotten into a fight with a tree, no?"

"You could say that."

"Well, they look mostly healed. You must have taken good care of the cuts. You won't need any more treatment for those." She holds each of my hands. "Flex." I do. "Make a fist." I do. "Wiggle your fingers." I do. "Yup. They look good. I think we're done here. Nice meeting you, Dylan. Good luck with the rest of it."

She walks out of the room, and Officer Stanton is waiting for me.

"I've got someone for you to talk to."

I figure they're going to make me speak to a psychiatrist or psychologist or something. Maybe the doctor reported the marks on my hands and thought I was dangerous. I tell myself to not get worked up. I'm bone tired, so it's hard to tap into my anger.

As we walk, the officer says, "You know we were supposed to dispatch to a different hospital."

"Okay." I've got no idea where this is going.

"Yeah. I brought you here, even though it was more than ten miles farther away."

"Huh."

He continues, "Rain Man is a legend on the trail for always helping people out. Everyone was so broken up when his wife died. She was a gem. They're good people, for sure."

I'm not sure why the officer is telling me this. I know it's for a particular reason, because he's slowed our pace, as if he's trying to build suspense, but I've got no idea why.

We take the elevator up to the third floor. The hallway smells of disinfectant and the floor is shiny, like it's just been waxed. Finally, we stop in front of a patient's room, which is weird, because I was sure we were walking to psych.

"What's…" Then I see her name on the wall. Sophie Mattox. I point. "Is that… Is she…"

"You earned this, kid."

CHAPTER 27

At first I'm worried to see her. I'm worried she'll be mad at me for leaving her and for going on to find Rain Man without her, even though I didn't have a choice.

"You going to go in, Dylan? It's not nice to keep a girl waiting."

Sophie's voice breaks through my reverie. "Dylan? My Dylan? Is that you?"

My Dylan. Before I know it, I'm rushing to her bedside.

Sophie's in a private room. The bed is lifted so she's at an incline, her foot is elevated in one of those trapeze things. I sort of forget about being careful about her injury and throw myself at her, which makes her laugh and yelp in pain at the same time. We hold the hug for a long time, maybe even a record time for me. Maybe even twelve whole seconds when I hear someone clear his throat behind me. I release Sophie and turn to see who's there.

An older guy, like Dad's age, who is really thin with curly hair and glasses says, "You must be Dylan." He's holding a coffee, which smells amazing. That's when my stomach goes nuts, growling loudly. I'm so embarrassed. The first impression I'm making on Sophie's dad is that I'm a pig. Wait, scratch that. The first thing he knows about me is that I let his daughter hike for days on a bad foot. Then when I see her again, I smother her and hurt her more.

He must not be too put off though, because he thrusts his hand out and I shake it. "I'm Sophie's dad. Mr. Mattox."

I square my shoulders. "Dylan Taggart."

"You hungry?" her dad asks.

I put my hand over my stomach. "Perpetually."

He takes his keys out and flips them around in his hand. "To be a teenage boy. You like hamburgers or pizza more?"

With the mention of food, my stomach does a marathon roar.

"I'll get both. Give you two a little time to talk. There's a place right around the corner, so I won't be long. You deserve real food, not hospital food."

He leaves and Sophie smiles at me. She pushes some of her hair behind her ear and sits up a little more. I see the IV attached to her arm along with the soft cast on her leg.

"It's an antibiotic. I've got an infection," she says.

Her hands point to her foot. "It's broken. I had compartment syndrome, which I guess is pretty serious. I've already had three surgeries. I might have more. They say you saved my life by removing the boot."

I hardly feel like a hero.

"I should've known to do that, but I guess..." she trails off.

"It's hard in the moment."

She nods. "They've got me on painkillers and antibiotics and a bunch of other stuff. I can't remember it all, probably because of the painkillers. They also make me puke, so that's been fun."

I sit in the chair her father probably sat in while he watched her recover from those surgeries. I think of how Dad's foot didn't heal properly after he injured it and how he didn't run anymore. Maybe that was one of the reasons he had the heart attack. I wonder how this will affect the rest of her life. She gives me her hand and I take it in mine. It's soft and feels so substantial.

"I heard you saved Rain Man," she whispers like it's a sacred secret. Sacred secret, two points. Then she says, "Hey, you okay?"

I want to tell her I almost bungled saving Rain Man, I want to tell her how sorry I am about her foot, but instead I kiss the inside of her wrist and let the tears come. They're grateful tears because she's okay, regretful tears because it's partly my fault she's here, and sad tears because I know soon Mom will be here to take me home, and I won't be with Sophie anymore.

"Aww, Dylan. I'm okay. Really."

"I was so worried about you." And for the first time I start to think about how awful it must have been for Mom all this time, how worried she must have been.

"But I'm fine. And you're here."

"I wasn't sure I'd even get to see you again."

"Those books you read me? They would never end like that... With us not being together again."

Us. That word makes the ones I wanted to say to Sophie jam the gates of my mind, but I sift through them carefully. "I should have made you go to the hospital sooner."

"It was my choice," she says simply.

"I should've pushed harder. Your foot…"

"It's going to be fine. It's already better. The reaction to the painkillers is the worst of it. They make me really tired too."

"So rest."

"I'm glad you came to see me. I was worried you wouldn't or couldn't. I was scared I'd never see you again."

My lips brush her hand. "I was worried you wouldn't want me to."

"That's ridiculous. 'You are the king of all wild things.' And even more than that to me," she says, then closes her eyes. They pop right back open. She takes her hand from mine and holds up a bossy finger. "Promise me you won't leave without saying goodbye."

I laugh. "Promise. Now go to sleep."

"Rain Man is okay?" she asks dreamily.

"I guess. I haven't seen him, but I'm not sure he's going to talk to me anymore, or even you. He was pretty mad."

She looks away from me. "I bet he will."

Then I remember the note he wrote her. "Hey, he sent you a note. It's uhhh…" I look at the bag of clothes on the floor.

"What did it say?"

"It basically said… Just to go on. Your mom would want that." She closes her eyes.

"Sophie, are you okay?"

"Yeah. Just tired. But why was he mad at you?"

"People don't always want help even if they need it."

"That's right," Mom's voice floats into the room. "They don't."

I've been dreading this very moment since I pushed the sat phone button, and now it has to happen here. In front of Sophie. Awesome.

CHAPTER 28

If I ever thought I had any control in the universe, that belief was completely unfounded. I'm still holding Sophie's hand, and I can't really see Mom's expression, because the room is dark and she's walking in from the bright hallway.

She takes a step into the room. Her hands are in front of her, a tissue balled in one fist. She stands stiffly, her head cocked slightly, like she's asking me a question. That gives me hope. Maybe she isn't only angry with me. Maybe she's angry and other emotions too. What are the best first words when seeing your mother in weeks after you ran away without so much as a goodbye? All I can come up with is one squeaky word: "Mom."

She's wearing her gardening jeans with tiny worn-away spots on the knees, the ones she only wears when she's working in the yard. It's like she got the call and drove straight here without changing, which makes my heart ache in ways I didn't know it could.

She reaches out to me, and I drop Sophie's and hand to go to her. Mom wraps me up in a fierce hug. She's crying and so am I. I don't know what else to say, but she must know what I'm thinking because she murmurs, "I know you're sorry. I'm sorry too."

The hug lasts and lasts, but I'm okay with that. I'm surprised by how much I missed Mom. Her perfume, Allure, the same kind she always wears. Her shampoo, Paul Mitchell, coconut scent. Her strong arms and hands with her trimmed nails painted in a neutral, pale white, called Bubble Bath, which Dad used to joke sounded too girlish for how sexy it looked. These tiny reminders pop through my head about all the things she did for me a specific way, because that's how I needed them done. I thought of how she made me food I could eat. Spaghetti was okay with sauce, but nothing else was. No lasagna. Even without the disgusting ricotta cheese. No potatoes. Although after being on the Trail, I'd probably eat just about anything.

I want to tell Mom that. I want to tell her about how I camped like Dad always wanted us to. I want to tell her how I cooked and filtered water and slept in different places, even without my Dramamine and my chants and drums. I want to tell her that I pooped in the freaking woods. I have all of these conversational streams running inside my head, but all I get out is, "I'm sorry I ran away," and then, "But Mom, it was amazing."

She nods and cries some more, and then Sophie's dad comes back carrying so much good-smelling food I don't even care that Mom's here to drag me home, or that I'm going to be in so much trouble, or even that there are things I don't want her to say in front of Sophie or her dad. There's no controlling the chaos that is unfolding in front of me.

Sophie's dad gives me a bag and a pizza box, and then extends his hand to Mom. "Reggie Mattox."

"Lilian Taggart," Mom replies.

I can feel my eyebrows lift. Lilian. Mom never uses her full name. Interesting.

The smell of grease is making me notice how empty my gut feels, but I feel like I should wait before diving into the food. This makes Mom's eyebrows lift. Guess she's not used to me considering others' feelings.

"Eat up, Dylan. It's all for you. Unless you want to share with your mother."

"Go ahead, hon," Mom says. "It's very nice of you to get him food." She takes her wallet out of her purse. "What do we owe you?"

Sophie's dad waves her away. "Are you kidding? Your son helped my daughter. He probably saved Sophie's life."

"Sophie?" Mom's eyebrows lift again, but at this point, I'm already digging into the hamburger and inhaling the fries.

"Hi, I'm Sophie."

Mom looks around her as if she's just now taking in everything that's going on and everyone who's in this room. "Oh, Sophie. Hi, I'm Dylan's mom."

"Yeah," she says, "the pain meds have me feeling kind of loopy, but I got that much." She smiles.

Because there aren't enough people in the room already, Officer Stanton knocks and enters. "I see you found him."

Mom nods.

The officer who gave me the doughnut and coffee earlier is also here, grinning widely like this is some kind of homecoming parade, like at any minute there will be cheerleaders and streamers and people eating popcorn and hot dogs, which were both on the pre–Appalachian Trail approved list of food I would eat. He keeps looking around the room, his eyes pinging from one person to the next. Has he forgotten that I evaded the law, or that Mom is going to go ape-shit once she gets over how worried she was about me? What about that I still don't want to go to that stupid school? Nothing has changed.

"You hear that Dylan's a hero?" Officer Nice Guy asks.

"Reggie was just telling me he saved Sophie's life."

I've got a mouthful of pizza, so I am not in the position to argue, but I should. I should argue my head off. I didn't save Sophie. Well, okay, I technically saved her, but then I pissed her off so much that she chased me in the middle of the night on her hurt foot and could have killed herself.

I hear Mom's voice telling Dad that he could've gotten a blood clot or worse, and Dad responding, *"But none of those things happened."* But now I get Mom's side. I do.

I don't even have a chance to offer my opinion when Officer Nice Guy says, "He also saved one of the most loved veteran hikers of all time."

Mom startles. "He did what?"

"He saved this guy called Rain Man. A hiker."

Mom aims her stare at me. "What happened?"

Officer Stanton steps forward. "Your son figured out that Rain Man was suicidal and followed him. He found him after he'd taken what would have been a lethal dose of tranquilizers had he not called it in."

Mom starts crying again. She doesn't even wipe the tears from her eyes. Big tears mean deep wounds, according to a hypothesis I haven't tested yet, but it is the one I postulated back when I made Emily cry. I start to recognize that I've made a lot of people cry over the years. I imagine a bar graph of the people I've made cry repeatedly.

And then I remember I'm supposed to be paying attention to Mom and why she's crying, and I'm distancing myself from these feelings again and that reminds me of how Emily used to smack me in the arm when I did stuff like this, when I missed the cues as to how to behave like a typical person. A person who gets social cues and doesn't stay in their head, but in the world with the rest of the people. This whole exchange makes me miss Emily so much I can't take it. I've got to do something, so I finally say to Mom, "Why are you crying?"

"Because you noticed other people, and you got involved with what they needed...and you went out of your way to help...and you....you're such a good kid, but sometimes you can be so..."

So I go forward and grab her hands that are starting to fly around. Mom's hands flying is never a good thing, and I hold them. "I know, Mom. It's emotional. You are mad at me because I worried you. I'm always worrying you or scaring you. But this time I scared you the worst and I'm sorry about that, but while I was doing this thing that was bad, I was also busy doing things that you always wished I would. I was putting others' needs before mine. On the trail, I had to get over my weird issues. I had to adapt, and I did. I even ate macaroni and cheese."

"And shrimp and grits," Sophie says from the bed.

Everyone laughs.

"Well, not to break up the fun, but we've got some paperwork to do at the station to release Dylan back to your custody, Mrs. Taggart," Officer Stanton says.

"Unless we don't actually bring him to the station?" Officer Nice Guy suggests.

"Nah. This isn't one of those cheesy good-time movies. The kid comes in, we do the paperwork, and he goes on his way. By the book."

"It's only a few months until he's eighteen," Sophie says.

Officer Stanton runs his hand over his stubble. "How many months?"

"Three-ish," I say. The weight of the consequences I could be facing now finally gets to me, and it settles in my stomach like a rock.

"Seems like a lot of paperwork for three months," Sophie's dad says.

"Let me make some calls and see what they recommend." Officer Stanton wipes his glasses with a cloth from his pocket. "But if the DA wants you to come downtown, that's what we do."

"Thanks," I say.

"Don't get all celebratory yet, we'll see what he says."

CHAPTER 29

At the airport, Mom and I sit at our gate waiting to board. I'm fidgeting, having just taken a Dramamine, counting the pulsing in my ears, waiting for it to kick in when Mom reaches into her purse and takes out my iPhone. My real phone, the one I used when I lived at home. "I almost forgot. It's charged for you."

She holds it out like one of many peace offerings that we will have to make with each other. Each one feels slightly less awkward than the previous, but it's still weird. "Thanks," I say without holding eye contact, which in this instance I think even my social skills teacher would forgive.

I flip through my screen, landing on my previous texts with Emily. My finger toggles over her name, and I want to text her. I have no idea what to say, so I scroll to my downloaded music and my heartbeat calms just seeing the chants. Drums. Sounds of nature. I slip in headphones and start listening. Man, that feels so good.

Soon, Mom prods my elbow, and I look up. It's time to board. We shuffle to the walkway and then board the plane. We are in seats 9A and 9B, a window and an aisle. In the past, this would have been a huge point of contention for me. I usually have to be on the aisle in an airplane, but Mom likes the aisle too. For years, she's given it to me, and she starts to again, but I say, "It's okay. I'll take the window."

She gives me an approving nod then goes to answer her phone. "Yup. I've got him. We're heading home. We'll get in around six." She smiles at me then mouths *your brother*. "He looks fine. Really good. Whatever you get is fine. Yes I'm sure he'd love that." Then to me. "Brad wants to know if Joey's Pizza is okay with you when we get home?"

"It's fine." I put the shade down and close my eyes. The emotions of the last few days have left me exhausted. It was crappy saying goodbye to Sophie.

Mom and Sophie's dad gave us a few minutes of "alone time."

"Alone time?" Sophie laughed. "What are we, five?"

I put my forehead against hers. "I've got like five hundred dorky things going through my mind right now."

"What does that look like?" she asked.

This girl. I pulled my head back, moved my chair closer to her bed, I reached for her hands. "Is this okay?" she nodded so I held both of her hands. "You really want to know?"

She nodded. "Plus you owe after digging up my notes."

I almost corrected her and said that debt was paid when she saw me lick spilled coffee grounds in the dirt. Instead I said, "It's like reading a comic or a graphic novel or manga. You ever read those?"

"*Death Note*."

"You and every other dewy-eyed teenager."

She punched me in the arm, the same way I've seen Emily punch boys. "So…"

"Ouch." I pretended to rub the sore area, and then said, "It's like how they have those speech bubbles in comics. I see them filled with things I could say or want to say or definitely should not say."

"How do you choose?"

"Well, I don't always choose carefully, as you have witnessed." She laughed. "True."

"But choosing first lines or last lines, that takes a special art. Like how you begin or end a book."

"This is not a last line. Just tell me you'll see me soon," she said.

"I will."

"I want that."

"Me too." I leaned my head against hers again. We stayed like that until Mom and her dad decided it was time for us to go.

Now sitting in the plane, I think about Sophie. I think of the notepad she gave me to write to the people I need to, packed away in my carry-on right now. I pull it out and start a note to Emily.

Em,

I know I've crossed the line so many times over all the years, and you always defended me. I know the boat thing was my fault. Not yours. Real-world consequences for the choices I made. I am so sorry for everything I've done. I love you.

Dylan

I sign it using my real name this time, not our fake names.

I fold it up into fourths. Then eighths. Then in half one more time. I pat Mom on the shoulder. She takes her headphones out.

"Can you get this to Em for me?"

"Of course."

I put my headphones back in and I think about my life back home, what it will look like, how it'll be, and how I will be. My eyes close, and I sleep the rest of the way to Connecticut.

———o———

Coming home is exactly as weird as I think it will be. Part of me hopes that Emily will be sitting in my living room, but only Brad is there. He must hear Mom's car pull up, and he meets us at the front door. I guess that means he's glad to see me, but I can't hide my disappointment when Brad and I untangle from our two-second man hug and go inside. My gaze sweeps the living room looking for her.

Mom puts her hand on my shoulder. "I thought it would just be us tonight. The rest of the family will come over this weekend."

When Mom leaves the room, Brad picks up on my mood

and says, "You know she'll get over this. She'll be over here soon. You two are close. She'll come around."

"Thanks, man. Hope so."

I nod. *Will Emily come or will she make some stupid excuse?* Then it hits me. This is the summer before she goes to college. It was supposed to be our last time together. And I ruined it. I think of all the plans we'd made. We were going to go back to the Cape house and make Uncle Bill take us parasailing and to see the seals at Chatham and going Banana Boating. All of the dorky touristy things we never did as a family. We were going to go into Boston and do a Duck Tour and walk the Liberty Trail. I ruined that. If only I could have stayed in school for two more months, April and May, I would have been able to spend an entire summer with Emily. We could have taken my boat out. My boat.

I am here now in this world I've made. My world without Dad. Without my boat. Without Emily.

Brad lumbers by with my gear. Mom makes a face. "Stick that in the garage for now, okay?" It *does* smell pretty bad.

We eat on paper plates in front of the television watching the first Harry Potter movie, because the first and the last are my favorites. But it makes my heart hurt, because I always, always did this with Emily.

So I send her a text. Hey Em. I'm home. And I'm sorry.

A calm comes over me. She'll get this. She'll text back. All will be fine. But for the entire movie, I keep checking my phone, but there are no messages. I try not to let Mom see me check.

I try to keep my mind on the movie. Sometimes you've got to fake it for other peoples' sakes.

I'm on my third slice of cheese and Brad is on his fourth when Mom gets up to make popcorn.

Brad tries to act like he's not stressed to be here instead of back at school. I try not to look like I wish my phone would beep. Mom comes back carrying a big bowl of popcorn with a shaker of parmesan cheese and a bowl of caramels. Emily and I have a long-standing argument about popcorn mix-ins. She's pro mix-in, and I'm con. At least when it comes to popcorn. There's nothing wrong with eating a piece of popcorn and *following* it with a caramel chaser. Why do you need to mix them?

I force myself to focus on the screen. My neck is tense, and my ears are listening for any sound of life from my phone. It's dark out now, and for me, the guy who just spent the last few weeks on the trail, this sends a strong signal to go to sleep.

When the movie finally ends, Brad stands, stretches. "Glad you're home, little brother," he calls from across the room. Then he gives Mom a hug. She holds it longer than she usually does. "I'll walk you out," she says.

I use that as my exit. "Going to bed," I call.

"Okay, Sweetie. Good night. So good to have you home."

It's been over twenty-four hours since Mom first walked into Sophie's hospital room, and neither of us has brought up the real issues that have to be ironed out. Like why I left, if I will run again, and what I'm going to do about school.

I don't know what to make of the cease-fire, but I think it's probably good we each have a cooling-off period. That way we can say the important things that people almost never say to each other before we start hammering out our demands and differences (two points) to find common ground.

I walk up the stairs to my room, my legs exhausted, like my mind. Once I walk in my room, the memories push me into a mess of sadness.

My gaze circles the room, taking the tour a second or two ahead of my heart. Straight ahead is my desk centered under the window. On either side of the window are white shelves with Harry Potter figurines, Star Wars Lego men, miniature stuffed Wild Things, and Lord of the Rings action figure sets.

My bed has one of the original stuffed animal Ewoks that Emily bought me on eBay for my thirteenth birthday. My bookshelves are arranged first by genre, then by author. I've got sci-fi on top, then mystery, then fantasy, then nonfiction. I have every single *Old Farmers' Almanac* since I was born. I have a collection of books on stars and constellations, and a book on frogs, because I used to be sort of obsessed with those. There's a small gap on that shelf, and I'm pretty sure a book on birds in the wild might fit perfectly.

I lie on my bed, the flannel sheets that smell like the lavender rinse Mom always uses. I bring the sheets to my nose and breathe in so strong I practically inhale the sheets. Tears well in my eyes. I press against them with the heels of my hands. I want to text Emily. I need to. So I do.

Em. C'mon. You can't stay mad at me forever.

It takes twenty-seven seconds for her to respond, which is ridiculously long for her, since she's sort of tethered to her phone. I'm pretty sure that means she's still pissed. Like she had to figure out to respond. Plus she only writes two words: I know.

I try not to let my annoyance get to me. I try to see it from her perspective. All of these possible replies dive-bomb my mind. My fingers itch to take direction from any one of them. They don't really care what they type or how the words will be received. Honestly, part of me is just as angry as Emily is, but being angry isn't going to help anyone. So I close my eyes and shut out the suggestions from my impulsive brain. I try to think with my heart about how I feel.

I feel really badly about how things went.

How so?

She's talking to me, so that's good, but I can read between the lines. So I write, I should have come home when you asked me to. Or at least written Mom.

Yes. You should have.

Will you forgive me?

Eventually.

But not now?

Not now.

Part of me is angry at her for being stubborn. But deep in my heart, I know I deserved that and more. So I type, I sent you a note. Mom's going to deliver it, and close my eyes, resting my phone on my chest.

The phone beeps again, and, because I'm not expecting it, I jump. Has she changed her mind? Has she forgiven me? But when I check the screen, it's not Emily who texted. It's Sophie.

Hey stranger.

Hey back.

Wrote you a note. But didn't bury it.

A smile lifts the corners of my mouth. Good. Because I wouldn't dig up your notes and read them again. That would be wrong.

Her next text makes me so happy. You made me laugh. For real.

That's my job.

Write me a note?

What kind?

I don't know. I'll text you my address tomorrow so you can send it. Promise you will?

Yes.

OK. Tired. Going to sleep.

Gnite. Sweet dreams.

Sweet dreams to you too. I sleep better when you are here.

Me too.

She sleeps better when I'm there. So that decides it. I have to be there as soon as I can. But I have to do it with Mom's blessing this time. That means I've got to finish high school. I put my phone back on my chest and let my body relax into the Tempur-Pedic bed my mother bought me because she read it helped kids like me sleep better. *Kids like me.* The ones who need labels. The angry. The out of control. Kids like me. But maybe if I use the things I learned on the trail, I can be less angry and less out of control. Maybe the school Mom wanted to send me to can teach me those things too.

CHAPTER 30

Mom is sitting at the breakfast table when I come downstairs. Her bowl of oatmeal is beside her, her hands are around a mug of coffee, and she's reading the paper. The smell of coffee is so compelling I want to pour myself a bowl of it, but I am sidetracked by Mom's comical expression.

"What are you doing up?" She taps her phone on the table. "It's early."

I run my hand through my hair. "Bad habit I picked up on the Trail."

She gets up from the table, walks to the cabinet, and takes out my favorite coffee mug and fills it for me. "I think I like that new habit." She opens the fridge and stops. "You still take cream and sugar?"

"If I can get it."

"You can."

I sit at the table as Mom serves me the coffee, which is not usually how breakfast goes in my house. It's usually help yourself, except on my birthday. The smell is incredible, But I resist the urge to guzzle it, letting the anticipation build.

"You hungry?" Mom asks, not understanding that she's interrupting my private moment with coffee. The old me would have growled at her or made a face. The new me puts my hand over my stomach. "Always."

"Oatmeal okay?"

"It's perfect, Mom."

I allow myself my first sip of coffee as Mom ladles the oatmeal into a bowl. Part of me believes I don't deserve this rock-star treatment, but another part of me screams to drink the coffee, so I do. Mom adds some butter and salt to the bowl, then she brings it to me and I think about how unfair to Mom I've been.

I stare at my phone, drink more coffee, stare some more. To text or not to text. Because I know Mom probably already got the note to Em. I stare at my phone. Should I?

So I do.

Emily. I sent you a note, which I'm pretty sure you got. You said last night you'd eventually forgive me. I feel like if I keep texting you, keep asking you to forgive me, that maybe I'm dismissing your feelings or being too pushy. So I won't. I'm sorry. And I want us to be good.

Meanwhile, Mom is busy preparing the rest of my oatmeal feast. First she fills another bowl with brown sugar and puts in the sugar spoon, the round one that I always used to eat with when I was little. I remember she told me it was my special spoon, because it was shaped like the full moon. I was dorky enough to believe her until my cousin, Abby, filled me in over one of our big summer breakfasts at the Cape. "It's a sugar spoon, you dork."

Aunt Mary smacked her across the arm. "What's wrong with you? Why can't you leave the little kids alone?"

Abby and Christian and Brad left, all riotous with laughter and Emily took my hand. "They're the dorks. We are awesome."

And we did a two-sugar-spoon salute and went back to eating.

Mom fills the creamer with half-and-half and adds it to the tray she's making for me. Golden raisins go in a small tea bowl. She looks at the pantry, cocks her head, and then sticks her hand in and comes out with raisins and slivered almonds. They each get their own bowl and small spoon. A warmth spreads over me as I remember all of the times she made me this exact breakfast. We used to call it a build-your-own. Mom figured out I would eat all sorts of things mixed together if I was the one who did the mixing. I add all of the toppings to my steaming oatmeal while she dusts cinnamon on top and I remind myself that I am so lucky to not only have a mom, but this one in particular.

The smell is insanely good. I take a swig of coffee and follow that immediately with a little bite of heaven that is this bowl of oatmeal.

Mom gets her coffee and sits across from me. I can see she's working on her crossword puzzle. It's a perfect peaceful moment. Warmth spreads inside me. I'm happy to be home. Really happy. Which is weird because no matter how tough or dangerous the trail was, I was happy there also. I think about telling Rain Man that. So I pull out that little notebook I've been carrying around with me since the trail, and I start a note to Rain Man.

Rain Man,

I'm sorry. I know you're probably angry
with me for what I did, but I think it was
the right thing.

Mom takes a sip of her coffee, looks at me writing, her eyebrows raised. "Everything good?"

"Yeah. I started writing to people about things I'm having a hard time saying."

"Another trail thing?"

"Yeah. And a Sophie thing."

"I like that girl," Mom says. "And in a weird way, I think the trail was good for you."

"Who are you writing to now? Sophie?"

"No. Rain Man. Although, I have no idea how to get this note to him."

"I'm pretty sure we can figure that out."

"Maybe. And one day you may get a note from me too, Mom."

"What will the note say?"

"Mostly that I'm sorry."

Her eyes glisten. She puts her hand on my head. "Me too."

I keep writing to Rain Man:

I hope you'll think that life is worth living
and that you and your family will make
up. I'm making up with mine. Person by
person. I also wanted to thank you. You

THE SECRETS WE BURY

*taught me to love shrimp and grits and how
to love the trail. Oh, and I still have your
socks. I hope to hike part of the trail next
year. And I hope I get to see you again.
Until then, I am really happy we met.*
Dylan.

She smiles. "That's good." She drinks some more coffee and
looks at her puzzle. "Seven-letter word that means—"

"Mom…" I start.

"No, seven-letter word that means—"

I interrupt again. "Mom. I think I should go to that school."

She looks up and almost knocks over her coffee.

"I mean it. I was wrong. I never should have run away. I'm
sorry. And I've been thinking that maybe I should try that new
school out. This summer, if possible."

"This summer?"

"Yeah. I want to finish my classes from last semester. I want
to graduate this year. Or even early."

"Early?"

"Yeah. I've been thinking I want to do something next May.
If it's okay with you."

Mom takes a drink. "The trail changed you."

"Yeah. It's about time I grew up, isn't it?"

Her eyes well up. "Your dad would be so…"

"Don't say it, Mom. Not until I've done everything I plan to
this year. Then say it when it's the perfect last line."

She nods. "I'll make some calls to see when you can start."

As Mom starts working the phones, as Em and I used to say, I stare at my cell and think about the trail. Mom said the trail changed me, and I think that's true. It's made me recognize how lucky I am with my family and my home. It reminded me that life is pretty fragile. It brought me Sophie, and I got to spend some time remembering Dad. At times it almost felt like he was with me.

My muscles got used to the regular exercise, and all of a sudden, I have a thought. Mom watches from her perch on one of the kitchen stools. Her lawyer voice is calmly explaining to the school board the nature of my issues and what she and I wanted to do next. I nod to her, thankful that I get to help make these decisions.

In my room I open the bottom drawer of my desk where I've stashed Dad's old running shorts. I put them on, knowing they'll be too big, I pin them so they'll stay on me. I put on my running shoes and go downstairs, just in time to get Em's text.

I forgive you. I guess.

Mom calls to me as I open the door. "Where…"

"Just going for a run. I'll be home soon."

"Aunt Mary just called. Everyone wants to come for dinner tonight. Okay with you?"

"Perfect." I let the door close behind me and plug my music in. Dad's favorite, Led Zeppelin's "Moby Dick" starts me off.

And I feel fine.

ACKNOWLEDGMENTS

Every book we write holds an untold story of the people who helped it along the way. Some of the players are always the same, will always be the same, but others insert themselves in special ways as the book is formed, takes hold, and eventually makes its way out into the world.

The same is true for *The Secrets We Bury*.

This is a very special book for me, as it relates to a lot of kids I've loved and cared for over the years. The book was initiated after a discussion with one of my coworkers. So the first person I need to thank is Brandie Horner, who urged me to write about some of "our kids."

Next, I need to thank Linda Rodriguez-Bernfeld, Dorian Cirrone, Rob Sanders and the rest of the Florida SCBWI team who invited my editor to the Mid-Year SCBWI Florida conference in Orlando in 2016. After taking the novel comprehensive with Jonathan Maberry and Lorin Oberweger, my head filled with their wise words and role-played pitch sessions, I pitched this book to my wonderful editor, Annette Pollert-Morgan, at dinner with my agent, Nicole Resciniti. And voilà! Sold! So huge props to the hardworking Florida SCBWI team, of course, and to Jonathan and Lorin specifically for teaching me how to do an emotional query. It worked!

To my fabulous editor, Annette, thank you so much for believing in me (again!) and trusting me to write this big book. Also ginormous thanks to Nicole Resciniti, who always makes me feel like I can do this incredibly difficult writing thing, who always shows up for me when I need her, and for suggesting wine with dinner that night!

Next on the thank-you list is Joyce Sweeney. She was there after that dinner to talk me through all of this, just as she's always been with me, this entire time.

While thanking my dependable and loyal writing tribe, I want to thank The Tuesdays, of course. They are my longest-lasting critique group and are part of every book I write. Tuesdays: best day of the week! While on the subject of critique groups, I'd be remiss if I didn't thank the PGAs, the Palm Springs group, and the Wellington Critique group. I am so lucky to have so many people who help me hone my craft. Thank you all!

Also on the I'm-always-thankful-for-them list are my writing besties, Steven dos Santos, Jonathan Rosen, and Jill Nadler. You guys pick me up when I need it, kick my butt when I need it, and celebrate with me when I've earned it. This writing life would not be the same without you!

My family is always supportive and instrumental in my writing. Bonnie, Mark, and Heidi, thanks for cheering me on from New England, with two of my nieces. Mike and Kelly, I appreciate the support from your side of the country with my other niece and two nephews. You all make up the heart of my books.

My mother-in-law, Kathy, has to cheer enough for all of the parents. Luckily she's not afraid to lend her voice and support at all times, including finding me research help on this difficult-to-write book.

To Vicky and Bill Hassel, you two have always loved my boys (plus one girl!), and anytime I write about boys, I think of you two. Thanks for being in my family's life. We heart you.

Finally I'd like to thank John (JKR) and my children who have had to do without my undivided attention and participation during some family card games and movie nights. I'd also like to thank my rescue doggies. No book is written without a furry friend by my side. Woof.

Oh, and one more group. Thanks so much to the Sourcebooks Fire team. You all rock.

ABOUT THE AUTHOR

Stacie Ramey learned to read at a very early age to escape the endless tormenting from her older siblings. She attended the University of Florida, where she majored in communication sciences, and Penn State, where she received a master of science degree in speech pathology. When she's not writing, she engages in Netflix wars with her children or beats her husband in Scrabble. She lives in Wellington, Florida, with her husband, three children, and two rescue dogs.

Who holds your secrets?

Allie trusted her older sister, Leah, with her deepest secrets...and then Leah betrayed her.

Read their story in Stacie Ramey's

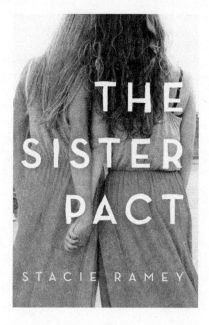

CHAPTER 1

The last thing we did as a family was bury my sister. That makes this meeting even harder to face.

I don't have to be a psychic to know what everyone thinks when they look at me. Why did she do it? Why didn't I? And the thing is, after all that happened, I'm not sure I know the answer to either.

Mom walks behind me, her hand gently curled around my bicep. Dad motions to show us where to sit, even though the guidance office is new ground for him.

I force myself to look into the faces of my judges and feel immediate relief. The principal, Mrs. Pendrick, smiles, warm and sweet, and the wrinkly skin around her eyes and lips lifts as she does. Mr. Hicks, my guidance counselor, the one the girls think is sort of cute, stands next to her. Where Mrs. Pendrick is all soft creases, he's wide shoulders, built for dealing with bad kids or bad parents, but he winks at me like he wants me to know he's on my side.

Mrs. Pendrick places a hand on mine. "It's nice to see you, Allie. We're so glad you're back."

Her hand is like an island of safe in a sea of danger. I smile at her so she thinks I'm okay. I smile so it looks like I'm not breaking. Like everything that happened was a mistake and I'm ready for a do-over.

Mr. Kispert, my art teacher, comes barreling into the room, carrying his iced coffee and my portfolio. "Sorry I'm late," he says. He nods at me and I try to nod back, but my body's kind of frozen. I had no idea he'd be here too.

"We were just getting started." Mrs. Pendrick opens a file, my name written on the tab. "I pulled Allie's records. She's on track for graduation next year, of course."

I tell myself to pay attention. I try to focus on Mrs. Pendrick, whose Southern accent makes her sound as misplaced as "the wrong Alice" in the new version of *Alice in Wonderland*, but it's hard.

"We may want to take a look at the courses she's chosen for this year." Mrs. Pendrick adjusts her reading glasses and flips through the pages.

My eyes hurt, the start of a migraine. I blink.

"We want to make certain we're not asking too much of her." Mr. Hicks shifts forward, his hands loosely steepled on the fake mahogany table in front of him.

The surface of the table is so shiny, I see my face in it, distorted and strange. I blink again. Caught somewhere between the blink and the reflection, I see her, Leah, in her black leotard and pink tights, like she's waiting in the wings for her cue.

Even though I realize it's just a trick of the light, I can't help staring at not-real-Leah, waiting to see if she's going to dance. I'm staring so hard, I must have stopped paying attention to what's going on around me because Dad's voice is stern. "Sit up, Allie. These people are here for you."

I square myself in my seat, horrified by the look of pity that crosses Mr. Hicks's face.

Mrs. Pendrick reaches across the table and takes my hand again, her touch soft as butter. "Are you okay, dear?"

"I'm fine. I just have a headache."

Dad shoots me a look like he wants me to behave, to make up for Leah. As if I could.

"Mr. Blackmore, we have to be patient with Allie," Mrs. Pendrick insists.

I should probably warn Mrs. Pendrick that Dad doesn't believe in being patient. It's all about domination and war games with him. He's the general. I'm the soldier he commands, and he will not lose this hill. No matter what. When I look at him, I see dried blood caked on his hands. Mom's. Leah's. Mine.

I shake that image out of my head and try to find my Happy. I think about everyone's colors. Mrs. Pendrick would be creamy yellow, icing pink, powder blue. And Mr. Hicks would be something easy too, like golf-course-turf green. I try to think about how I would paint them if I still painted. And just like that, Happy has left the building. Like Leah did.

"It's her junior year." Dad leans forward, his not-giving-an-inch stance making my stomach knot. I already know his colors: muddy brown, gray black, the color of pissed. "We need to get her back on track."

"We understand that." Mr. Hicks folds his hands again like a tent. "But this is going to be a very hard year for Allie."

It *is* going to be a hard year. And no meeting is going to change that. So instead of listening to them, I close my eyes and call to my mind the sound of Leah's ballet shoes shuffling against the floor. Eight weeks after, I can still hear them, but who knows for how long? Right now, I'm so grateful for the soft slide, slide, slide that is so real and strong that it fills me with unreasonable hope. Maybe she hasn't left me. Maybe it didn't happen. Maybe she'll forgive me.

"Maybe we could keep just two of the AP classes?" Mom suggests.

I open my eyes and pray I'm not crazy. It's hard to know if you are. Nobody really thinks they are. But I can almost hear Leah laughing with me—so like her to laugh when I'm in the hot seat and she's not.

Mr. Kispert takes out my portfolio and lays it on the table next to a brochure from the Rhode Island School of Design. The requirements are highlighted in crime-scene-tape yellow. "Allie should keep her AP Studio Art class. I'll supervise her. She'll do fine, and she needs it to work on her application."

Reading upside down, I can make out all the things I need to do to make that happen. Last year it all seemed easy. Now each step feels like a mountain I'm not equipped to climb. Mr. Kispert looks at me and winks. I smile back, even though I feel like a complete fake. I can't do art anymore, and I don't know how to tell him.

Mom puts her hand out to take the brochure, and it shakes. *Please don't let Dad notice. Please.* Dad grunts and takes it instead. "I'm not giving up on my daughter. Even if you guys are."

"Nobody's giving up on her," Mr. Hicks says. "We just want her to be okay."

"She wants to go to RISD. How do you expect her to get into a top art school if you don't give her the right classes?" His voice strains, and for a second I think he's going to cry, which I've never seen him do—except when we buried Leah.

"David, please." Mom says.

He slams the table hard. "Goddammit, Karen, this is what you do, what you always do. You give into the girls." He clears his throat. "Her. You give into her."

Mom's eyes well at Dad's obvious stumble. They've been calling Leah and I *them* or *the girls* for so long. It must be hard to adjust, but seeing Dad struggle with the math makes me feel horrible. We did this. We cut his regiment in half. Maybe his heart too. I want to reach out to him. I want to tell him I'm sorry. That I didn't think she meant it. That I definitely didn't—until I did. But that's a cop-out. Truth is, I don't remember most of that night.

Dad's voice sounds like he's surrendering. "What do you want me to do, Karen? Let her fail? That's not exactly going to fix her, is it?"

Everybody gets quiet. I can feel the silence like a noose around my neck. Dad's pain radiates off him. Mom's shame makes her sink into the chair. Mr. Hicks and Mrs. Pendrick sit, waiting for the right thing to say to heal this family. But there isn't anything to be said after all this. After what Leah did and what I almost did.

I close my eyes and wish Leah were here. I wish so hard,

I can almost feel her holding my hand. Sometimes she did that when Mom and Dad fought. Sometimes she held my hand and I'd play with her silver flower ring, the one she always wore. They buried her with that ring. Mom said she wanted to give it to me, but I wanted Leah to have it. I lay my head on the table, the cool feeling enough to calm me for a minute.

"Jesus, Allie, can you try to focus?" I lift my head to see Dad close his eyes, and I know I've pushed him too hard. He shakes his head like a bull. He does that when he's done. He stares at the ceiling. "Is this how it's going to be now? Are you going to give up?"

And just like that he makes me want to disappear, makes me wish I could be wherever Leah is now, away from him and his shit. Away from everyone's expectations. Away from his stupid war with Mom.

And more than ever, I wish Leah were here. If she were here, really here, she'd stop Dad from being a jerk. She'd make Mom sit up straight and actually have an opinion. She'd take over this meeting and make them stop talking about my life as if I'm not even in it. Leah could totally do that. She was epic.

Until she killed herself.

Mrs. Pendrick clears her throat. "I understand your concerns, Mr. Blackmore. Junior year *is* a very important year. But Allie needs to heal."

We Blackmores? We don't heal. We patch up and make do. We Blackmores move on. It's in some contract that Dad made us sign when we were born. Leah's in breach. Now I'm the one in the spotlight. Thanks, Sis.

"Allie's seeing someone." Dad clears his throat. "A psychiatrist."

Mom nods quickly to show they're on the same page, which has been a ridiculously rare occurrence since Mom's Xanax addiction made the scene. Or since Dad's girlfriend, Danielle, did. The one that has texted him three times since he picked Mom and me up today. I guess she was mad he didn't let her come. To *my* meeting. My head starts pounding. I reach into my backpack and pull out an Excedrin pack and a Gatorade.

"What are you doing?" Mom's face gets red.

"I have a headache," I explain.

"You're supposed to tell me, and I give it to you." She shuffles around in her purse.

"It's just Excedrin." Does she honestly want to become my personal med vending machine? Like a human PEZ dispenser? I rip open the packet and put the pills on my tongue. Everyone gets quiet and looks at me like I just bit the head off a bat.

This is so outrageous. I can't deal with it alone. Leah should be facing this horrible aftermath with me. Every suicide pact needs a fallback for prisoners of war. Apparently.

Dad's hand goes on Mom's. It's a small gesture but so foreign in their full-scale battle that I can't pull my eyes from the spectacle. Mom puts her purse back on the arm of her chair. I'm not sure if I've imagined it, but I think I hear the sound of the pills rattling in their bottles, and that worries me greatly. Now that Leah's gone AWOL, I don't think I'd follow her, but if I'm so solid, why the hell am I wondering how many pills Mom has on her?

"I want to hear how Allie feels," Mr. Hicks says, breaking my reverie.

I swallow hard. How do I feel? I feel like I'm breaking inside. I can't see colors anymore. It's like when Leah left, she took the best of me. I feel like if one of us should have lived, it should have been her. She'd be way better in the role of surviving sister than I am. She'd have better hair too.

"Allie?" Dad prompts. "Mr. Hicks asked you a question. How do you feel?"

Sometimes I feel like I'm no more here than Leah is. Sometimes I forget. I think it didn't happen. I wait for my cell to ring. I think she's going to burst into the room, full of life and pissed at me for having borrowed one of her things. But then I remember. And it's like that night all over again. And I get mad—at her for going, and them for not even knowing that I'm not just mad she went, but also that she didn't take me with her. Like she promised. Like we promised each other.

"Allie?" Dad's voice gets tighter.

But I can't tell them any of that. They don't want to hear about that. Everyone's so sick of death, they want me to lighten the mood. It's up to me. I'm on stage now. Dad's beating the drum. Mom's cowering. My teachers and the guidance counselors are waiting like revival attendees ready to be preached to, ready to clap. I can't disappoint them. So I try to be like Leah. I sit up tall. I "dance." "It's fine." I look at Mom so she'll know I mean it. Mostly. "AP art classes. Everything else honors."

"You sure you can do that, sweetie?" I hear the relief in

Mom's voice. She wants to believe it's all over. I guess I can't really blame her.

Mrs. Pendrick's face screws up. "I think this is a mistake."

"I agree," Mr. Hicks says. "But let's do this. How about we move forward with that schedule and keep an eye on you, Allie? That sound okay? We're here whenever you need."

"Perfect." Dad stands.

Mom follows his lead.

I stand too, not wanting to break rank, especially when there's been a break in the fighting. It's not that I think it's so perfect, but I'm playing the part of the foot soldier, as usual. We soldiers march and follow orders. We soldiers act like it's all good. Hup, two, three, four. Even when we're breaking.